PETTIFYR

ON THE ROCKS

A.P. THOMPSON

First published 2018.

The moral right of A.P. Thompson to be identified
as the author of this work has been asserted.

ISBN 978 1 7908 5188 1

PETTIFYR

ON THE ROCKS

www.pettifyr.biz

In Loving Memory

of

Howard & Doreen Davies

(She loved a bit of tea and swearing)

Foreword

by the Reverend Nicholas J. Allbrighton
St Mary's Parish, Essex.

Given the notoriety in the popular press (not to mention half of the broadsheet lot) of the so-called 'Bursands Affair', it was with some trepidation that I agreed to introduce this first published account of young Jennifer Pettifyr's exploits in Devon.

Now what, you might be asking, does a crusty old vicar from an uncharted backwater in Essex know about it? What, precisely, does this old fart bring to the party? Well, in short, not very much. I wasn't there. I didn't see, hear or say anything to contribute to those events whatsoever. I am, however, the only person whom the youngest Pettifyr girl could successfully strong-arm into providing a reference.

The lady does, you see, have an unfortunate aptitude for rubbing people up the wrong way. Now, I say this from a position of staunch affection for Jennifer. I have known her since she was but a bouncing baby little pup, urinating enthusiastically over my kitchen floor, all the way through to her emergence into fully-grown (and having started this rather unfortunate dog metaphor I had probably better finish it) bitch-hood.

I say unfortunate but writing this has reminded me that on her eighteenth birthday I again found her urinating in my home and completely avoiding, I might add, the rather helpful litter tray placed down at five o'clock once I discovered she was on the cider. So, she can take that one on the chin. I spend enough time on my knees, thank you very much, without wasting a whole weekend trying to eradicate her tenacious whiff of asparagus.

Anyway, to summarise. The lady may be small. She may be verbally offensive. She may also be physically offensive (not unattractive, you understand, just liable to hit you at speed). She remains however, to my mind at least, one of the finest examples of the human species it has ever been my privilege to encounter. I would not hesitate to take a bullet for her. Three years ago, I watched her take one herself. Jennifer saved the life of my daughter, without a single thought for her own welfare and in circumstances (not relevant to this Devon business, by the way) under which any normal person would have happily crossed to the safer side of the street. That is, to 'get down' with the children for one horrible moment, just how she rolls.

I would simply encourage you not to judge a Pettifyr purely by appearance. As a family, they have hidden depths and the youngest of them, despite her quite spectacularly wide-ranging fault set, remains my favourite. This is in spite of her language, which is (and let's get this clear from the outset) rather dreadful.

Chapter One
"The Crown vs Pettifyr J."

Having spent most of his life buggering around, day-dreaming at his desk and basically fantasising about something slightly more interesting coming his way, Simon Martin was now discovering that it really does pay to be a little bit careful what you wish for.

Simon had parked up at the Butcher's Apron pub, two hours earlier, and made his way into the bar (having to bypass, in the process, a shiny vintage Triumph motorcycle which somebody had chosen to deposit entirely across the main entrance) with very few cares in the world and something of a spring in his twenty four year-old step.

Once inside he had been confronted by a powerful and assertive pair of legs straddling, cowboy-fashion, a small wooden chair drawn up in front of a large, central table. It was, by any standard, a very nice view indeed. The owner of the legs was poring over a set of Ordnance Survey maps which appeared, to Simon, to be in a state of some emotional distress.

The lady herself sported a fetching pair of red leather boots, tight blue jeans and a bottle-green leather biker jacket. Above the jacket sprouted a vicious eruption of wild red hair, being tossed around as its owner appeared to be attempting to fashion an origami swan out of a long stretch of coastline and a small plastic clothes peg. Next door to the redhead a small family of three was squeezed up together. The sour-faced matriarch, if the expression on her face was anything to go by, was clearly put out by the single woman's hogging of the large central table.

"Bollocks" grunted the curls suddenly, after wrestling her swan to the ground with the assistance of a strategically-placed pint of beer. The expletive was delivered in such an incongruously well-educated voice and Simon found it to be rather amusing, although he was guilty of judging the book purely by the quality of its denim-clad backside.

The lady's neighbour however, sitting with her boy of early junior school age, looked somewhat less impressed with the table-hogger adding a potty-mouth to her list of offences. She shot the lady in the jeans a sour look and a middle-class disapproving tut. Simon fetched himself a drink from the bar and sat down to peruse the menu. He rather fancied a cheeseburger.

"Oh, for fuck's sake!" The lady with the red hair necked the remains of her pint whilst simultaneously swinging a shapely leg up and over her chair, propelling herself up for a re-fill. This smooth yet complicated manoeuvre resulted in her impressive backside ending up approximately ten centimetres from the face of the father next-door.

To be fair, he didn't seem to mind this one little bit. Vinegar tits next to him, however, had clearly had enough. "Excuse me" she squawked, "but would you mind not swearing, please?"

Now, to those uninitiated in the modus operandi of the Pettifyr ladies, this might sound like a perfectly reasonable request. Any acquaintance of Jennifer Pettifyr, however, would point out that she would have more luck asking a nun for a condom.

"What? Was that directed at me, then?"

The offender at the bar cocked up an eyebrow from behind a set of brutally expensive sunglasses. Undaunted by this intimidation, the mother pressed on. "There are children present ..."

She indicated, with a bony index finger, towards her little boy who was now looking around for a hole to jump into. The redhead shifted her gaze to the child, briefly, before returning her attention to the lady.

"What's its name?" she barked, jabbing a nail at the youngster.

"*His* name is William! And I would appreciate it if you could tone your language down, please. He's only ten!"

The redhead pushed off from the bar and then shot out an arm towards the child like a karate chop. This generated much flinching all around until it dawned upon the group that the gesture was actually intended as a handshake rather than a punch to the child's face.

"Pleased to meet you" said Jennifer Pettifyr, peering down at the boy. "Are you a Willy, a Billy or a Jeff then?"

She received a rather perplexed expression in response.

"Who's Jeff?" asked the youngster.

The redhead ducked the question and glared at the little boy instead. "Not you then? Fine. Anyway, enough chat, let's cut to the chase shall we? Are you (jab of finger toward youngster's nose) offended, at all, by my swearing? Because…" The lady paused. "If so, well… I'll try to tone it down a bit."

After her long-winded run up this final delivery seemed rather conciliatory and disappointingly tame. Had Simon known Jennifer better he would have realised, of course, that she had not actually started her run up. Jennifer Pettifyr was still just rubbing the ball on her trouser leg.

"Although, in my humble defence, m'lud, I would just draw the attention of the jury to the fact, and some might feel this to be a tad obvious but we'll throw it out there anyway, that this is a pub. A public house, yes? A drinking establishment for, and this rather gets to the nub of my defence, adults. Grown-ups, you know?"

She paused, presumably for breath as much as effect. "It is not a crèche, nor indeed…" Jennifer glanced down her nose at the lemon-sucker's choice of beverage, "a coffee shop. So, as my dear mother used to tell me, if you will insist on playing on the beach, Jennifer, don't come a crying when you get sand up your crack."

Spitting his drink at this point brought Simon to the woman's attention and he found himself the subject of a disturbingly prolonged appraisal from across the bar. She poked a finger at him which he could almost feel from the other side of the room.

"Tissues in the toilet friend, unless Derek (thumb towards the barman, who was keeping his head well down by this stage) has been playing with himself again. Or has the shits."

The lady considered her horrible statement before adding, for reasons best known to herself, that the two possibilities were not mutually exclusive. Leaving Simon to ponder on that one, she swivelled back to the youngster.

"Anyway, let us return to the case of the Crown versus Pettifyr J. Now, I am quite sure that you hear far worse things at school every day, don't you?" She cocked her head expectantly and, clearly feeling under pressure to respond, young William emerged nervously from the pavilion and made his way to the crease. "Well, Gavin Watkins did call Mr Jenkins a cunt in Geography..."

Jennifer Pettifyr, who was a lady always well-pleased to have her opinions validated by others, opened her arms out like a television evangelist. This was a more positive reaction, it must be said, than that of the lad's mother who just gave him a very sharp smack to the ear. Smelling the blood in the water, Jennifer went in for the kill. "Exactly, William, and I'm sure that Mr Jenkins appreciated the feedback. Anyway, the point is that's FAR worse than my dropping a good-natured F-bomb, isn't it?"

She grinned like a Cheshire cat and tapped the boy's nose with her fingernail. "Don't let me catch you swearing again, though" she added, with quite spectacular unfairness. "However, if you will insist upon it, try calling Gavin Watkins a..."

The money shot of this particular piece of advice was sadly lost upon Simon as it was whispered very quietly into young William's right ear. Whatever it was, however, it caused the small person to giggle violently, turn beetroot red and then gaze up in wonder at his new best friend.

"After all," Jennifer stood up, brightly. "I think we can all do a little bit better than the C word, can't we? Vulgar." She put her hands on her hips and Simon noticed the logo on her black t-shirt which, in faded white letters, appeared to say "I don't need sex. The government fucks me every day." He might have misread it. He hoped so. Seizing the opportunity for a tactical toilet break, he headed off past the fruit machine to locate the facilities. After a minute or two spent losing his way through a rabbit-warren of passageways he was about to return to the bar when a surprisingly velvety voice piped up in his ear, making him jump.

"Straight down the end, handsome. Turn left at the tits."

Good deed for the day sorted, Jennifer Pettifyr swaggered her backside back to the bar. The somewhat peculiar instructions left Simon wondering about the nature of the establishment he had wandered into, however all became clear when the full-length portrait of "Lady with Candle" loomed into view between the usual gender-specific door signs. The artist was clearly a breast man, Simon reflected, as he relieved himself at the urinal before washing his hands and remembering to pocket some toilet roll to deal with the drink spillage. Back in the bar, the family had left (presumably on the basis that too much of a good thing, that good thing being verbal abuse from Jennifer Pettifyr, might actually be bad for you).

Simon used the opportunity to take a closer look at the lady with the maps. She looked extremely fit. Her feisty red curls had the air of a violent offender out on day release with only an elderly green head-band protecting the public.

Finishing his drink Simon reluctantly considered making a move. The road to the coast was extremely slow and he realised that he was unlikely to reach Bursands before dark. As he was rising to his feet to leave the little redhead suddenly emitted a loud grunt of disgust and slammed her head down onto the table.

"I don't suppose" came a small muffled voice, "that anyone here has heard of a place called Bursands?"

Chapter Two

"Pasty ginger twat"

After trying to explain the route to Jennifer in the pub and
discovering, quite quickly, that finding South Devon on a large
map of Scotland is a little bit challenging, Simon had given up and
suggested that it would probably be easier if she just came with
him. Jennifer had put away her maps (managing entirely to avoid
the manufacturer's quite helpful pre-designated folds) and left her
Triumph motorcycle in the capable hands of Derek the barman.
("If anything happens to that machine, Derek, you're fucking
dead... and do not even THINK about sniffing my pillion"). They
set off in Simon's silver car with Jennifer tucked up in the
passenger seat and her expensive Italian hold-all stuffed into the
well between her feet.

Over the course of the journey it emerged that Jennifer
Pettifyr's skill-set does not extend very far at all into the realms of
polite small talk. That is not to suggest that she is quiet. She is just
not very polite.

"So, you do actually have a cottage in this Bursands place then? I'm only asking because, well, I'd just heard that it's bit of a dreary shit-hole." Simon had never actually been to Bursands before but, before he was able to relay this, Jennifer poked him in the ribs. "Also, whilst we're at it - and please pay close attention to this part - if this is actually just an elaborate attempt at a pick up on your part then we will not, in the manner of Queen Victoria, be very amused. We won't be amused to the extent that we will give your testicles a very good battering, before proceeding to remove them with the aid of a rusty blunt fish knife."

More than a little disturbed by the direction in which this conversation seemed to be travelling, Simon suddenly found himself facing into a very large, very red and very angry-looking tractor. He braked the roadster hard to a standstill before reversing, very slowly, back up the country lane.

The car might have stopped, but Jennifer Pettifyr hadn't.

"Then we batter your balls with flour, deep-fry the little buggers to within an inch of their life and then, finally, we serve them up together with a nice little pot of garlic aioli. Down on the quay at lovely Bursands!" She prodded him in the ribs again. "Ever had deep-fried bollocks in Bursands? Because that's where you and I are cruising, if this is you trying to put one over on little Jennifer." She gave him a hard look, then smiled sweetly. Simon returned his eyes to the road but Jennifer poked him in the ribs again to get his attention back. "Twice-battered… do you get it?"

Simon didn't.

Receiving no response Jennifer inspected her nails instead. They were painted in a rather garish shade of purple. Blissful silence continued until, fifteen minutes later, she turned and gave him another sharp poke, this time to his arm.

"Like triple-cooked chips, yes?"

Bloody hell, thought Simon, however as the testicle-threat seemed to have receded he decided to risk another conversational skirmish. "I'm Simon, by the way."

"Pleased to meet you, Simon. Jennifer, here. Jennifer Pettifyr. That's me." She pronounced her surname with the same Nellie the Elephant cadence as her first. "Of the Brentwood Pettifyrs" she added. "From… Brentwood. Essex, you know." She tailed off then, having apparently taken a wrong turn into a verbal cul de sac. Simon waited for a safe stretch of road before looking at her again.

"Aren't you a little pale for an Essex girl?"

His passenger's face lit up like a Christmas tree.

"Banter! Well, fuck me. Hang on." Jennifer began to scrabble around in the foot-well to reach her bag. "I've got a notebook in here somewhere. I'm going to write that one down, if you don't mind. Comedy gold." Jennifer continued to rummage. "Definitely got a pencil in here somewhere..." The curly head popped up, eventually, brandishing a stubby little HB. "Here we go. Right! I'm ready." She licked the end of her pencil. "What was it again? Something about my being a pasty ginger twat, wasn't it?" She began to write, extremely slowly, keen as mustard to demonstrate to Simon that he was in absolutely no danger of being misquoted.

"Hang on… I didn't mention your hair!?"

"And a fucking good job too, Simon. Anyone would think you know, with the way that you're carrying on, that you actually enjoy having your bollocks bashed!" She fixed him with another stare. Simon found himself wondering why she was still wearing her sunglasses. The sun had dropped away and it was now starting to get dark. She was still banging on.

"Although, just hang on there a minute! Maybe you do? Yes. That would explain everything, wouldn't it Simon?" Jennifer dropped her voice lower and tapped him on the arm a few times. "So, as well as being a stand-up fucking comedian, are you also one of those pervies who gets off on having their nuts battered in May? Because if so, well…"

She paused, for a bit more tapping. "You should be careful what you wish for, Simon. Jennifer Jane kicks very hard, you know. Very hard indeed."

Unsure quite how they had returned to this theme so quickly, Simon decided to tread more carefully. Normally he would be right up for his nethers being the centre of a lady's attention, but not this lunatic. Despite her looks, Simon's brain was strongly advising him to offload her at the next available opportunity (i.e. a hedge).

He decided, however, to be a gentleman. It was a long drive and it didn't make much sense to fall out with her. Besides which, she looked more than strong enough to chuck him out of the car if he tried anything. Opting to keep his knackers intact, Simon decided to play nicely.

"Pleased to meet you, Jennifer. For the tape, this is not a kidnap attempt." Jennifer nodded sagely.

"Pleased to meet you too, Simon. Oh, and to your earlier question, I'm wearing these to hide the rather impressive shiner which little Jennifer is currently sporting above her right eye. No need to frighten the horses and all that."

"Did somebody hit you?"

"No, Simon, I punch myself in the face every morning just to save the rest of the world the fucking job." With that, she settled back to get some rest. Well, thought Simon, fuck you too.

By the time around an hour later, however, that the first signpost appeared for the small coastal village of Bursands and the road gently blended away into a dirt track ending at the waterfront, his animosity towards his passenger had softened. Simon pulled up into a small car park at the western end of a pretty quayside and sat, for a few moments, just enjoying the feeling of Jennifer's sleeping head, which was now snoring softly, as it rested against his shoulder. She smelt faintly of cherries. Her sleeping face had lost some of its natural contrariness and she looked rather sweet, and peaceful, as she snuffled up against him.

A slight bruise was visible above her eye and he found himself wondering how she had received it. Being preoccupied with that, Simon would later say, was why it did not occur to him to wonder how Jennifer had known that he was thinking about her sunglasses in the first place. He nudged her awake, gently.

"We're here" he said softly.

Jennifer opened her eyes, sleepily, and stretched out her arms like a fat ginger tom-cat. She yawned, widely, before looking at Simon as if seeing him for the first time. Then she frowned.

"Oh it's you. Right, where did we get to then? Oh yes!" She sat up. "Do you prefer a surprise kick, or should I be taking a run-up?"

Chapter Three
"Rubber gloves"

"Right. So, just to be clear, you have no money, don't know anybody here and have nowhere to stay? Fantastic." Simon's patience was wearing a little thin as, two minutes after waking, Jennifer Pettifyr had become seriously annoying without really having to stretch herself. "Where, if you don't mind my asking, were you planning to stay tonight?"

"I don't know, Simon. I thought I'd get a room or something. It's not my fault you took so fucking long to get here, is it? Don't shout at me. I've got credit cards you know, I'm not a complete tool... and anyway," the lady looked around, "what sort of two-bit piece of shit town doesn't have a hotel?"

"This one, and it's late, so keep your bloody voice down!" Simon's irritation really stemmed from his absolute certainty that, not only was he about to cave in and offer this woman his spare room (because, deep down, he was not a complete shit) but also that his passenger had sussed this out and was, therefore, just finding the whole situation extremely funny.

"Calm down, Simon." Jennifer hefted her bag out of the car and gave the roadster's door an almighty and unnecessary slam just to annoy its owner a little further. "Your sofa will be fine. Thank you very much for your kind offer. Anyway, I won't be staying long." Too fucking right you won't, thought Simon.

They stomped along the quay in silence until, after one hundred yards, Simon had to resist a powerful urge to punch Jennifer in the face when she enquired, loudly, whether he should have put some coins into the parking meter. It was at this point, for the record, that Jennifer's black eye ceased to be conceptually difficult for him.

Reaching the end of the quay, in pitch darkness now, they located a small cluster of holiday cottages. After some very slow progress, not really helped by Jennifer chuntering on about a new-fangled gadget she had read about, somewhere, called a fucking torch, Simon got them to the furthest cottage at the back. Fumbling in his pocket, for the envelope containing the keys, after a few false starts he got them inside.

The front door of the cottage opened directly into a small sitting-room containing a neat little sofa, with its back running along the left-hand wall, beneath an ornate gold-framed mirror. A comfy armchair sat in the corner, whilst the centre of the room was taken up by a long, low wooden coffee table. A half-dropped dining table and a couple of wooden chairs stood quietly against the far wall.

Simon put down his bag and located a side-lamp. A warm glow of light flooded into the room, making it instantly more inviting.

"Cocoa please!" barked Jennifer, dumping her bag and bottom down onto the sofa. Simon stared at her.

"I don't have any bloody cocoa! We've only just got here!" Jennifer raised an elegant middle finger in response and suggested, sweetly, that he might like to check out the kitchen cupboards.

Simon did so with ill grace and was annoyed to discover, along with a few basic staples presumably provided by the letting company, a small tin of drinking chocolate sitting smugly on the shelf. He took a deep breath, boiled the kettle and located a couple of mugs. Absolutely no thoughts about rat poison passed through his mind.

Mercifully, once mollified with a hot beverage, Simon's guest proved herself to be remarkably low maintenance. Jennifer hauled off her red leather boots and sprawled back onto the old sofa, leading Simon to register once again that she was an extremely good-looking woman. At least, when her mouth was not moving. He found himself wondering what the hell she was doing in such a remote part of Devon. Jennifer, for her part, was content just to wriggle her toes and, having also extricated herself from her green leather jacket (giving Simon his first view of an unexpectedly muscular pair of arms), she stretched herself out and yawned like the Dartford tunnel. She gazed across at her host.

"I'm here on business" she stated, a feat of mind-reading which almost caused Simon to drop his drink. Reaching into her back pocket (at least that was where he hoped it had come from) Jennifer whipped out a small rectangle of card and flicked it, with frightening accuracy, over the room onto Simon's lap.

He picked it up and was confronted with a business card.

Pettifyr's Preternatural Investigations

This meant less than nothing to him. On the back was a London telephone number and a random coat of arms containing a Latin inscription which Simon was too rusty to decipher.

"So, what brings you to Devon? Bursands is a pretty remote place and you don't, well, you don't exactly look like a tourist." What was he saying? That was exactly what she looked like. Every B&B owner's worst nightmare.

"I told you, Simon" she said lightly. "Business. I'm here on a case." Jennifer consulted her nails and, finding one of them letting the side down, tutted and began to hunt through her bag for some gadgetry to rectify the problem. Simon did his best to ignore the eclectic assortment of tampons, vodka miniatures and animal print underwear being scattered across the floor.

"What do you investigate then?" asked Simon. Frankly, he found it difficult to credit the creature in front of him (which, having located its quarry, had begun to apply an offensive shade onto an elevated middle finger which, incidentally, seemed very much at home in that position) with the attention span, never mind the social graces, required to hold down employment.

Jennifer looked up and, for the first time, Simon was unsettled by the expression on her face. She became almost unnaturally still. Her emerald green eyes fixed him with a look of such obvious, undisguised, intelligence that it quite silenced him.

"Things that go bump in the night, Simon" she said shortly. "And I'm not talking about your headboard."

She returned to her nails.

"What. Ghosts?!"

"Yeah, right." The redhead got up from the sofa and began to tidy her things back into her bag. "Obviously, there's nothing that little Jennifer loves more than dragging her sporty little arse around the British countryside chasing ghoulies, goblins and generally pandering to the fantasies of the great unwashed, attention-seeking, low-IQ British public."

She looked up and pointed at him. "That was ghoulies with an 'h', by the way, just in case you're hoping that we're back on your balls again. Yes, Simon, obviously that's how I like to spend my time."

Rant seemingly over, Jennifer jumped up from the floor and back onto the sofa, slightly overestimating its strength and underestimating her own weight in the process. Both parties survived the encounter intact but remained more respectful of each other thereafter.

"So you're *not* a ghost hunter then?"

Clarification seemed worth the risk of another caustic put-down but Jennifer displayed a rare moment of mercy. Perhaps, Simon wondered, she had used up her quota of sarcasm for the day. Had he known her better he would have realised that something was definitely up, as the concept of little Jennifer passing up an opportunity to put in the verbal boot was quite unheard of in the Pettifyr household.

"No Simon. I am not a ghost hunter. Neither, incidentally before you go there, is it anything to do with babies" she added bizarrely.

"Babies??"

"Gynaecology."

"What? You're a gynaecologist?"

Simon stared at her. She looked much more like a tourist now.

"No! Bloody hell, why do I bother? No, Simon, I don't play around with girls' bits for a living nor, as we're on the subject, in my spare time either despite what my mother tells her friends. I only mentioned it because, well, a lot of people do not appear to understand what 'preternatural' means and, instead, they book appointments for me to 'take a quick look at their bump'. I don't know why this is. I just get it a lot."

Jennifer stuck her arms behind her head and looked pensive. She consulted her nails again and gave him another stare. "I presume it's because most people are fucking ignoramuses!"

"Ah. I see" said Simon. Some light was finally beginning to penetrate through the dark murky fog of Jennifer's verbal diarrhoea. "Pre-natal, perhaps? Rather than ante-natal? Maybe that's their confusion? Anyway, so you're basically just a lesbian lady-parts doctor then?"

Jennifer balled a fist.

"That was a joke" Simon said hurriedly. "I will confess to not knowing what preternatural means though. Ignoramus I can manage, being one."

"Right. Well. OK then." Jennifer's fist stood down.

"I was forgetting your legendary sense of humour. Anyway, just to close this question off, once and for all, I do *not* make a living from putting my hands inside pregnant ladies despite, I might add, their best efforts at enticing me into it."

She rested her arms behind her head.

"I tried it for about a month as, well, the girls had bothered to make the trip and I do like to be helpful but, really you know Simon, I do think that you need a bit of training to do that kind of thing properly. The rubber gloves were expensive too…" Simon looked aghast. Jennifer frowned at him. "That, also, was a joke. Better than yours too, if we're keeping score. Which I am, incidentally, because I like to win."

Jennifer pulled her knees up to her chin and, looking suddenly much younger than her actual twenty-nine years, gazed across at Simon with a mischievous twinkle in her elfin green eyes.

"I look into things which don't make sense, Simon. Anything which doesn't, at face value at least, have an obvious explanation. In short," she looked serious for a moment, "I stick my little nose in. I'm like that monkey-typewriter thing, Simon. If I irritate enough people, for a long enough period of time, I usually find out what's going on."

She scratched her nose.

"Which, nine times out of ten, is sweet fuck-all."

"And the one time out of ten?"

"I don't know, Simon. This is my tenth case." Jennifer yawned. "If I include the pregnancies. Now, where's the toilet please? I need a wee."

Whilst the lady relieved herself (rather noisily) in the downstairs lavatory, Simon tactfully decided to check out the upstairs. Thankfully, after heading up a short creaking wooden staircase, he was confronted by two separate bedrooms, both of which had been made up with fresh linen and towels. Whilst Simon was starting to warm to his lady visitor, he had not entirely forgotten her apparent side-interest in testicular punishment. A locked door, he surmised, would definitely help him to sleep more soundly.

Hearing a flush, he returned to the sitting room to find Jennifer lying back on the sofa with her strong arms now folded behind her head and her firm legs crossed and up on the arm-rest. The combination of her obvious physical strength and the faint bruise above her eye lent her an animalistic air which Simon, somewhat to his surprise, found rather arousing.

"So, what is your case then?" he asked.

Jennifer had closed her eyes. He watched her for a few seconds, unsure whether she had fallen asleep. Then she spoke. "Come with me tomorrow and find out for yourself. I don't suppose you have a blanket, do you?"

It took Simon a few seconds to realise that she was expecting to be sleeping on the sofa for the night. "Oh. Sorry. No, you can come upstairs. You don't have to sleep down here…"

Jennifer looked at him, warily, and he realised the interpretation that she may have placed upon his words. "I mean, sorry, there are two bedrooms. Upstairs. You have your own room. The one on the left has a sea view, if you want that one?"

Simon pointed to the stairs and they looked at each other for a few moments until Jennifer got up, hoisting her bag from the floor. They parried briefly at the foot of the staircase before Jennifer took the initiative and trotted up first. Outside her room she turned though and, clutching her bag to her chest, she suddenly bounced up onto her tip-toes.

"Thank you" she said quietly.

With that, they bade each other good-night.

Chapter Four

"Clandestine excrement"

This is, perhaps, a sensible point at which to cover off a few salient matters of which Simon was quite unaware. Firstly, Jennifer was, as she had informed him, down in Devon on business Secondly, the lady was expecting trouble. That would be why, buried beneath her spare pants and the other miscellaneous crap in her Italian overnight bag, she was carrying a small and rather unusual pearl-handled revolver named Jessica. Trouble, you see, was very much Ms Pettifyr's business.

A few days earlier, the lady in question could be found ensconced, in the warm embrace of a deep red leather armchair, in the quietest corner of a frighteningly exclusive private members' club located a few streets back from Piccadilly Circus. She cut a curious figure with her fiery red curls, black trouser-suit tailored beautifully to her athletic body, smart black heels and a vicious brute of a black eye which was hiding discretely behind a rather piratical eye patch. Her heels sat quietly next to her chair like an obedient dog whilst their owner, legs tucked beneath her, nursed an over-sized scotch and listened intently to the man sitting opposite.

Her companion was a well-dressed, handsome and rather elegant middle-aged man with dark hair slicked neatly back behind his ears. He wore a well-tailored, dark-blue three piece suit carrying the faintest of pinstripe, and spoke with an accent that was pure English public school but with none of the natural arrogance which so often accompanies it.

"I'm afraid that the reports are quite compelling" the man said, taking a delicate sip of his drink. "Our mutual friend is very much alive, I'm afraid." This statement caused Jennifer to stir and roll her eyes upwards towards the heavy portraits adorning the racing green walls above her companion's head. She bit her lip and swirled the ice around in her glass.

"That's unfortunate. I thought I'd finished off the little shit." Her companion smiled, amused as he always was by the lady's colourful choice of language. He had been dealing with her for about two years and had grown rather fond of his most informal, and certainly most unpredictable, sometime agent.

"You handled yourself extremely well in Venice. We were," he took a sip of whisky, "extremely satisfied with the outcome. It is a little unfortunate that our friend did not, in fact, meet his maker but that in no way detracts from the success of your efforts."

Jennifer snorted. "I made a pig's ear of it."

Her companion smiled. Knowing the facts of the case, he was well aware that the lady was being more than a little hard on herself. "Whatever you made, it worked. I am also extremely glad that you managed to get out in one piece yourself. It was looking… problematic. How is the eye, by the way?"

Jennifer wafted away his concern like cigar smoke. If they thought so bloody highly of her, she thought wryly, how about a little more cold, hard cash for putting her sporty little booty on the line then? She took another sip of her drink, appreciating its quality, and hitched her legs up more tightly underneath herself.

"So, what's the flap this time?"

"Well now, Mr Collins has received some rather disturbing information this morning which has put him right off his tea and toast and, as you are aware, he is not a man generally prone to overreaction." Jennifer nodded. On the rare occasions upon which he had graced her with his presence, Collins had appeared to be the human embodiment of not so much a cold fish as a three-week dead turbot with a personality disorder. His intelligence, however, was second to none. Brinkley, the man sitting across from her, was certainly the more socially-acceptable face of whichever government body the pair of them represented. To Jennifer they referred to themselves simply as Trinity, leading her to wonder whether a third party operated somewhere in the background. He was speaking again. "How familiar are you with the Devon coast, Miss Pettifyr? The south in particular."

Jennifer shook her fiery head.

"Arse-end of nowhere, isn't it?" she responded, hoping that he wasn't a local. He had exactly the type of expensive accent which someone trying to lose their own might acquire.

"You're thinking of Cornwall."

Brinkley paused to allow Jennifer to enjoy his joke, however the lady was a harsh crowd. He pressed on.

"There is a small operation, on the south coast down there, which is currently engaged on the development of some rather sensitive bits and bobs for our masters up the food chain." Jennifer caught his drift and tapped her nose conspiratorially.

"Secret shit?"

"Precisely. Clandestine, as you say, excrement. Now, whilst the detail of their work is, predictably, beyond all of our pay grades I can say that, in the broadest terms, the institute is engaged in electronics." He paused for another sip. "Miniaturisation. Giving the Japanese a run for their money. Anyway, we all know how cagey these scientific johnnies can be when it actually comes to committing themselves to anything. Slippery as eels in a bucket of jelly. Let us just say, Miss Pettifyr, that the recent results of their work have been positive."

"Oh, bloody hell, we're not all going to have to start carrying telephones around with us are we?" Jennifer found the constant pestering from her mother on the land-line difficult enough. At least she could lie and say she was out.

Brinkley smiled. "Nothing quite that awful. Anyway, the work itself is not actually the problem. It is one particular aspect of the latest report which has Mr Collins worried. It appears that there has been some… interference." He took another sip of his scotch.

"Interference?"

"Disruption, Jennifer. May I call you Jennifer, by the way?"

"Call me what you like" responded Jennifer. "I don't answer to twat-face, though. That's my sister." Brinkley raised an eyebrow.

"Right… Jennifer. Unexplained accidents. Breakages. Graffiti."

"It wasn't me."

"The institute is an extremely small and self-contained unit. It would appear, unless something truly bizarre is going on, that there is a rotten apple in their barrel. We would like the disturbances to stop. Our masters, shall we say, wish to protect their not inconsiderable investment."

"A rotten apple. You want me to do a bit of bobbing around and fish it out?" Jennifer went to sip her drink but, finding her glass to be empty, waggled it up in the air to attract the attention of the bartender. Once contact was established, she returned her attention to Brinkley.

"In a word, yes. If you are not otherwise engaged, of course."

Given that all Jennifer currently had in her social diary was the continual avoidance of her mother and putting off a visit to the dentist, a trip to Devon sounded like Disneyland. "Oh, go on then."

A waiter quietly stepped up to replenish their drinks. It was the form at Brinkley's club for drinks to be constructed table-side, rather than at the ornate art deco bar. Jennifer approved of this, firstly, because she enjoyed the theatre of cocktail construction. Secondly, it gave her a chance to snaffle the bottle.

She treated the man to what was (in her eyes, at least) her finest trouser-stiffening eyelash flutter. "Just leave the bottle, chum. We're here for the long haul." The waiter nodded politely. After a glance towards Brinkley (not from any sexist stand-point but because, when push came to invoice, it was he and not the lady boxer who would be footing the bill), he parked the horrifically-expensive spirit down on the table next to Jennifer's right hand.

Result. Brinkley then brought Jennifer up to speed.

The Bursands Institute was located on a small outcrop of land a short distance along the coast from the village from which it took its name. The outcrop was connected to the mainland via a half-mile or so stretch of beach which apparently flooded at high-tide. An old wartime hospital had been converted into a laboratory together with living quarters for the small group of scientists based there. Food and provisions were brought over each week either by boat or driven across the sand during low-tide.

The last report from the institute had revealed that a series of breakages, accidents and graffiti had been disrupting the work for several months. The Director of the Institute had tried to manage the problem locally but had now asked whether some form of independent investigation could be undertaken, discreetly of course, in order to put an end to the disturbances and, hopefully, to exonerate the scientists from any suggestion of complicity. Brinkley and Collins had thought of Jennifer.

At the end of all this Jennifer Pettifyr stood up and, half in jest, made to sweep the whisky bottle into her bag. Brinkley nodded at her. "Take it, please. Keep in touch through the usual channels. By the way," he glanced up, "the usual rates have been increased. Also, if you run into trouble down there, don't try to go it alone."

Jennifer, busily trying to fit the whisky bottle into her bag without breaking either it or her perfume, nodded. Once baby was safely in its cot she shook Brinkley's hand with her curiously formal handshake.

"Right then," she said sweetly. "Let's do this shit."

Chapter Five

"Biscuit"

Jennifer slept lightly in the cottage but was well-rested by the time she awoke at eight o'clock on the following morning. She luxuriated in the warm bed for a few minutes, enjoying her unfamiliar surroundings and thinking about the rather handsome man in the next room. It did not sound as if he was awake yet. She briefly contemplated tip-toeing in and smacking him in the face with a pillow but thought better of it. Jennifer was sufficiently self-aware to know that most people utterly failed to appreciate her rather warped sense of humour. Her joking about his balls in the car had certainly fallen flat.

Needing a wee, she clambered out of bed and slung on her jeans before making her way downstairs for a nosey around. After using the downstairs loo and splashing some cold water onto her face, Jennifer located the cottage key on the mantelpiece and popped outside for a bit of fresh air.

The cottage was set back forty yards from a rather pretty quayside. It was at the end of a cluster of similar dwellings painted in an assortment of complementary pastel shades. Further down the quayside Jennifer could make out Simon's car (which, thankfully, did not appear to be clamped) and an old pub with a scattering of wooden tables outside. There was also a small, blue shack serving, presumably, food to the tourists.

Behind the cottage was a field. Jennifer spotted a narrow dirt track winding up through the ferns which presumably connected the village to the cliff-top coastal path. She struck off towards the track and, after fifteen minutes of hard climbing (and fourteen minutes of wishing she had put her fucking jacket on) Jennifer Pettifyr reached the top of the cliffs.

Pausing briefly to catch her breath, she looked around and was faintly surprised to spot the ruins of what appeared to be some sort of ancient chapel. It was roughly thirty feet long with a once-grand archway at one end and a small, narrow window at the other. Any of its original wood or glass had long been removed or had rotted away. The roof looked considerably holier than the building itself which just squatted unpleasantly in the shadows. Jennifer gave the gloomy structure a wide berth as she walked over to the cliff edge for a better view.

The climb had been worth the effort. The shining sea beneath her was dazzling. Bursands and its quay lay down to her left, whilst on the right she could see for miles along the coastline. In the very far distance sat a modern white lighthouse, hazy and peaceful, basking in the morning sunlight.

Jennifer looked down. Beneath her was a vertical drop of about a hundred feet to the crashing waves below. A vicious cluster of wickedly sharp rocks stuck out of the surf up towards her like the arms of drowning sailors. In the haze of the morning, and the swirl of the boiling foam, they almost appeared to be in motion, swaying and beckoning up to her.

Halfway between her current position and the far lighthouse lay what Jennifer had come up to the cliffs to get her first proper look at. A small outcrop jutted out into the sea and, from her position, Jennifer could make out a squat, white building at its centre with a few similar blocks dotted around it like Lego bricks. The tide was out and Jennifer could make out the stretch of golden causeway which Brinkley had described in London. It was a spectacular setting. Nipple-numbingly breezy, but spectacular.

As Jennifer turned around to make her way back down the path she discovered, suddenly, that she was not alone. A young man was now leaning against the wall of the stone chapel, watching her and smoking a cigarette. He appeared to be in his early-twenties with long, lank black hair and a pale, gaunt face. Thin and tall, he was slouching back against the masonry in a pair of faded black jeans and a dark leather jacket.

Jennifer walked back to the track and could feel the man's eyes following her. It was not a pleasant sensation. She almost expected him to say something, as she drew level, but he did not. As she continued however, still feeling his eyes on her back, she heard him emit a low but very distinct wolf-whistle followed by some muttered words which she did not catch.

Fucking locals, she thought to herself, and made her way back to the cottage. Thankfully, the man did not follow her. Unsettled, Jennifer checked the path behind her intermittently as she made her way down. Back on the waterfront, however, the incident was forgotten. Jennifer stopped at a small grocery store to acquire some food and the wherewithal to construct a decent cup of coffee (essentials, Jennifer!) before letting herself back into the cottage to find that Simon was now up, about and pottering around in the front room. Nice legs, she noted. Very nice thighs indeed. Pretty fit and still, she reflected, tall and handsome. Little Jennifer's day, she decided, was definitely looking up.

Simon, oblivious to being sized-up, was still half-asleep and craving caffeine so when Jennifer extracted a bag of coffee and a shiny little cafetiere from her shopping bag he could actually have kissed her. Remembering his manners and her interest in physical violence, however, he restrained himself. He took the bags and disappeared off to the kitchen. Jennifer still swears blindly that she did not, in any way, use this opportunity to take a good long look at his arse. That lady, it should be noted, lies about a great many things.

Breakfast was spent working out a plan of attack for the day. Simon had intended to motor over to the pretty coastal town of Shercombe however the prospect of accompanying Jennifer on her first visit to the bizarre little island rather appealed to him. He was, quite frankly, curious about what the hell she did for a living. He was also not quite such a bastard as to bugger off in the car leaving Jennifer at the mercy of the local bus service.

At ten o'clock, having driven the short stretch of the coastal road, they parked up outside a decent-sized pub located practically on the edge of the causeway. Jennifer noted that it also had rooms to rent which might be useful if she found herself suddenly needing accommodation. She had no false modesty about her ability to find herself turfed out of Simon's cottage, at minimal notice, for being a twat.

The tide was still out and they stood together on the front, listening to the seagulls and simply gazing out across the impressive arc of wet golden sand as it glistened warmly under the sunshine. A smattering of hikers and dog-walkers were striding out across it with long canes. After a tactical pit stop in the public toilets (these are real people, yes? Real people do have to urinate at reasonably regular intervals) they hit the slipway and struck out onto the beach.

The gloomy rock of the island loomed larger and darker in their vision as they approached it across what turned out to be a deceptively-long stretch of sand. It was a good twenty minutes before they arrived at the slipway on the other side and headed up a short tarmac path to a wire perimeter gate which was guarded by a metal box, mounted at waist-height, demanding a sequence of numbers in order to gain entry.

A small booth, matching the vintage white of the hospital, sat next to the barrier. Jennifer popped her head inside a soulless little office containing a wooden desk and chair, a metal filing cabinet and absolutely bugger-all to help her get through the gate. On the back wall was a large map of the Devon coast.

Re-joining Simon, Jennifer mulled over whether this was a good opportunity to indulge in a light spot of one of her favourite activities, namely breaking and entering. She had not walked for twenty minutes over a bloody beach just to be defeated by a locked gate. She chose to ignore Simon's observation, really quite crass and unhelpful as it was, that perhaps she should have telephoned ahead.

Pondering whether to turn back and telephone ahead and, if so, how to achieve this without it looking like Captain Smug's idea, the situation thankfully resolved itself in Jennifer's favour. A door suddenly opened in the distance, emitting a woman in a white coat who stomped over towards the gate.

She was heavy-set, with a bird's nest of grey hair thatched firmly onto the roof of an extremely high forehead. Jennifer found herself confronted by a pair of intelligent blue eyes nestling behind a thick pair of NHS spectacles. Under her coat the lady sported a dark brown pair of corduroy jeans, brown brogues and a mustard-yellow knitted jumper.

"Hello, hello!" she boomed in a deep voice. "Are you from the Ministry?" Simon looked at Jennifer. Ministry? Were his taxes paying for this?

"That's me!" replied Jennifer brightly, having frankly no idea. She might be from the Ministry. Jennifer was never entirely sure of her status when on Brinkley's business and she suspected, quite rightly as it happens, that this enabled him to deny all responsibility for her when she inevitably fucked things up. Extracting a business card, she poked it through the fence.

"Pettifyr. Jennifer Pettifyr. This," thumbing to the boy next-door, "is my glamorous assistant Simone." The lab-coat tittered at this and studied the card through her thick lenses. She peered at Jennifer as if she were an unfamiliar animal in a zoo.

"An interesting quotation, Miss Pettifyr. I will try to bear it in mind. Right then, let's get you inside and get a pot of tea on, shall we?" She manhandled the gate open, with some polite assistance from Simon, then led them up to the front door of the white building they had seen across the causeway.

Inside was a dark and musty corridor which reminded Simon very strongly of his old grammar school. Photographs on the old wooden walls gave a sense of the building's history. Amongst the stills of medical practitioners and photographs of the site during the war Jennifer noted some more modern shots of laboratory equipment. One picture showed the former Prime Minister cutting a tape on the front steps.

They were ushered briskly into a small office containing a well-stocked bookcase, a large wooden desk and a battered but comfortable-looking brown leather sofa. "Margaret Nicholson. Director. Pleased to meet you both." The lady gestured to the sofa. "Make yourself comfy, dears. I'll scare up some tea." Jennifer began to tell her not to go to any trouble but was swatted away. "I'm thirsty, even if you're not…" the deep voice echoed back to them as the little doctor stomped off down the corridor.

Jennifer inspected the bookcases. They took up an entire wall and were extensively stocked with scientific textbooks, medical journals and a few local histories.

In one corner there was a limited but significantly better-thumbed selection of pot-boilers, thrillers and a smattering of erotic fiction. Simon's attention was drawn to the desk, where a large, framed photograph of a handsome black Labrador took pride of place. He sat down and stretched his legs.

"Ministry?" he enquired towards Jennifer, who appeared to be thumbing straight to the juicy bits of one of the more salacious paperbacks.

"Need to know basis, darling. I could tell you, but then I'd have to…" Jennifer consulted the novel as if for inspiration. "Put your balls in a blender." She snapped the book shut and popped it back onto the shelf at the sound of returning footsteps. The little doctor bustled back in and dumped her significant backside onto her chair, splaying her feet wide for maximum stability. The chair appeared to be less stable than its owner and the manoeuvre looked, to Simon, like a very well-practised one.

"Right then, tea and biscuits are on the way." She indicated the door with a nod of her head. "Nancy had a fag to finish. God help us all if we interfere with that." She peered at Jennifer with interest. "Now, what can we do for you Miss Pettifyr? Or, perhaps more pertinently, what can you do to help us?"

Jennifer, looking far from saviour-like, was busily scratching away at her ankle. Bloody gnat bite! Where the arse had that come from? Poncing around in the ferns, presumably. She looked over at the scientist.

"Well, firstly, the basics, you know? Who you are, who does what, who's shagging whose dog, that kind of stuff."

Simon coughed and tried to avoid glancing at the photo on the desk. Jennifer glided on. "Also, the disturbances. In particular, which little weasel you think is responsible for them." Nicholson nodded vigorously at this but, before she could go any further, they were interrupted by the distinctive sound of a pair of heels coming along the wooden corridor outside. Presumably, this marked the arrival of their tea.

A moment later, a young woman walked into the room.

The first thing Simon noticed, from his advantageous seated position, was possibly the longest and most beautiful pair of legs that he had ever set eyes upon. They belonged to a striking-looking girl, of perhaps twenty years of age, with rich coal-black hair flowing down onto her shoulders. Her face was intense, slightly angular, with a prominent set of beautifully high cheekbones. She stared at Simon with the eyes of a large, wild cat. Stalking into the room, feline and untamed, she drew Simon's gaze to her like an industrial magnet.

Above a traffic-hazard of a skirt, the girl sported an equally dangerous tight white blouse. She was carrying a heavy silver tray, upon which sat three blue mugs and an open packet of chocolate digestives. Maintaining eye contact with Simon throughout, the girl made a show of leaning forward and depositing the tray down onto the coffee table treating him, as she did so, to a prolonged display of a cleavage into which empires and ancient civilisations may have fallen and burned into dust. A brief, slightly crooked, smile flashed at him, revealing a beautifully-even set of white teeth.

Simon was then hit with the scent of her perfume, which teased into his nostrils and which, combined with the faintest whiff of her cigarette smoke, took him straight back to school and fooling around with Michelle Cartwright behind the bike sheds. The things that girl could do with her...

"Biscuit please." A painful prod in the ribs interrupted him.

Simon frowned and passed Jennifer the packet. The dark-haired girl cast a disparaging look at the redhead before, having established that no further services were required of her (Simon could think of a few), taking her legs back to wherever angels choose to sit when not dispensing beverages. The room became a shade less exotic upon her departure, although her scent remained in the air to tantalise him.

Nicholson took a biscuit from the plate. She nibbled away, like a pensive hamster, and looked uncomfortably at Jennifer. "It's all a bit of a mess, really" she said, quietly. "In the cold light of day, I suspect that it just sounds a bit silly. I do wonder, you know, if I am just making a big fuss about nothing by reporting it?" Jennifer said nothing, allowing the woman to continue. This was not a tactical ploy, she just had a biscuit stuffed in her mouth.

The institute, Nicholson explained, had been running for five years. She had stepped up to the leadership role, eight months earlier, following the untimely death of her predecessor, a French scientist called Martine Dupuis. Dupuis had committed suicide.

Two months after this tragedy, when work and life had according to Nicholson been settling back to normal, a strange incident had occurred.

A fire had started, overnight, in the refectory.

It was highly fortunate that it had not spread any further because the alarm in the room had, quite deliberately, been disabled. At first, Nicholson had put the incident down to someone playing a silly practical joke which had gotten out of hand. Nobody had admitted responsibility and, to be honest, she could not imagine any of the staff doing anything quite so stupid or irresponsible.

If that had been the end of it, Nicholson told them, she would have forgotten all about it and chalked it up as a one-off piece of idiocy gone wrong. A few weeks later, however, graffiti had started to appear on the walls.

"This ought to be an exciting time, Miss Pettifyr." The little woman looked distraught. "I can't believe that one of us would want to spoil it. It's also rather frightening because, you see, the things on the walls were… well… vicious. We're a just little family here. The thought that one of us could be responsible for that filth, well… it's rather horrible."

She stopped and looked out of the window.

Jennifer felt rather sorry for her. Not quite so sorry that it stopped her inhaling a fourth biscuit. She sipped her tea which was, annoyingly as she had taken a quite instant dislike to the sharp-faced brunette, quite excellent.

Nicholson was still banging on.

"Five of us live here full-time. Myself, of course, then John and Linda are our head scientists. The Leightons." She noticed Jennifer's puzzled expression.

"Married, dear. Then there's Nigel Whittaker who is, well, I suppose you would describe him as an audio specialist. I've known Nige for donkeys' years. Absolute wizard. Then there's Barbara Porter, our radio expert. We're the full-timers. Oh, we also have a visitor. Martin MacKenzie is with us at the moment from Edinburgh. The professor. He has been conducting some research into our, erm, well he believes we may have a..."

The director looked uncomfortable.

Jennifer helped her out.

"A ghost, presumably. He's rather well-known in his field."

Nicholson nodded.

"Well, yes. Although, God knows what he expects to find here. Stuff and nonsense, Miss Pettifyr." Nicholson looked down her nose. "The only spirits on this island, I can assure you, are in that cupboard over there!"

She pointed towards the far corner of the room. Jennifer made a mental note as this was, to her mind, the first even vaguely important piece of intelligence that she had gathered so far. It also reminded her that it was nearly eleven o'clock and she mulled over whether it was unprofessional to ask for a G&T.

Along with the location of the alcohol Jennifer found Nicholson's attitude equally interesting. She pondered whether Nicholson was aware that, by rubbishing the supernatural, she was pointing the finger of blame quite squarely in the direction of her own colleagues. After all, the existence of a spirit-hand might have let one of the slightly less-deceased members of the household off the hook very nicely indeed.

"Finally, there's young Nancy. You just met her (legs eleven, thought Simon) but she lives on the mainland and only comes over to help out. Far too attractive for her own good, I dare say, but I don't think it's right to judge against a girl on that front. She's reliable enough. She's never been here when any of the trouble has happened. During the night, I mean."

They finished their tea and, still alcohol-free, went for a tour of the facility. Nicholson led them along the wooden corridor towards a set of double swing doors which opened out into a large hall. The room inside was lit by three overhead electric lamps. Four rectangular trestle tables, each covered with gingham cloth, occupied the centre of the room supported by a rag-tag assortment of mismatched wooden chairs. The walls supported Nicholson's graffiti story as it was clear that they had recently been scrubbed clean and certain sections re-painted. One of the corners was blackened, presumably by fire. At the far end there was an alcove and Jennifer poked her head inside.

It was a small kitchen containing a stove top, oven and free-standing refrigerator. A selection of enamel mugs sat draining, quietly, on the side of a large white porcelain sink. Not enough time to check the fridge for vodka, that would look suspicious. Gain their trust first. She re-joined the others and a side door took them out onto the gravel which surrounded all of the buildings.

The wind had picked up as they walked past a low, stone structure with a squat metal door before reaching another building. It was painted in the same uniform white as the hospital but was more modern, constructed from floor to ceiling in glass and wood.

As they approached, a rotund man was letting himself out of the front door. He was short with wavy blond hair and a pair of round spectacles perched upon a pudgy nose. Underneath a similar coat to Nicholson's, Jennifer noted a rather incongruous heavy metal band t-shirt.

"What's up Doc!" he waved at them. "How goes the battle?"

"Reinforcements have arrived!" bellowed Nicholson back. The fat man joined them. "Nigel, this is Miss Pettifyr from the Ministry and her assistant..."

"Simon. Pleased to meet you." He got straight in to block any further piss-taking from Jennifer Pettifyr and to save Nicholson the embarrassment of not being able to remember his name.

"They are here to... err, to help you know."

"Oh, I see. Excellent." The man's tone left Simon with the faint impression that fat Nigel Whittaker was not overly happy about their presence although he might simply be shy. He was certainly spending more time looking at his trainers than at them. "Let me know if I can help, won't you? Just nipping to the bathroom" said Whittaker, backing away.

"Weak bladder..." Nicholson apologised once he had gone. "Right, let's meet the others, shall we?" She held open the heavy glass door and ushered them through into a small foyer containing a water cooler, a small red fire extinguisher and not much else worth noting.

A long corridor led away to the left, ending at a gun-metal door. Ignoring it, Nicholson opened a second door immediately in front of them and led the way in.

The room had the air of a tatty student common-room. One leather armchair was occupied by a grizzly, grey-haired old man sporting a monumental set of moustaches. He was tapping away with his foot whilst nursing what appeared to be an enormous glass of scotch (a bit early for that, thought Simon, precisely mirroring Jennifer Pettifyr's own thoughts on the subject. A mirror, of course, reflecting the opposite of whatever you place in front of it). A cable connected the monster's head into a square metal box, presumably emitting sounds of some kind. He might have been plugged in for a recharge ten years earlier and left to gather dust.

Standing by the bookcase was a short, smart woman in a brown skirt, cream blouse and shoes so sensible that Simon would have trusted his baby sister with them. Her mousey hair was fashioned into a short bob and, like Nicholson, she sported a thick pair of spectacles. They could, thought Simon, be related.

On the sofa, reading a broadsheet newspaper, was a good-looking man with a lean, brown face and longish-dark hair swept rakishly over which seemed constantly at risk of falling down across his eyes. A faint suggestion of stubble troubled at his cheeks and chin. He was wearing dark chinos, a casual white shirt and a brown sports jacket. He continued holding his newspaper but looked up sharply as they entered.

The newspaper man was introduced as the first of the Doctor Leightons whilst the lady by the books was not his wife but Barbara Porter, the radio bod. She gave a wave which the redhead failed to notice as her attention was concentrated firmly upon the scotch. For fuck's sake, it was practically midday.

The gargoyle in the chair turned out to be Professor MacKenzie of ghost-hunting fame. The old codger growled and removed his headphones. Leaning forward, rather than getting up from the chair, he wafted his glass at them presumably in greeting although he might just have been requesting a re-fill.

The fumes confirmed Simon's suspicion about the scotch and he felt rather nauseated. Jennifer just thought that the old bastard was rubbing it in.

Suddenly the old man jerked into life.

"Totty!" he leered up wolfishly at Jennifer.

Nicholson was unamused.

"This lady is from the Ministry, actually, Martin." This was stated loudly and slowly enough to make it crystal-clear to everybody what she thought of both his mental faculties and his gender politics. "I'd say that our reputation here is poor enough right now without you adding sexual harassment into the mix, wouldn't you?" MacKenzie pulled a face as if somebody had shot his pet gerbil.

"No offence intended! Bark's worse than my bite."

The professor then offered up a horrible rictus grin, presumably by way of apology, which exposed an evil set of yellow-stained teeth and receding gums. The expression in no way suggested that he was either remotely sorry or that he wouldn't happily bury his teeth into Jennifer's buttocks the second that her back was turned.

Coughing, the old man then decided to indulge in what was, presumably, intended as a bit of low-level flirtation with the redhead. It wasn't the subtlest opening gambit.

"If I were thirty years younger I'd give you something to bite on…" Nicholson went nuclear. Confiscating his scotch and passing it to Jennifer for safe-keeping she bundled MacKenzie out of his chair, and out of the room, with a series of good hard verbal boots up his backside together with a few physical shoves to his back for good measure.

On her return, however, something strange had occurred. The scotch had disappeared. The empty glass was now sitting neatly upon the table. Jennifer looked around, hoping that Nicholson would chalk it up as just another mysterious event. Don't breathe on her, Jennie, and you've got away with that one.

A diversion was required though.

Jennifer clapped her hands.

"Right! How about a quick poke then?"

She pointed at Simon, who had raised an eyebrow.

"Around, I mean. Not sex. A tour, yes? Not a sex-tour either. Anyway, Simone can amuse herself whilst we're gone, can't you darling?"

Chapter Six

"Sad little ex-urinated husk"

One hour later, following a whistle-stop (and entirely sex-free) tour culminating in her being left alone in the laboratory, Jennifer Pettifyr was rather annoyed to admit to herself that she had, so far, managed to come up with precisely jack shit.

The place seemed entirely normal, dull even, and populated simply by a small group of nerds, none of whom Jennifer could imagine creeping about in the dead of night throwing books around, spraying graffiti or starting fires. She had taken against the girl Nancy right off the bat, but Jennifer was self-aware enough to know that this was for entirely personal reasons. Simon obviously fancied her anyway. Well, her big fat chest. Fucking men. As a result, Jennifer Pettifyr was now in a bad mood.

Her search had been ruthlessly thorough and utterly fruitless, revealing no hidden passages, creaking floorboards or anything else which might have explained the falling objects in the laboratory.

She bobbed up from the floor where she had been lying, face down, to inspect the underside of a metal cabinet. The lab was clean. Never a lady to remain depressed for too long, Jennifer decided to return to the common room for a bit of a re-think.

At that point, something rather unusual did happen.

On the bench at the back of the lab a glass boiling tube, which had been quietly minding its own business on a rack with its colleagues, decided to fall over and roll its way down from its previously satisfactory perch. It smashed loudly onto the bench below. Jennifer jumped at the noise and stared at the back of the room. Apart from her, it was completely empty. She went over to the bench and inspected the mess.

The shattered tube lay in sorry-looking pieces, clearly embarrassed by both its clumsiness and its sudden blatant disregard for the laws of physics. Jennifer collected up the broken glass and deposited it into a waste bin. After a brief inspection of the rack, satisfying herself that it was not about to offload the remainder of its occupants, she went back to the common room.

Things there were largely unchanged. Little Barbara Porter was now engrossed in a racy paperback thriller which had clearly, from its dog-eared state, seen a fair degree of active service. Probably, thought Jennifer, because of the heavy dungeon bondage scene on page ninety-five (Jennifer isn't clairvoyant, incidentally, she just happens to own the book. Her copy falls open at page ninety-five. Don't ask her why, or what the stains are. It was like that, apparently, when she stole it from the library). Leighton was still reading his paper but had made it through to the sports pages.

Jennifer coughed politely. "I'm afraid," she stated, "that some glass has broken in the laboratory. A test-tube or something. It fell down, you know…" The final bit was just to reassure them that she was not some sort of irresponsible little thug who enjoys going around to strange houses and breaking stuff. As noted earlier, Jennifer Pettifyr does tend to lie quite a lot. She loves breaking shit. Barbara Porter lifted her nose out of her book.

"Oh, don't worry yourself about that Miss Pettyjohn. That's just Matron." The scientist's nose returned to its paperback.

"Pettifyr" Jennifer corrected her, "and the room was empty. Does somebody else live here besides your team?"

The little scientist gave a snort of laughter.

"Not live, exactly. Matron's our resident spirit."

"Oh, for God's sake!"

John Leighton had been silent up until this point but now rolled his eyes and, slinging his newspaper violently onto the sofa, looked over grimly at his colleague. He offered a brief smile to Jennifer by way of apology. "Sorry, but thanks to my illustrious colleague over here (thumbing Barbara Porter) we've now been invaded by the mad drunken Scotsman and all of his technical quackery. It's bloody tiresome." He gave Porter a dark look. "It also reflects, rather poorly, on our reputations as scientists." Point made, he picked up his paper. "It's a crock of shit."

Barbara Porter, to be fair, wasn't about to take that kind of abuse lying down. "Oh really? The graffiti, then? Or when Linda got shoved down the stairs?" You go girl, thought Jennifer, who loved a good bitch-fight. Should have brought some popcorn.

"Barbara!" Leighton shook his head. "She wasn't pushed, she just fell over her bloody slippers! You know this. How many times? Unbe-fucking-lievable."

The position of his newspaper temporarily obscured Barbara Porter from John Leighton's view so he failed to benefit fully from the middle finger standing sweetly up in his direction. "Whatever, dick-head." Porter returned to her book. "Don't come running to me when something falls on your bloody head." Leighton muttered something offensive under his breath and got up to leave.

"I put the glass in the waste bin" Jennifer called to his retreating back, adding "Love to Matron!" just to wind him up. Barbara Porter chuckled. The two ladies were now alone together. Jennifer took Leighton's seat and, hoping to nick a cheeky one on the quiet, was annoyed to find that some killjoy had cleared away the scotch bottle. She looked over at the mouse and her paperback.

"Were you being serious just then? About the ghost, I mean?"

"Of course!" Barbara Porter put down her book (slightly reluctantly as she had reached page ninety-four) and gave Jennifer her full attention. "There's something wrong in that lab. It's creepy. I was in there once, height of summer, and my bloody breath started frosting! It smells rank sometimes too… enough to make you throw up." Jennifer thought, privately, that old MacKenzie might be responsible for that before remembering that he had only recently arrived. "The others might laugh, but you try and get one of that lot to spend a night alone in the lab. They would, pardon my French, shit their knickers. Myself included."

The little doctor came and sat next to Jennifer on the sofa.

"I'm not an idiot, despite what knob-head thinks. Objects, Miss Pettifyr, do not fall off flat shelves without the application of energy. Agreed?"

Jennifer nodded thoughtfully.

"That's fair enough, but what makes you think that it's the dearly departed doing the pushing?"

Porter warmed to what was clearly her favourite theme. "It's classic! I've been going all over this with Mac. Don't mind him, by the way. You get used to his bullshit. He's an old darling, really, terribly knowledgeable about ghosts and stuff. Anyway, this building..." she waved her arms around like a windsock, nearly smacking Jennifer in the face. "There have been reports of activity here for decades, long before we turned up. This was an old hospital you know. I mean, can you imagine how much pain, misery and suffering has been endured within these walls?"

"Tea was quite good." Jennifer said distractedly. She was wondering where a dead nurse would get hold of an aerosol can.

Porter frowned at her.

"Don't take the piss out of me, Miss Whatever-your-name-is! Bollocks to the Ministry. You've been here for five minutes. I've lived here for months and I've seen things which would turn your hair curl..."

She glanced at Jennifer's thick red locks.

"Straight!"

Jennifer reached into her back pocket and removed the last of her business cards, making a mental note to re-stock her bum cupboard. She handed it over to Porter.

"Actually, chum, I don't work for the Ministry. They just use my services occasionally and, to correct your earlier statement, I wasn't taking the piss. Believe me, if I had been then you would currently be a sad little ex-urinated husk on the floor because I don't indulge in half-measures."

Porter looked at the card and considered Jennifer afresh.

"Is ex-urinated a word? Really?" She peered at the card again. "Pettifyr's Preternatural Investigations. PPI. I like that, quite catchy. Anyway, whether you believe it or not, bloody peculiar things have been going on around here. So what, little Miss Smart-Bollocks, are you going to do about it?"

Chapter Seven

"Siren"

Left to his own devices (really quite rudely, he thought) Simon had decided to use his time productively by doing some exploring. The island had a few short stretches of cliff-top from which the views should be something quite special. As the alternative was to be stuck drinking tea with the nerds, whilst Jennifer did whatever a Jennifer does in these situations, a stroll in the sun had seemed like the much better option.

Getting his bearings outside, Simon had been surprised to notice a squat little lighthouse on the far side of the island. It was coated in faded stripes of red and white paint and was, presumably, disused. A more modern beacon had been flashing, further down the coast, when he and Jennifer had arrived on the previous evening. Rounding the corner of the main building, he had been very pleasantly surprised to discover the young woman who had served them tea in the doctor's office.

She had acquired a large pair of sunglasses and was now leaning back, casually, against the washed-out white wall smoking a cigarette. She inclined her head in his direction at the crunching of the gravel but showed no sign of embarrassment or any inclination to stop. Instead, she remained very still, watching him as he approached. Her long legs and heels made her very nearly as tall as Simon himself. He nodded a greeting.

"Nice day for it." Not his best line, to be fair. Quite a shit line, to be really fair. In his defence, it was sunny (so give him marks for factual accuracy) and he was distracted by the legs.

The girl didn't move her body at all but spoke quite clearly in response. "It's a lovely day for it. Stuck at work though, aren't I?" she purred like a kitten. The somewhat suggestive sentence hung, along with the cigarette smoke, in the air between them. The girl spoke very slowly and with a strong local accent. The sing-song lilt of her voice, Simon thought, could make the shipping forecast sound filthy. After taking another sensual drag, she offered him her cigarette. "Fancy a go on it?" she asked.

Simon hadn't smoked since school, but he took an exploratory drag trying, quite spectacularly unsuccessfully, to look like James Dean. Predictably, he just coughed his guts up. The girl laughed loudly and took the poisonous object back, before depositing some ash onto the gravel with a sharp tap.

"You're not very good, are you Mister London?" she said lightly. "Need some practice, I reckon." Stamping the butt onto the ground with her heel, she tapped him on the forearm. "Come on, handsome. Follow me."

She began to stalk her way towards the cliff-top, affording Simon an unashamed view of her legs and a voluptuous backside imprisoned, presumably for the safety of wider society, within the confines of her short black skirt. Simon followed, watching her hips as they swung from side to side with the grace and confidence of a professional model.

The girl stopped at the edge of the cliff and stood still, for a moment, enjoying the sunshine. They looked out in silence at the dark blue-green spray of the surf and the slow progress of the assorted little boats going about their business on the water. A seagull, swooping low, cried out as it soared down towards the water before settling itself onto the surface. It was some time before the girl spoke again. "I'm Nancy."

Simon introduced himself, but the girl cut him off with a touch on his arm which, in its casual intimacy, felt like an electric shock. "I know who you are" she said softly, moving closer so that once again he received the perfume and nicotine hit to his groin. "I asked as soon as I saw you, Simon. We don't get many good-looking men around here. A girl could go mad in these parts..."

"A beautiful lady like yourself must get a lot of attention."

Simon was distracted by her scent, her hypnotic voice and the sheer power of her physical proximity. Nancy removed her sunglasses and looked directly at him. She was the most naturally-beautiful girl that Simon had ever seen. Her eyes were dark, enormous and accentuated the angles cut by her elegant high cheekbones. It was quite impossible to draw his eyes away from her face, so he did not try.

"Beautiful, am I?"

A playful smile touched the faintly crooked line of her full lips. Her chest was almost touching him now and a simple gold chain around her neck pulled his eyes downwards. At the end of the chain a small gold key nestled contentedly at the summit of her cleavage. She was tanned summer-brown beneath the open collar of her bright white shirt and a small scar, about an inch in length, ran along the part of her throat which would be most natural for him to bend down and kiss.

Embarrassed, Simon raised his eyes back to her face and back into the fierce intensity of her animal eyes. In the bright sunlight they were as raven-black as her hair but remained no more readable than when hidden behind her glasses.

The wind had picked up again. As they stood still, looking at each other, it began to whip the long strands of Nancy's black hair around both of their faces. The girl's expression seemed to invite him to action but Simon was instinctively wary. Her siren lips made him think of the beautiful razor-sharp rocks swirling and boiling in the surf beneath their feet. He imagined himself diving down and being torn apart on them.

Chapter Eight

"Government Health Warning"

Jennifer took her leave of Barbara Porter (after the little scientist, consulting her wristwatch, had sworn loudly and rushed off back to the lab). Alone in the common room, she hunched down into the old sofa and mulled over what she had learned.

The bones of Porter's account mirrored what Brinkley had told her in London although there was a subtlety. Jennifer noted that the glass breakages had all taken place in the laboratory, whereas the 'proper' damage (in her eyes, anyway, being a bit of a connoisseur when it came to wanton destruction), the fire and graffiti, all happened in the main building. Jennifer was unsure what, if anything, that meant. Probably, she decided, arse-all.

Porter had mentioned that the island had a long and turbulent history which had fascinated local scholars for decades if never quite generating any national interest. Its story dated back at least as far as the eighteenth century, where legend had the island down as the epicentre of local smuggling activities at the turn of that century. Bollocks to all that, though. It was the graffiti which bothered Jennifer.

In addition to the refectory fire, various obscene and threatening messages had been scrawled in yellow paint onto the walls of the refectory. To Jennifer's mind, the other events might be attributable to structural quirks or simply to an over-active imagination. Spraying filth onto a wall, however, required a very much not-dead hand holding an aerosol can. One of these nerdy little fuckers was lying through their bottom and, worse than that, might be potentially dangerous.

Porter had also told her more about Linda Leighton falling down the stairs. Nancy, apparently, had been cleaning the bedrooms and heard a shout from the stairwell. Barbara Porter had found Linda in a heap at the foot of the stairs. Porter insisted that she had said something like "pushed me" but Linda later insisted that she had tripped over her own feet. This event, although seemingly unrelated to the graffiti, was the only daytime incident of note.

The last of the scientists, the second Doctor Leighton of staircase fame, Jennifer had encountered briefly whilst the laboratory was being cleared for her. The married lady was a tall, slender blonde in her mid-thirties and quite good-looking if a bit drippy-bohemian. Quasi-normal anyway, thought Jennifer. For a scientist. Jennifer's main takeaway from the whole morning was that the island was a fucking damp and depressing place. Most disturbingly of all she had still not been offered a proper drink.

Restless, Jennifer got to her feet. She had agreed to return the following day and stay overnight (and bring a fucking bottle, yes? Mental note, Jennie).

Privately, she was unconvinced what good her presence would achieve (many people, incidentally, have had exactly the same thought over the years, usually when compiling the invitation list for parties). All the little vandal had to do to escape detection was to sit on his or her greasy little hands for a few days. Jennifer's best hope was if the culprit were such an arrogant little sod as to act whilst she was actually in situ. In any event, the longer she stayed the better chance she had to get to know the residents. That, if nothing else, might reveal something.

There was also, she remembered, her appointment in Shercombe that afternoon which might bear some fruit of its own. Jennifer consulted her watch. Plenty of time if Simon got his bloody arse back. Where was he? She needed his car. Jennifer liked Simon. She didn't show it, but she liked him very much indeed. Not exactly Brain of Britain but he was bloody good-looking and he didn't seem to object, unlike most of humanity, to her stupid sense of humour. A bit young, she thought, but there could be something there. Maybe she should ask him out on a date. Presumably he lived in London. She smiled, happily, wondering where the nice man in question had taken himself off to.

Jennifer did not have to wonder for long as, looking out of the window, she was faced with the sight of the cheating bastard himself walking back towards her with a big fat grin plastered onto his cheating big face, arm in arm and deep in conversation with, who fucking else, but tea-bitch.

Calm yourself, Jennie, she told herself.

Over-reaction helps nobody.

"And where the exact fuck have you been?"

Jennifer's warm welcome took place approximately thirty seconds after window-gate once the turd had the temerity to walk into the common room as if butter wouldn't melt in his mouth. At least, Jennifer noted, Nancy had fucked off out of her warpath. Presumably the little twat had returned to the refectory to get back to as little bloody work as she could get away with.

"What? I've been out walking. Has something happened?"

"We're leaving."

Jennifer stomped out.

Ever since her deeply unhappy boarding school days during which she had endured years of quite relentless bullying by the older, prettier and less-ginger girls, Jennifer Pettifyr had never had many friends. She had developed, through necessity, a very thick skin and a monstrously powerful right hook as a consequence of her upbringing but she had never quite mastered the difficult art of holding her emotions in check.

Jennifer's inability to articulate her feelings was very much the main reason why she had never, really, had a proper boyfriend. That and the constant threat of impending physical violence that seemed to travel around with her. Her few attempted relationships had all ended badly, for Jennifer at least, with her being dumped unceremoniously onto her athletic backside. She always got up again (she was a Pettifyr girl, after all, and those little fuckers never stay down for long) but she had picked up a few bumps and bruises from the canvas.

The sulking Jennifer walked straight out of the front door, down through the perimeter gate and down to the concrete slipway. She hit the causeway with long strides and a black mood. Keeping a safe distance behind, unsure quite how he had managed to piss on her chips this time, Simon followed cautiously. Having seen her arm muscles he did not really fancy being on the receiving end of a Pettifyr knuckle-sandwich. Guiltily, as he was genuinely concerned about the redhead being upset, his thoughts strayed back to Nancy. The muskiness of her scent and the intensity of her eyes… the thrill of being up close to her body… her lips.

Simon's timing was unfortunate, as Jennifer had actually stopped walking to enable him to catch up. He cannoned straight into her bum and barrelled her down onto the sand. This went down really, really well.

"Fucking HELL Simon!" she bellowed up at him, backside firmly beached. Simon apologised and tried to help her up but Jennifer was so strong that she nearly dragged both of them down.

Finally, getting her upright, he ended up with the top of her fiery head pressing into his chest. His hand was supporting her lower back and it was an unexpectedly intimate position. Holding on to her, Simon could feel the considerable strength in her compact frame. She was breathing heavily. To his surprise, Jennifer made no immediate move to disengage. Instead she nestled, panting like an ageing red setter, until after about a minute she popped her head up.

Simon found himself looking down into a very moist pair of green eyes which were now no longer angry at all. Just very sad.

"Sorry" Jennifer said, quietly. "Tantrum."

She looked so childlike and vulnerable that Simon was caught quite completely off-guard. "That's OK" he said. "I'm sorry too." Being this close to Jennifer was totally different to his encounter on the cliffs with Nancy. Simon felt, again, a tug of attraction towards the rather strange woman. The instinct to run his fingers through her flaming red hair was suddenly almost irresistible.

"Ha!" squeaked Jennifer, popping out of his embrace. "Friends again, then?" Simon accepted her curious formal handshake. Then he frowned. "I'm rather afraid," he said sombrely, "that you've got sand all over your arse."

"Well you shouldn't be looking at my arse, should you Simon? It comes with a government health warning." Jennifer twisted her neck to inspect the posterior damage. "Anyway, shall we save the 'Jennifer gets a sandy crack' scene for after we've solved the case, yes? You don't find James Bond with his arse in the sand before he blows up the enemy base, do you Simon? No" Jennifer asserted, with possibly the most factually-incorrect statement ever uttered by anybody.

"That's because he's always on top."

"You're a very dirty boy. Now, come along."

She bounced off happily.

As the pair of them made their way back to the car park they were unaware that their progress across the sand was being observed from a tiny, upper window of the sadly-derelict lighthouse on the island behind them.

A figure stood motionless in the window, watching them as the tide, which would shortly seal off the island from the mainland for the afternoon, began gently to lap across the golden arc of sand, creating ripples across its glittering surface. As Jennifer Pettifyr made her way back to shore, the figure drew out the knife it had been fingering in its pocket and began, very slowly, to lick the blade.

Chapter Nine
"Difficult customer role-play"

After a pit stop at the pub for Jennifer to address the worst of her wardrobe problem (and for yet another wee) Simon drove them back to the cottage. They showered and consumed a delicious lunch of Devon crab and crusty bread which Jennifer had conjured up out of nowhere ('nowhere' being a spot of hard flirting and queue-jumping at the seafood shack on the quayside) whilst Simon was in the shower.

One hour later the pair were driving (ball-achingly slowly in Jennifer's opinion, which she was helpfully sharing) back to the coastal road. With the roof down, the lady's hair was billowing so fiercely that a good hard push on the accelerator would probably para-glide her right out of the vehicle. Unless she shut up about his driving, Simon was tempted to try it.

"Destination Shercombe!" Jennifer boomed loudly into his left ear, nearly causing him to crash into a hedge. His corrective action was firm enough to smack Jennifer's head into the window pane, giving Simon at least (and this does reflect poorly upon his character) some payback for her constant carping. He wasn't quite stupid enough to share his amusement with the lady herself.

"Watch the road, numb nuts!" Jennifer bellowed.

"Perhaps if you stopped shouting, I could concentrate…"

"Perhaps if you grew a pair and became less shit I wouldn't need to?!" shouted Jennifer above the road noise. "Seriously, Simon, you drive like I make love."

The redhead sat back and folded her arms.

"Too close to the car in front?"

"No, Simon, infrequently and with dog-shit technique." Now, Jennifer could have just left that one out in the wind but she felt the need to expand. "Obviously, you think you're brilliant but, really, you're just putting lives at risk." She huffed on. "Nobody ever wants to get in twice. Despite your having invested in all the fancy equipment."

Jennifer gestured, with her arm, around the cabin of car.

"Like that stereo, for example."

"You're more than welcome to drive…"

Simon's olive branch, however, was flaccid today.

"Don't start getting all Mrs Pissy-Pants with me, Simon. I've had a rather difficult few days, you see, and I'm on a very short fuse right now. Rocket Jennifer, you might say, is nearing take-off and she is pointing right up your arse right now!"

There was a small pause.

"And…" she carried on, "she is one of those old-school sharp pointy ones, yes?" Simon just said nothing. He was starting to learn. "Not like the space shuttle. Which is smooth, you know…" Nearly there, hopefully. "Until the wings, obviously. The wings would bite like a bitch."

Simon drove on grimly, wondering what, exactly, he had done wrong in a previous life. Ten minutes later his companion piped up though and came out with what was, with the benefit of hindsight, the only comment during the entire journey which actually made any sense.

"Anyway, if you're driving I can get shitted."

The sun was shining brightly in Shercombe as Simon found a small car park in the centre of town. Jennifer's mood had also lifted and the redhead had bounced out like a puppy released from kennels. She had even opened Simon's door for him. As he got out, however, she didn't (as would have been normal for a normal person) move backwards to leave any room for him.

This absence of movement resulted in his exiting the car straight into Jennifer Pettifyr's personal space, which many will tell you is not an area generally considered advisable to loiter in. His guard went straight up.

"Everything... OK?"

They were practically at kissing distance. Perspective is, of course, everything as he was also within ball-breaking distance and, given his experiences to date, that really should have been his first concern. Eye-balling him, Jennifer put her sunglasses on, very slowly, and prodded his chest with a painted forefinger.

"You see, Simon, I'm just a pussy-cat really."

She was very close to him now.

"Oh yes?"

"Yes, Simon."

She poked him in the chest again.

"There's nothing I like better than taking a shit on somebody else's lawn. Let's get to work, shall we?" Jennifer strode off across the tarmac until, after a hundred yards, she again suggested he go back and put some money on the meter. This time however, very much to his surprise, Simon was rather aroused by the bossiness.

Failing miserably to stop at the ice cream shop (which Simon noted purely because he fancied an ice cream) Jennifer bustled down the street at a rate of knots, her thick red hair bouncing in the breeze. Once the car was sorted, Simon jogged to catch up.

This was easy to do because the lady had stopped, half-way down the street, and was peering intently through the window of a small local spirits shop.

She consulted her wrist watch.

"We're early. Come on, let's kill some time. I'm thirsty."

Jennifer ducked up a side alley and into a building behind the shop. Taking the chic industrial stairs two at a time, she located the bar in approximately two seconds flat. The females of the Pettifyr brood, incidentally, seem to have a quite superhuman ability to do this kind of thing. Some attribute it to a sense of hearing attuned, over centuries, to the clinking of ice cubes. Others point to a sense of smell so well-developed that they can sniff out some juniper from a hundred paces.

Either way, the member of staff with the misfortune to be on duty that afternoon turned around from glass-washing to find Jennifer Pettifyr, still sporting her sunglasses, perusing the drinks menu.

"Can I get you a drink, madam?"

This is perhaps another sensible point at which to provide some further colour to flesh out the reader's understanding of the customer at the bar. The concern being that, taken purely at face value, she might just appear to be a bit of a sarcastic cow. Which, playing devil's advocate for a moment, she is. I mean, totally.

Behind the rudeness, however, there is often motive. There is frequently planning and usually misdirection. One may find oneself asking, perhaps, is this a character that she is playing? Is she intending to provoke a reaction? I'll leave that with you to ponder.

In any event, as a life-long lover of *film noir*, Jennifer Pettifyr was firmly of the opinion that a monumental pain in the arse is not something that you can be judiciously unless you keep in practice. On this occasion, therefore, she was just being a sarcastic cow.

"Well, I was just wondering whose criminally-hip, small-batch distillery I needed to wet my knickers over around here to get a decent pint?" she asked sweetly. Simon, who had just that moment arrived at the bar, groaned inwardly and suddenly found his shoes to be just that little bit more fascinating.

The girl behind the bar, to be fair, wasn't fazed in the slightest. Truth be told, she was quite game for this kind of thing. After sitting through umpteen staff training courses she had no problem recognising a difficult customer role-play when a gob-shite little ginger one tried to bite her on the bottom.

"Ha! Yes, well that would be ours! Ha ha. Well we have these beers here…"

She smiled at Jennifer (reminding herself that the customer is always right, even when she is a sarcastic little prick, plus this one could easily be a mystery shopper).

The girl gave a jaunty wave of the wrist toward a selection of pump clips located right under Jennifer's nose which were displaying a small but diverse selection of tasty local ales.

Jennifer still had her nose stuck in the menu.

"Actually, I'll try one of your martinis."

She prodded at the top of the list.

"Large please. With a twist of lemon."

She dumped the menu back down.

"As my mother always says to me, Jennifer, when life gives you lemons, don't be a wanker and start banging on about pink grapefruit." She beamed at Simon but was disappointed to find him staring at his shoes. Jennifer found herself wondering, not for the first time in her life, why boys did not find her very funny. Or girls, for that matter. Well, bollocks to the lot of them. She turned back to the bar.

"Laughing boy here will have a Diet Coke."

Jennifer made the internationally recognised gesture of holding her arms out in front of her and jerking her hands violently from side to side.

"Driving?" ventured the staff.

"Incontinent" Jennifer replied. "Can't keep it in. Also, he gets a bit frisky once he's had a couple. Half a shandy and, frankly, he's like an octopus on Viagra."

"Ha ha! Well, aren't we all!" Definitely a mystery shopper.

Jennifer thumbed Simon to go outside and bag a table, before he could refute any of these allegations, whilst she settled up. Given that he had half expected to be stuck with the bill, Simon felt that he had been let off quite lightly.

"I love your jacket!" twittered the bartender, determined to apply a final dusting of icing sugar onto the perfect chocolate brownie that was her handling of Jennifer to date. Simon left them to their love-in and went outside to secure two seats on a pretty terrace overlooking the water.

Jennifer appeared shortly afterwards. Slipping off the aforementioned jacket, she sat her bum down and crossed a firm leg. "Nice view!" she said, looking around at the little boats and the pretty backdrop of cottages and meandering side streets. Simon, surreptitiously taking in Jennifer's smooth but powerful arm muscles, was inclined to agree.

"Do you sail?" he asked.

"No, Simon, I do not sail and I'll thank you not to raise that subject again." Jennifer swung her strong legs up onto the table (taking up far more than her fair share of it) and waggled a red-booted foot in Simon's face. "Little Jennifer and boats do not mix. The examples are many and varied but, generally, boil down to some combination of vomiting and violence." She looked at him seriously. "Neither of which, I would suggest, is ideally performed on the water."

Their drinks arrived and Jennifer received hers with the expression of a child unwrapping a Christmas present larger than its own head.

After a further round of twitter concerning the Pettifyr boots, they were left alone in the sunshine again. Jennifer leant over her glass and began to push the little twist of lemon peel around with the tip of her finger, like a cat with a captive mouse. She took a deep drag on the cocktail then sat back.

"Now, you may have been wondering, unless you're a completely disinterested waste of space and, let's be brutal, Simon, the jury's still very much out on that one, why we're here today." Jennifer tapped her boot on the table, to get Simon's full attention, and lowered her sunglasses. "It's not for the view Simon. Not. For. The. View." She returned to her drink.

Simon had been operating under the assumption that, like him, Jennifer had just fancied a bit of sightseeing. He had thought, basically, that she was slacking off the job for a few hours as the weather was nice. He took the opportunity to appreciate the view again (mainly the boats but with the occasional appraising glance at the Pettifyr legs which did not go unnoticed by the lady but, unusually, did go entirely uncommented upon).

"How's the drink?" he enquired, slightly more passive-aggressively than was really called for, because he quite fancied one of his own. What was particularly irritating, the more he thought about it, was that whilst saddling him as designated driver she had then spent the entire trip bitching about his lack of speed.

"Not bad at all, thank you, Simon. Not. Bad. At. All." Jennifer didn't offer him a sip which would have enabled him to form his own opinion. "Obviously not a patch on a Pettifyr Martini, but definitely not shit in any substantial way."

Sensing that this statement had been deliberately left hanging for him to ask the obvious follow up, Simon decided to oblige the lady. Otherwise, he suspected, they might be there all afternoon.

"What's a Pettifyr Martini, then?"

Simon had expected Jennifer to trot out a convoluted and deeply involved recipe requiring ingredients found only in a small village in Russia being combined with the technical expertise of a nuclear physicist. "What? Oh, basically anything nice and cold really" was her rather underwhelming response.

"Thrown very hard into somebody's face."

Jennifer returned to her drink, sucking at it with unladylike relish before, apparently deciding it was getting a bit warm, she necked the remainder in two gulps and shoved her glass over towards Simon's three-quarter full Coke.

"Your round."

"What?"

"What what? Same again please. No rush. Oh, I'll try the pink grapefruit this time. After all, If you can't beat a hipster around the face with a sturdy truncheon you might as well join him on his mismatched chairs, don't you think?" Shaking his head, Simon went and did the honours. As he didn't actually need to use the toilet, the bartender's loud and insistent instructions as to its location left him equally perplexed.

Finally, drinks consumed and watch consulted, apparently this time to Jennifer's satisfaction, the pair struck back out onto the streets with Simon still none the wiser as to their intentions for the afternoon.

Jennifer navigated her way around the groups of Japanese tourists heading down towards the waterfront until, just when Simon was about to enquire for the third time where they were actually going, she pre-empted the question by ducking off into a side-street.

The redhead strode purposefully to the end of an alley which opened out into a small square, one side of which was taken up by a large, official-looking red brick building. Jennifer marched up to the front door upon which a poster had been stuck up with four pins. It read as follows:

LECTURE TODAY

by prominent local businessman and entrepreneur

Mr Jack Kendell. 2pm.

The title of the talk appeared to be 'Making My First Million' which, in Simon's opinion, made the man sound like a bit of a bell-end before they had even got through the door.

"You are joking?" he asked, but sadly the redhead appeared to be serious. Jennifer pushed in through the big door and set about acquiring a couple of tickets from a fat, red-faced lady sitting at a table inside the door. She gestured to the double doors at the back with a nod of her head.

"The lecture has just started, dear. You two head on in and help yourselves to some tea and coffee. The biscuits have probably all gone though. Bloody Gannets..."

Simon followed Jennifer inside and found himself in a large room bearing a strong resemblance to his old school hall. At one end, on a small raised stage, stood a thick set middle-aged man with a quiff of long dark hair. He was wearing a sharply-cut, but ostentatious, three-piece suit matched with a shiny pair of brown shoes. Simon thought that he looked like a used car salesman. He fetched himself a coffee and verified that the biscuits, had they ever existed, had indeed all gone.

The man on the stage, presumably the Jack Kendell referred to on the poster, was talking loudly into a microphone to an assorted group of people. Most of them, it seemed to Simon, were over the age of sixty but there were a few pockets of younger student-types scattered about. Kendell's name sounded vaguely familiar to Simon, but he could not place from where. He assumed that he must have come across the entrepreneur in the press, or in some work context.

He found Jennifer, who had deposited her firm bottom onto a wooden chair on the back row and decided, for God knows whatever reason (and Simon was giving up trying to work out the thought processes behind Jennifer Pettifyr's life decisions) to leave her sunglasses on, giving herself the clear and unambiguous air of a woman with mental health issues, a hangover or probably both.

The next hour was, Simon maintains, the dullest of his life, which is a bold statement from a man who works in a solicitors' office. To be fair, the talk itself might have been vaguely interesting, but to Simon it just sounded like a man who had done very nicely for himself simply rubbing it in to the rest of us.

It was also a very hot day and the room was extremely stuffy. Simon wondered what Jennifer's game was. A horrible suspicion began to grow in his mind that she was actually just after some advice on how to get her business off the ground.

The lady, for her part, had spent a highly productive hour re-applying a fresh coat of varnish to her fingernails and, in a performance displaying an impressive degree of flexibility in a confined space, to her toenails. The latter activity meant that Simon spent the final twenty minutes of the lecture trying to avoid being kicked in the head, as a contorted Jennifer Pettifyr waggled her feet dry. After what felt to Simon like half a day in a ski-sit, the man on the stage finally finished banging on.

Jack Kendell paused and looked around the audience.

"So, does anybody have any questions?" he asked.

Simon really hoped to fuck that nobody did because he wanted an ice cream quite badly now. He deserved an ice cream for sitting through this shit. Jennifer Pettifyr, officially, owed him a fucking ice cream. After a brief pause and much to his dismay (although he really could and should have seen this one coming) Jennifer popped her bright little hand into the air.

"I have a question!" she barked from the back.

Chapter Ten

"Bikini season"

Jack Kendell grinned and clapped his hands together. A couple of the crumblies at the front attempted to turn around in their seats. Tectonic plates have moved faster.

"Hello! Yes love? What would you like to know then?"

He beamed broadly.

"Do you give many of these talks then?" asked Jennifer, loudly.

"Well, not as many as I would like!" Kendell grinned to the front row. "As you can imagine, I'm a very busy boy these days." This elicited a few laughs from the oldsters, particularly the ladies, who clearly appreciated a bit of the Kendell rough-diamond cheeky-chappie persona. "What, with the businesses and the Council… and the charity work and all that but," he opened his arms expansively, "I always try to give something back, you know? Help the little fella get on, by passing on some of the stuff I've learned the hard way, that they don't teach you in school or the textbooks."

He smiled at Jennifer, who was nodding along with him.

"Well personally I found it so boring I could feel my pubes turning grey" announced Jennifer loudly. "At least, they would have done if it wasn't bikini season."

Nobody in the hall spoke. An octogenarian lady, three rows in front, slowly creaked herself around and fixed Jennifer with what was clearly intended as a glare of disapproval but which the redhead seemed to interpret as a request for clarification.

"Shaaay-ven!" Jennifer mouthed at her, gesturing downstairs.

"Well love," said Kendell, thrown slightly off his stride by the feedback, "I'm very sorry to hear that. I mean, the bit about the talk, yes? Not the other bit. Anyway, I'm quite happy to give you a refund if..." Jennifer cut him off.

"I do have a serious question actually Mr Kendell. Jack? OK to call you Jack? Lovely. Yes, well, my question is Jack..." Jennifer continued loudly, "just how did you expect to get away with it?"

Jennifer was sitting very still now and staring at Kendell through her sunglasses. This, together with her very clear and well-educated voice, began to cause something of a stir amongst the audience who realised that something was clearly up. Jennifer continued.

"I am, of course, referring to the rather bizarre circumstances surrounding your acquisition of the North Moor estate. Specifically, Jack, just to be crystal-clear you understand, I am referring to the murder of Martine Dupuis."

Now this did get a reaction. Starting as a murmur of tutting, it grew steadily into a wave of disapproval directed squarely towards the offensive stranger on the back row.

Jennifer, however, did not seem to notice the animosity. She just sat back and continued to stare at the man on the stage. "I mean, Jackie" she continued loudly, "it's all a bit fishy, isn't it? Isn't it true that Martine Dupuis' property stood in the way of your developing a multi-million pound retail park on the outskirts of town?"

"Err... no" said Kendell but Jennifer was bulldozing on.

"Then, splash, next day she's dead in the water - literally - having rather conveniently decided to leave her house to you in her will?" Simon looked at Jennifer. Where was all this coming from?

"Suicide my left arse cheek!"

With that, Jennifer sat back, folded her arms and contemplated her nails. On-stage, Jack Kendell was gripping the lectern so hard that his knuckles had turned white. He looked physically sick and took some time gathering himself together.

"Young woman," he finally said, hoarsely, "I don't know where you've got that idea from but it's the biggest load of crap I've ever heard in my life. I'll have you up in court for slander if you ever repeat it! Are we clear on that!?" He was clearly struggling to contain his temper but there was something else though. Simon thought that he detected a different emotion in Kendell's body language. The man was genuinely distressed.

"Alright!" Jennifer held up her hands in mock surrender. "I'm only telling you what everybody else is thinking, though." She waved her arms around to embrace the group of puzzled pensioners (who, for the record, weren't thinking any such thing. Most of them just wanted the toilet).

"No need to shit the bed Jacko. We're leaving."

Jennifer got up and, collecting Simon with a cocked finger, sauntered out of the hall leaving the rather stunned pensioners behind her. Simon, after a few seconds, got up and, having first returned his cup to the side table (not wanting to compound the slander with being untidy), followed her out.

Jennifer was in the foyer, having a quiet word with the lady at the desk who had sold them their tickets. The woman was nodding to her, then Jennifer trotted out into the sunshine. Simon found her outside, stretching her arms up to the sky on the stone steps. She had a big smile on her face.

After their departure, Jack Kendell remained stationary for a long time with a deeply perplexed expression on his weather-beaten face. He stared at the doorway, scratching his head. An elderly gentleman (with, incidentally, a genuine if grindingly-dull question about tax planning) decided, on balance, not to bother him. The older man sensed that the interruption would not be welcome. Also, he really did need the toilet.

Once everybody had left the hall, Kendell went back into the small office he was using for the day and downed a large glass of water. Sweating, he loosened his shirt collar, undid his cuffs and checked his pulse. He made a few telephone calls but found himself completely unable to concentrate. Ten minutes later, the lady from the front desk brought him in a cup of tea, some biscuits (from her own stash, safe from the great unwashed) and a small rectangular object which made Jack Kendell's afternoon even stranger still.

Chapter Eleven

"Flake"

"What the hell was all that?"

Simon, who was generally a patient soul, was reaching if not the end of his tether then somewhere along its final straight. Jennifer was just chuckling away to herself.

"That, Simon, was little Jennifer shaking the tree. Now we wait and see whether anything juicy falls out." Simon found himself wondering, not for the first time since arriving in Devon, which particular secure institution was currently missing its red-headed star occupant.

"What have you got against Jack Kendell, anyway? Isn't he a bit of a local bigwig?" Simon pointed the question at Jennifer's back as he followed it, through the tourists, back through the streets towards the car park.

"Nothing!" the redhead shouted back over her shoulder. Then, spotting the ice cream stand, she began to squeal loudly and to jump up and down like a small child on steroids.

It might be noted here that, in her youth, Jennifer Pettifyr had actually been praised at school for her conciseness of speech. She had been praised for precious little else and, in truth, the brevity bit only limped its way into the final draft of her report out of utter desperation on the part of her headmistress to "get something positive in there." Up until that point, a rather lame assertion that the junior Pettifyr was "a strong girl" and "gifted at sports, if a little agricultural with her challenges" had been the best that could be said.

Urban legend has it that the first draft had Pettifyr J down as "the most contrary, foul-mouthed and feral little bitch this institution has ever had the misfortune to have to kennel" however, after the fire, no evidence remains of that. The involvement of said feral Pettifyr in the starting of that fire, it goes without saying, remains similarly unproven.

The now fully grown-up (never knowingly mature) Jennifer was now standing in a sunny Shercombe street and waiting, impatiently, whilst Simon dug out the coins required to supply them both with a restorative ice cream cone.

Jennifer was feeling inordinately pleased with herself, a state which manifested itself in her bouncing up and down on her toes and throwing in the occasional star jump to frighten the tourists. Her bright red hair glistened in the sunshine and she looked every inch the small child on her summer holidays. Simon handed her a large Mr Whippy topped liberally, as instructed, with chocolate sauce and nuts.

"Where's my fucking flake?"

Two minutes later, having finally signed off on her cone, Jennifer perched her firm backside onto a stone wall and began to devour it with such lascivious tongue work that Simon had to stop watching her or risk getting an erection.

Five minutes later, back in the car, Jennifer attempted to get her thoughts in order. She had been telling Simon the truth. She had nothing concrete against Jack Kendell whatsoever. What she knew from Brinkley, however, was that shortly before Nicholson's predecessor, the ill-fated Martine Dupuis, had taken a long walk to the top of the island's old lighthouse and thrown herself to her death, she had made a will.

That will had left all of her worldly possessions to one Jack Jason Kendell, and those possessions just happened to include her house, mortgage-free due to a windfall on the death of her parents. The house (and this was the bit which, to Jennifer, stank like a turd wrapped in pilchards) was part of a development which was owned entirely by Kendell's construction company. Its acquisition was the final part of a jigsaw which freed up the land for development and would, potentially, make Jack Kendell millions. So, Jennifer had decided to make a nuisance of herself and see how cool a cucumber Mr Kendell actually was.

She relayed the gist of this to Simon, who shot her a look.

"Well, it does sound a bit fishy when you put it like that."

He rounded another corner at snail speed whilst Jennifer rested her arms back behind her head.

"It's a bit of a stretch to say that he was involved in her death though? I thought she killed herself in the night."

"Oh, he didn't push her, if that's what you mean. Oh no. He's got a watertight alibi and he couldn't have got onto the island anyway. Not without a boat, at least. The tide was in." Jennifer extracted a compact mirror from her bag and inspected her make-up. Simon looked at her sharply.

"So, why the hell did you just imply that he did? Err, to his face, and in front of a room full of people!?" Simon was incredulous. "He could sue you. He's got the money."

Jennifer pouted into the mirror and began to re-apply lipstick.

"What? Oh whatever. How the fuck else was I supposed to raise it then, clever bollocks? Book a fucking meeting?"

"Well, yes!? Like a normal person!?"

Simon's reply was a bit aggressive as he did think, actually, that a quiet meeting with Kendell might have been marginally more sensible than just rocking up, on spec, and giving the poor bastard both barrels in public.

"A normal person? Oh right. Thanks. Thanks for that."

"I didn't mean…"

"Let's just leave it there, shall we?"

The rest of the journey passed in a rather stony and awkward silence. Assuming that Jennifer would cool off, after a bit of time to herself, Simon reflected that it was probably a good thing that they would have some time apart that evening.

He did, after all, have a date.

Chapter Twelve

"Extra-curricular"

Later that evening as the sun, having broken the back of its work for the day, began its lazy journey down to the horizon, activity at the Bursands Institute was similarly winding up for the day. Old MacKenzie, having finally chivvied the scientists out of the main laboratory, was manhandling a heavy cardboard box into the room. Pausing for breath, he unpacked an assortment of multi-coloured cables and metal contraptions, separating them into various piles on the hard linoleum floor. He rubbed his pudgy hands together. A good night's work lay ahead.

John and Linda Leighton, sceptical of both the Scotsman and his line of work, walked together down the darkening corridor from the laboratory and, after a brief stop in the common room for Linda to pick up a paperback, they went out into the cool evening breeze where a light but not unpleasant drizzle hung in the air and moistened their faces. John Leighton put his arm around his wife's slender shoulders and gave them an affectionate squeeze.

"I'm sorry, darling. It's only for a couple of days and I will be getting paid for it." Leighton shot his wife an apologetic glance. Linda looked completely worn out. She was also losing weight. Working too hard still and not eating properly.

"It's fine, John. Is it London again?"

"I'm afraid so. Look, I know these conferences are a bloody pain in the arse, but I can do a bit of networking with the Japanese this time. There should be some faces over from the States, too. I might even be able to wangle us a job overseas." His wife's face lit up at this suggestion and it reminded him how long it had been since he had seen her smiling. She looked at him hopefully.

"Really? That would be wonderful. I guess we should be looking ahead. This project can't go on forever."

"Let's see how things go. We're not going to be stuck on this bloody rock forever. Anyway, I'm sorry to be going away again. Will you stay here tonight?"

"Worried about me?" Linda Leighton knew that, if she asked him not to go, her husband would not travel to London. He would stay with her if she was worried some harm might come to her in his absence.

Harm. She thought again about why that short, unpleasant word was at the forefront of her mind so much these days. She shivered. Her husband was speaking again.

"Why don't you visit your mother for the weekend? She'd love to see you. It must be her birthday soon."

"Fine. Yes."

Linda's mind was very much elsewhere and she certainly had no desire to spend any more time at home being grilled about her career decisions and lack of parental ambition. "Maybe. Don't worry, anyway. I'll find something to do." The couple entered the residential block and went upstairs.

In the common room, Barbara Porter sat finishing her novel and making a mental note to order a few more on the quiet. She had re-read the juicy stuff so much the thrills were wearing a bit thin. A bit more page ninety-five, please. Nigel Whittaker sat opposite her, next to the radio, wearing a pair of black headphones and enjoying God knows what music he was into at the moment. She always got the genres wrong. He was playing with an album cover which looked like the collected works of Aleister Crowley.

Barbara thought again about the unusual lady from the Ministry. She had an instinctive loathing of government types but the redhead had been rather amusing. Not a snobby little London suit at all. Hopefully she might come back and liven the place up a bit. They might even get to be friends. At least, thought Barbara, the bloody woman had actually listened to her. Nobody else did. Nobody seemed to understand that something on the island was very, very wrong.

Barbara's main concern, as it had been for several weeks now, was the graffiti. She was not a fool and, whilst she was certain that something supernatural or (she had been rather taken with Jennifer's business card) preternatural inhabited the old hospital, she did not believe that its activities stretched to daubing the obscenities which had been sprayed onto the wall of the refectory.

She could not imagine one of her colleagues doing it either but her thoughts just ended up taking her around in circles. Despite knowing them so well, with the possible exception of MacKenzie but he was harmless and had only recently arrived, she had reached the inevitable conclusion that one of them must be responsible. Barbara Porter was frightened. She looked over at Nigel, bashing his head up and down playing air guitar, lost in his own little world. Fat Nigel stealing down in the dead of night to scrawl filth on the walls? Hardly. He might sneak down for a chocolate bar.

The Leightons? There was definitely more going on between that couple than met the eye, of that she was certain. John Leighton seemed to be spending more and more time away. Conferences, apparently. Yeah, right. Pull the other one, John. Barbara Porter had a naturally suspicious mind. Perhaps their marriage was in trouble and John was playing away. Linda was a bit on the ditch-water dull side. All she ever did in her spare time was bugger off with her camera for hours on end.

Frankly, she couldn't blame John Leighton if he was off having a bit of naughty extra-curricular. Barbara wished she was getting some herself. Page ninety-five was all very well, but a nice warm man in her bed would sort her nerves out very nicely indeed. She dragged her over-active mind back from the bondage onto the matter in hand. John Leighton dipping his dirty bits in somebody else's ink-pot wouldn't explain the graffiti. They would both have to be in on it, for starters, as they shared a room. The thought of the flower-like Linda Leighton holding a spray-can was genuinely laughable.

Even less likely though, in Barbara's opinion, was Margaret Nicholson. She was like a mother to them. Since Martine's death, a cloud had hung over the whole bloody place. Barbara had known Martine quite well, at least as well as any of them had as the beautiful Frenchwoman had been something of an enigma. She had been horrified when she had taken her life. Barbara shuddered just thinking back to those times. To go out in the dead of night and, of all places, to the old lighthouse. It was horrible.

Anyway, Nicholson had lifted that cloud and saved the institute from imploding in the fallout from the suicide. She was the heart and soul of the whole place, giving them back their enthusiasm and a genuine reason to keep going on. Margaret Nicholson didn't have a malicious bone in her body, Barbara was convinced of that. Also, if she was the phantom filth-sprayer, why on earth would she have insisted upon involving the Ministry and Miss Pettifyr which, surely, would be the last thing the perpetrator would want.

Barbara remained puzzled. Puzzled and unhappy. She got up, deciding to get changed before coming back for a cocktail with the others. No good, she sensed, was going to come out of this business. No good at all. She thought again about Jennifer Pettifyr and wondered when, if at all, she would be returning. She hoped it would be soon.

Which, in fact, it was. Sooner than any of them expected.

Chapter Thirteen
"Self-harming stuck record"

Jennifer had said nothing further in the car and it was with tears in her eyes that she had clambered out at the headland car park before stomping off down to the causeway, without either thanking Simon or acknowledging his attempt to arrange a time to see her the following morning. By the time she was half-way across she was, of course, regretting her childish behaviour. She turned around, contemplating running back to the car to apologise. Simon and his car had gone though. She was on her own.

She had been horrible to him and now she hated herself for it.

Always her own worst enemy, Jennifer had sulked all the way back from Shercombe and then buggered off, on her own, for a long walk to clear her head. On returning she had felt so guilty and contrite that she had gone straight to the village shop and bought a massive assortment of bread, cheese, cold meat and bottles of red wine. She had hurried back to the cottage, desperately wanting to apologise and make it up with a cosy evening talking over the day's events and, basically, showing him that she was not just a complete A-hole. Well, not all of the time.

Then he had dropped his 'oh, I'm really sorry, but I've got a date' bombshell.

That had been bad enough but, of course, it had to be with Nancy the pneumatic tea-goddess with the legs up to her fucking armpits. Bloody men. Jennifer re-played the horrible scene in her head like a self-harming stuck record. She had pretty much told him to fuck off, or at least to fuck off once he had kindly dropped her off at the causeway so that her evening would not be completely wasted. She had phoned Nicholson and asked, frostily, if she could stay the night. Purely, you understand, for investigative purposes. Not, in any way, to get away from shit-head and having to listen to his bastard headboard banging away all night

Jennifer felt wretched now. What was wrong with her anyway? She never got this mental over men. Well, she admitted, that was possibly a lie but she certainly did not choose or enjoy the experience. Feeling suitably miserable, with her stomach hurting horribly, she stomped across the sand trying very hard not to cry.

The sky was darker now and the old white hospital stood out bleakly against the skyline. The plaintive sound of seagulls accompanied Jennifer as she trudged up the concrete slipway which she and Simon had attacked, together, earlier in the day. She stood in the gloom and wondered what she was doing there, alone. She wondered, looking briefly back towards the headland where the warm lights of the pub were faintly visible, what the hell she was doing with her life.

Jennifer found it hard not to feel Simon's absence as she re-performed the identical actions of the morning, although at least she now knew the code for the gate.

Punching it in, she made her way up to the main building. Inside, the musty corridor was now unpleasantly dark however a puddle of warm light was spilling out from the office half-way down, presumably from a desk lamp. Jennifer navigated towards it gratefully and peeped nervously around the jamb. Margaret Nicholson was sitting at her desk, fiddling with a small transistor radio. She looked up as Jennifer tapped on the open door.

"Aha! Hello my dear!" she boomed. "You've made it, then! I was rather worried that you might have changed your mind. The walk across is a bit grim in the evening." Her warm, friendly face gave Jennifer a surge of confidence. The larger woman got up and gave her a brief but much-appreciated hug.

"I'm afraid you're stuck with me for the night. Sorry for the zero notice." Jennifer stepped sheepishly into the office. The warm glow from the lamp did make her feel a little less unhappy though.

She could, she told herself, do this.

"Nonsense, my dear. It's a pleasure to have you. Between you and I, Miss Pettifyr, most of our nights here are bloody dreadful. Tedious as. Anyway, let's get you settled and then we can all have a nice drink." Result, thought Jennifer, who had also been kicking herself for forgetting to bring any booze. They headed outside, over the gravel, to the residential quarters. After a bit of small talk about the deteriorating weather, Nicholson punched the now-familiar digits into the lock and they entered a small foyer which was brightly-lit by a single, exposed bulb.

"Right. Well, we have some washing facilities through here…"

Nicholson pointed to a small alcove within which sat an old-fashioned washing machine and a large set of drying racks. "The bedrooms are this way. I'm afraid, and this is a bit of a kicker Miss Pettifyr, there are no toilet facilities in this block. If you need the loo in the night you have to brave it across in the dark to the main building... although" she pushed her thick spectacles up her nose, "there is a sink in your room. I am not linking those two statements you understand. We are both women of the world."

She led Jennifer up a narrow flight of stairs into a long, hotel-like corridor. "Right, here we are!" They arrived at room number nine. "As they have both buggered off for the weekend, I'm putting you in the Leightons' room rather than on a camp bed in the office. Don't panic, I have changed the sheets."

Nicholson unlocked the door and ushered Jennifer into a tidy but spacious bedroom. A double bed with bedside tables was at one end, with a desk and a sofa at the other. A small television set and video recorder stood in the corner next to a large free-standing mahogany wardrobe. The legendary low sink sat to the left of the wardrobe. Jennifer put her bag down onto the bed.

Nicholson clapped her hands.

"You freshen up then come and find me in my office when you fancy a drink. I've got a nice big fat bottle of gin that we need to get through."

She left with a wave and Jennifer heard her stomping down the corridor and down the stairs. Jennifer looked around. An assortment of personal possessions nestled in clusters on the various surfaces of the functional furniture.

The most interesting feature of the room was a series of large, framed black and white photographs mounted across the wall above the bed. These depicted different views of the dramatic Devon coastline and the photographer clearly had a good eye. The shadows and compositions were striking and unusual. She pulled back the duvet and the linen looked fresh and inviting.

Being a naturally nosey little bugger, Jennifer could not resist having a peek into the wardrobe where she found various further signs of habitation. Suits and dresses were organised neatly into male on the left and female on the right. An assortment of shoes sat tidily in one corner. The back of the wardrobe comprised a full-length mirror in which Jennifer regarded herself critically. A few toiletries were on the upper shelf, supplementing a pair of toothbrushes and a tube of toothpaste which sat in a small mug next to the sink.

Jennifer changed into a dark pair of jeans and a comfortable sweater before making her way back downstairs. The rest of the block was silent and nobody was around. Thinking about Simon, and wondering what he was doing, she made her way back to the main building.

It was eight o'clock.

Chapter Fourteen

"Colditz!"

Simon, at that precise moment, was in a bad mood but trying to snap himself out of it. Still irritated with Jennifer, but more annoyed with himself for allowing her maniacal mood-swings to affect him so much, he was making his way on foot around the pretty back-streets of Bursands which wound up and away from the waterfront.

He walked for twenty minutes, through clusters of colourful cottages, until he reached a small church on a village green. Nestled next-door, exactly where Nancy had told him it would be, was an attractive little pub with a thatched roof. Light spilled out warmly from its windows onto a couple of locals who sat nursing pints of beer on an old wooden bench on the pavement.

Simon went inside. The bar had a low-beamed ceiling and was about half-full of beer-drinkers. He ordered himself a pint of the local ale. There was no sign of Nancy, so he found a free bench outside to enjoy the evening breeze and his pint. Five minutes later he heard footsteps in the lane.

Nancy was dressed more conservatively than earlier, with very little of her nut-brown flesh on display, however her tight black jeans and sweater complemented her physique superbly. She sported a small black bag and her ubiquitous black heels. Her curves were sublime and Simon could not take his eyes from her as she stalked up towards the tables. Curiously however, given that Nancy was so remarkably eye-catching, the two local men at the next table looked at her only once before, very quickly, returning their eyes to their beer. They stopped talking and avoided any further eye-contact with the girl.

Simon got a blast of heady perfume again as Nancy smiled and kissed him on the cheek. Her face was more made-up than during the daytime but with nothing extreme that did anything other than enhance her naturally striking features. Her slightly crooked mouth smiled and she wore the same teasing expression as she had by the cliff-top. Her long black hair now sported a slight wave in it.

"Didn't stand me up, then?"

The voice was like velvet soaked in sex.

"As if I would dare. Would you like a drink?"

"Vodka tonic, please. Lots of ice." Simon went inside to order. When he returned, the two locals had disappeared and Nancy was alone, perching like a puma and exuding a similar air of disdain.

The warm light from the windows played across her face as Simon handed her the drink. She sipped it very slowly and stared at him in silence.

"Enough ice?" he asked.

He almost expected her to start licking her paws.

"Perfect…" she eventually burred before extricating a packet of cigarettes and a blue-plastic lighter from her bag. Nancy lit-up and took a long, slow drag before exposing her throat and blowing out the smoke in a continuous upward stream. Simon was not quite so naive as to imagine that this elaborate routine had not been very well rehearsed for maximum seductive effect, however he was appreciative of its ruthless effectiveness.

Nancy continued to stare at him with the same unnerving intensity that she had displayed on the cliff edge that morning. She tapped the ash from her cigarette onto the floor, quite deliberately ignoring an ashtray that was within easy reach on the table. After her long silence, it was almost a surprise when she suddenly spoke. She leant forward towards him.

"Did your little ginger friend find anything today, then?"

The sudden reference to Jennifer gave Simon an irrational pang of guilt. He found himself, despite his senses being overloaded by Nancy's physical presence, wondering what the little redhead was up to. Getting shit-faced and punching somebody, most probably. The thought made him smile. He realised that Nancy was watching him intently and waiting for an answer.

"What? Oh yes… but nothing too worrying. Just a cantankerous old Scotsman and a beautiful local nymph."

The girl laughed and took another drag on her cigarette. Unsure quite why, Simon felt relieved to move the subject away from Jennifer Pettifyr.

"I'm not a witch at least then." She giggled softly. "A nymph, am I? Not sure as I like that, Simon. Makes me sound easy, which…" She tap-tapped her cigarette and ran a discreet hand through her black hair. "I am most certainly not. I am, in fact, a very demanding girl…"

She stopped tapping.

"Hours of work required, I'll have you know…"

Simon sipped his beer thoughtfully.

He might, he thought, have to move to Devon.

Meanwhile, darkness had now set in outside the Institute and the tide had finished its remorseless job of shutting the island off from the mainland for the night.

Jennifer let herself back into the main building and walked down to Nicholson's office. The corridor was cold and she was gratified to see that the warm shaft of light which had greeted her earlier was still spilling out from Nicholson's room. She stuck her head around the door again, rapping her knuckles on the frame to announce her presence.

Things had progressed.

The owner of the office was now gleefully decanting multiple measures of gin into an enormous silver cocktail shaker. She looked up brightly at Jennifer's knock and waggled the shiny shaker at her.

"Miss Pettifyr! At last" said the doctor. "I say, could you be an absolute treasure and fetch me some ice, please? Bottom drawer of the freezer!"

Jennifer nodded and bobbed along to the refectory and made her way through the gloom to the small kitchen at the back. Nobody was around. Opening the refrigerator, she was confronted with an assortment of cold meats, cheeses, milk and vegetables. In the lower section she located an ice box and decanted an entire tray of cubes into a stainless-steel bucket from the draining board. A seasoned habitual drinker, she re-filled the ice tray from the tap and returned it automatically to the freezer.

"Good girl. Let's get these over the road then" said the little doctor on her return. Jennifer held the door open and they crunched across the gravel to the laboratory block, with Jennifer in charge of the ice bucket. A breeze had picked up and it had also begun to rain. Nicholson let them in to the dark foyer and led the way into the common room, from which Jennifer could hear the low murmur of voices.

Inside it was lovely and cosy. Jennifer felt the warmth from the little oil heater in the corner and the room was illuminated softly by three low-wattage desk lamps placed strategically around the room. A low fire was burning softly by the bookcase, throwing out additional light and heat. Barbara Porter was sitting on the bashed-up old sofa next to the Scotsman, MacKenzie. Nigel Whittaker, who was now sporting a different black T-shirt but was otherwise unchanged, was sitting in the chair which had been occupied by the Scotsman that morning.

A radio on the side was playing old-fashioned jazz at a low background volume and lending the scene a quaint and timeless appearance as, Jennifer reflected, none of the occupants were exactly on the cutting-edge when it came to fashion (not, she reflected, that she could talk). MacKenzie raised his glass in greeting and Barbara Porter actually bounced up and down in her seat and waved enthusiastically which, given Jennifer's current state of mind, instantly elevated her to best-friend status.

The old Scotsman, who seemed to be on better behaviour at the moment (early days, thought Jennifer, he's probably not pissed yet) pushed himself up onto his feet and bullied over to where she and Nicholson were standing.

"Evening lassie! Unexpected pleasure. Have a seat now."

He had clearly managed to recover his scotch bottle though, Jennifer noted, as a half-full tumbler of liquid gold was clutched in his pudgy right hand. Jennifer parried his attempted kiss on the cheek and, judo-style, diverted his energy into sending him straight back into his chair.

Barbara Porter, by whom the neat little manoeuvre had gone neither unnoticed nor unappreciated, got up and helped Nicholson before relieving Jennifer of the heavy ice bucket. She gave Jennifer a hug and pointed to the seat.

"Sit down Jennifer. I'll shake us up something dirty!"

She's been on ninety-five then, thought Jennifer.

The redhead sat herself down and then proceeded to pass what was, very much to her surprise, one of the most enjoyable evenings that she could remember.

Porter and Nicholson turned out to be hilarious raconteurs, as well as cocktail lovers, and Jennifer found herself laughing heartily as they took turns trying to out-do each other with tall tales from school, centred mostly around mishaps in the laboratory and the chasing of unsuitable males. Nicholson, leading by example, won the prize for most outrageous night-out having burnt down her science lab after a short-lived foray into explosives. She had merely been proving, quite successfully as she pointed out, that girls were better at science than boys.

After several further drinks (which were quite impressively bastard-strong, thought Jennifer, even by her high standards. What the hell was Porter making them with, petrol?) with a break for some underwhelming sandwiches, old Professor MacKenzie turned down the lights and attempted to scare them all shitless by firelight with a dark tale of torture from a remote Scottish castle. Clearly a ninety-fiver as well, thought Jennifer, who just kept a beady eye on where the old letch thought his hands were wandering in the dark.

The most surprising part of the evening was the revelation of Nigel Whittaker. Painfully shy at first, after a few stiff cocktails he came out brightly as a keen music-lover. He entertained them at length, firstly simply by fiddling about with the radio before, after rummaging around in a cupboard for twenty minutes, digging out a set of old vinyl records whilst trying not to knock over his fourth martini. To get at the records he had also managed to unearth a large, rectangular cardboard box, in dark-blue, with a rather sinister picture of a castle on its front. Far more disturbing was the even larger swastika emblazoned upon its lid.

Jennifer clocked the box and her eyes lit up like a Christmas tree. "Colditz!" she squealed excitedly.

"Now then, I didn't think that we were quite that grim dear" observed Nicholson drily. Jennifer picked up the box.

"Can we have a game? Please?"

She looked around the little group hopefully. She loved Escape from Colditz. "I'll set it up! Don't worry." The others looked at each other, dubiously, and shrugged. She was from the Ministry, after all. If they didn't let her play she could probably have them all banged up in Colditz, or whatever the current equivalent was. Probably best to go along with her.

A resigned Nigel opened the box and helped Jennifer to set out the board on the coffee table, together with its various assorted playing pieces. Barbara Porter took the opportunity to replenish their drinks and to crack open another bag of crisps into the large bowl on the table.

Five minutes later, they were ready for the off.

"So!" said MacKenzie, clapping his hands. "First things first. Who is going to be the Nazis? Shall we roll for it?" Jennifer looked at him, then around the group, then back at the Scotsman. She peered around the group again, just to make sure that she was not missing something obvious, then looked back at MacKenzie.

"Well… it's me isn't it" she said.

MacKenzie looked at her and raised his eyebrows.

"Well.., I think we should roll for it, lassie."

"I have to be the Nazis. It's in the rules."

"What?" MacKenzie was confused.

Jennifer rolled her eyes. She knew his type. Jennifer often found her world sadly blighted by people who talked a good board game but turned out to be all mouth. She took a deep breath and explained patiently.

"I'm the youngest, so I'm the Nazis."

"What?" This, now, from Barbara Porter. Seriously?

"It's the rules" Jennifer stated patiently.

"Have you played this game before, dear?" Nicholson leant forward and peered at Jennifer, with renewed curiosity, through her thick lenses.

"Yes of course I have!" said Jennifer, hotly, in response to that frankly outrageous question and actually quite livid that anybody might have the brass neck to question her Colditz credentials. "We play it every Christmas Day!"

"And you're always the Nazis?" asked the Director. "Every time?" Jennifer stared at her. For a scientist, the woman was being more than a little bit thick now.

"Yes! I'm the youngest at home, too." Frankly, this was all just getting a bit ridiculous. "It's in the rules. The youngest player is the Nazis and I'm the youngest player."

"That's not actually in the rules…"

Nigel Whittaker had dug out the paperwork from the bottom of the box and had been busily reading the small print.

"What?"

"The youngest player being the Nazis. It's not actually in the rules." Nigel passed the document across to Jennifer.

Some awkward time passed.

Jennifer sat quietly working her way through the pages, running her fingernail along the lines, until eventually she passed the paper back to Nigel.

"Oh. Right."

Jennifer looked so utterly bewildered that Nicholson felt the need to lean over and pat her warmly on the knees.

"Do you want to be a prisoner instead?" she asked kindly.

"I don't know how to be a prisoner" said Jennifer quietly. "I've only ever been the Nazis." MacKenzie clapped his hands together at this and decided, for God knows what reason, that this was clearly a really good time to crack out a truly spectacularly bad German accent.

"Vee ver juzt obeying zee orderz!" he barked gleefully, before catching a ball-shrivelling glare from Nicholson which shut him up smartish.

Barbara Porter snuck a look at Nigel Whittaker and received a nervous shrug of the shoulders in response. Maybe, they thought, it was some form of Ministry test.

"Can I be the Nazis... please?" came a small voice from the end of the table. Jennifer looked around the group. "I can't play otherwise. I don't know what to do."

Nicholson leaned over and, using the same voice which used to do the trick with her beloved Labrador Fergus, gave reassurance.

"Yes of course you can!"

She rubbed Jennifer's thighs vigorously as encouragement, which made the young lady brighten a little and so, sides finally settled, they set off.

The next two hours were spent in deep concentration as the little group of scientists worked their way around the board devising and attempting to execute a series of increasingly-devious escape manoeuvres only to have their every effort thwarted by an increasingly-gleeful Commandant Pettifyr, whose level of sadistic cruelty seemed to increase directly in proportion to her martini intake.

Twenty minutes in, she was also doing the German accent.

Finally, once Jennifer had succeeded in killing off the last of the small band of plucky prisoners (along with, she explained at length, all remaining hopes of the western allies) the party decided that, perhaps, it was time to call it a night.

"Awesome!" said Jennifer brightly, removing the makeshift swastika armband which she had knocked up at half-time to get into character. "What's next?"

MacKenzie peered at her sleepily,

"Well, it's nearly bedtime I reckon, lassie, however I could use a wee bit of help before retiring."

"Going to the toilet?" asked Jennifer blankly, causing Barbara Porter almost to wet herself. This woman was priceless.

"No, Miss Pettifyr" the professor said tartly, although Jennifer was pretty sure that the old goat would have loved a helping-hand with it. "I was thinking more along the lines of helping me to set up my equipment next door." This had piqued Jennifer's interest and so, twenty minutes later, she and Professor MacKenzie ('Mac', as the old man had insisted she call him) were getting up from their hands and knees and checking out the fruits of their labour.

The laboratory floor was now criss-crossed with slender wires connecting a series of small metal boxes. Each box had a row of lights on the front which were currently green. A larger machine, with a quivering needle dial, sat plugged-in on the front bench.

"So, the youngest player is actually allowed to own a hotel?"

The night was proving a bit of a challenge to poor Jennifer.

"YES! Who on earth told you otherwise, ya daft wee brush?"

"Right." said the redhead quietly, making a mental note to bugger her sisters with pineapples. She'd make page ninety-five look like a fucking nursery rhyme.

The professor escorted Jennifer out and, locking the door behind them, lifted up a small, hand-held, radio transmitter. Extracting the aerial, he pressed a large red button on the front of the unit. In the laboratory, the lights on the boxes all blinked and turned red.

They had spent their time setting up the professor's spirit detection equipment and Jennifer had been rather fascinated by it all. In the event of any localised sudden changes in air temperature, or movement, in the laboratory the alarms would trigger. In addition, the unit on the front bench was monitoring electro-magnetic energy and would activate in the event of any significant changes.

The final piece of equipment was a large video camera, on a tripod, which would switch itself on in the event of any of the other equipment triggering (Mac knew that the camera worked as he had, surreptitiously, tested it whilst Jennifer was on all fours fiddling with a connecting wire. What a rump!)

Having collected the others from the common room, the little party trooped out together and back towards the residential block, in high spirits, to retire for the night.

Whilst crossing the gravel, Jennifer caught a small movement in her peripheral vision. She turned her head but, in the darkness, it was impossible to see anything distinctive. After a couple of seconds, a seagull launched itself up from the ground and, with a plaintive cry, disappeared off into the night sky. Before Jennifer could think any more about it, they were inside.

It was eleven o'clock.

Chapter Fifteen

"Secrets"

Back in the village, Simon settled the bill with the over-attentive Italian waiter who had felt the need to treat them like royalty all evening rather than just leaving them in peace to enjoy a quiet meal. He was having a good night though.

Nancy had gone ahead for a cigarette outside. She was, Simon reflected, as sexy as a hell-cat. The food had been good, despite the obsequious service, and he was looking forward to walking her back to the taxi rank. She lived further down the coast, apparently very close to the island causeway, and walked to work when the tide was out. Tip done, he walked out of the little bistro and joined her in the road. Nancy smiled at him and stubbed her cigarette out onto the tarmac. "All good?" she burred.

"Lovely." Simon looked at her and appreciated, again, the impact of her tight black ensemble. As they walked, arm in arm, down the road the closeness of her body and her scent made him shiver. They reached the taxi rank far sooner than he would have liked. Nancy spoke briefly to the driver then turned to him.

"Maybe I'll see you again tomorrow, then... Mister London."

She moved in and kissed him, very slowly, on the mouth. Her body pressed itself up and Simon felt himself responding but, suddenly, she pulled back and with a brief laugh was inside the taxi and gone. Simon watched as the car trundled off along the edge of the green until it finally disappeared around the corner behind the church.

He walked back down through the village to the quayside and, twenty minutes later, he reached the waterfront and stopped for a moment to look over to where, in the distance, the lights of the old hospital were twinkling on the little island outcrop. The tide, he noted, was in. He thought again about Jennifer Pettifyr, as he had done intermittently throughout the evening, and wondered what she was doing.

To his surprise, given how he had been spending his evening, Simon realised that he was missing her. As he stood there, watching, the lights on the island suddenly went out. Simon remained still for another couple of minutes, looking out across the dark water, trying to understand the uneasy sense of foreboding which he now felt. Eventually, however, the chill of the night air encouraged him back into the warmth of his cottage and to bed. He lay awake for some time, thinking. It was midnight.

In the back of her taxi, Nancy settled back contentedly and, putting her hand into her clutch bag, extracted a bright-red lipstick which she began expertly to apply to her mouth with the aid of a compact mirror.

Once satisfied with the result, she leaned forward and tapped on the window. "Majestic Hotel, please." The driver inclined his head slightly in acknowledgement.

Fifteen minutes later, the taxi pulled up outside the front entrance of a smart hotel in the main square of the next major town along the coast from Bursands. Nancy got out and paid the driver. She stalked up the steps through to the entrance foyer and, with a brief nod to the concierge, bypassed the lifts and made her way slowly up the red-carpeted central staircase. Reaching the second floor, she walked along the corridor until she arrived at a room at the very far end. A 'do not disturb' card hung quietly on the door handle. Extracting a fobbed key from her bag, she let herself in and closed the door firmly behind her.

The hotel room was exactly as she had left it earlier that evening. The single bedside lamp threw out a soft, low-level glow which created rich dark shadows on the walls. Nancy sat down in an armchair and, slowly, unlaced her shoes before removing them and placing them neatly under the chair. Standing up, she held the hem of her black sweater and pulled it up and off over her breasts in a single motion. Underneath she wore an expensive black brassiere. She began to unbutton her jeans.

"I told you I wouldn't be long…"

The naked, handcuffed and blindfolded figure splayed out on the bed was just as Nancy had left it. The figure stirred at the sound of her voice. Nancy finished peeling off her jeans and, now in just her underwear, she moved onto the bed. Giggling, she straddled the naked body.

Gazing down, she reached over and removed the blindfold, causing her prisoner to blink at the sudden in-rush of light. "Nancy... we can't do this" the figure stuttered, "we can't do this anymore. We have to stop. This is wrong..." The words were cut short by a sharp slap to the face, followed immediately by a soothing caress. Nancy smiled down, coldly. Reaching behind her with one hand, she unhooked her brassiere and let it fall away. Leaning over, she gave the face beneath her another little slap, more tenderly this time, as she allowed her exposed breasts to brush lightly against the figure's lips.

"I don't think so. I think, we're going to keep doing this whenever, and wherever, I tell you because, until I get bored of my little game and say so, you belong to me. I own you. Isn't that right, darling?" She reached back and the figure gasped as Nancy's hand found what it wanted and began to play. She placed her other hand lightly, but quite meaningfully, around the figure's throat. "After all," Nancy burred softly, "I know all of your little secrets, don't I... Doctor?"

Chapter Sixteen
"Shit on toast"

At one o'clock in the morning Jennifer Pettifyr lay awake on the sofa in Doctor Nicholson's office, in a rather fetching set of red silk pyjamas, working her way through one of the more lurid thrillers from the bookshelf. After about an hour in her bed in the residential block the cocktails had caught up with her and she had felt the need for the loo. She had given serious consideration to just squatting over the sink in her room however the Pettifyr pride overcame that temptation so she had made her way, together with her toilet bag, quietly down the stairs.

The residential block had been silent. Everyone else, it appeared, was sleeping soundly. Jennifer had gone outside into the cold night air and the main building was in darkness as she had made her way over and let herself in through the front door. It was gloomy and unsettling being alone in the dark, so Jennifer had quickly used the toilet without switching on the light and then decided, given that it was conveniently next to the toilets, to spend the remainder of the night in Doctor Nicholson's office. The key was on the inside of the door so Jennifer had locked herself in and settled down for the night.

Jennifer was trying not to think about Simon but the image of him and Nancy having fun on their date together would not leave her alone. She knew that she was being utterly ridiculous. She had only met him yesterday (well technically the day before she told herself, after realising the time, so a long-term relationship then). Not being generally very good with boys, Jennifer was painfully aware that she had behaved badly and had quite royally fucked it right up.

She hoped that she would get a chance to see him again to apologise. In fact, she resolved to visit him in the morning to do just that.

Restless, Jennifer got up from the sofa and poured herself a glass of water from the jug which she had placed on the desk. The uber-strong martinis had taken their toll and she splashed some water onto her face before adjusting her hair into a makeshift ponytail to keep it out of her eyes.

She extracted a small mirror from her bag and considered her reflection critically. A few laughter lines were appearing around her eyes and mouth. She pouted at herself and snapped it shut. Then she stopped moving.

Jennifer wasn't even certain if she had actually heard a noise. It was just that something had alerted her. She stood, stock still, in the centre of the room. The curtains were closed and the light next to the sofa was so low that she was confident that nobody outside the locked door would perceive that the room was occupied. She remained still and listened. After about ten seconds, she froze.

A subtle clicking sound was coming from the doorway.

Being unable to identify its origin Jennifer's subconscious immediately began, really quite unhelpfully, to suggest all manner of horrors such as psychotic knife-men, undead surgeons or canvassing politicians. Horrible.

As the sound continued, Jennifer was slowly able to narrow down its source to the door handle. This did not really help with her fear levels, however, because someone was, quite definitely indeed, quietly rocking the handle back and forth and attempting to get in.

Shit on toast.

Jennifer crouched down low and crept in her bare feet across the carpet so that she could take up a position behind the door in case her luck should be out (and Jennifer's luck, in her view, definitely had a better social life than she did) and mister creepy person in the corridor turn out to be in possession of a second key. After a bit more low-level rattling, confirming to a thankful Jennifer that a second key, if one existed, was not currently in the game, everything went quiet.

Jennifer switched off the little light and waited silently for about ten minutes before, hearing no further sounds with her ear pressed up against the door, she slipped her key into the lock and, trying to be as silent as possible, worked the mechanism open. She slipped the door open a crack and peeked out cautiously.

The dark corridor was empty and nobody, thankfully, was lurking with a chainsaw. Jennifer slipped out quietly and closed the door behind her, not bothering to lock it. She might, she reflected nervously, need to return in a hurry and lock herself back in.

Crouching low, the little redhead moved along the corridor towards the swing double doors of the refectory and peered in through the small glass window. There was nothing obviously amiss and nobody appeared to be in the main eating area. The tables and chairs looked undisturbed.

She slowly opened one side of the door and slipped inside, holding and pushing the door back into place to prevent it swinging after her and telegraphing her entry. Jennifer then slipped down behind a back table and waited, listening intently, for any indication of an intruder.

A noise, like a faint whisper, came across to her from the far side of the room. She peered through the darkness towards the small archway that led into the kitchen area. The noise came again. It was so familiar, but Jennifer struggled immediately to place it. Then it came to her. The refrigerator. Someone had just opened and closed it in the kitchen.

The possibility that one of the residents had simply popped down for a midnight snack crossed Jennifer's mind but she discounted it swiftly. Firstly, one of the residents would surely have switched the kitchen light on and would also have had no legitimate reason to be trying to access Nicholson's office. Secondly, who the fuck would be brave enough to come all the way across from the warm residential block, over the wet gravel and into a dreary old blacked-out potentially haunted hospital at one o'clock in the morning just for some cold milk and a sandwich? Jennifer wouldn't, and she loved a good sandwich.

The answer to her question came sooner than expected.

Jennifer held her breath as a dark figure emerged from the kitchen carrying a bottle of milk and what looked like various items of cold meat under its arm. The silhouette was hard to make out in the darkness. Jennifer could not tell if it was a man or woman. It might have been a bulky physique or merely a more slender person wearing a padded, hooded coat. She stayed silent, and low as the dark shape moved purposefully across towards the side door which Jennifer had expected to be locked. This did not appear to be the case, however, as the figure slipped easily through it and dissolved into the darkness outside, leaving Jennifer alone in the refectory. She got up and looked out of the window, but it was too wet and dark outside to see anything.

Unable to do any good on the gravel in bare feet, Jennifer made her way quietly back to the office and put on her fluffy pink pig slippers. Feeling sufficiently ridiculous, she returned to the refectory and took a cautious look out through the side door.

Nobody was around so she went outside. Not wanting to risk drawing attention to herself, Jennifer skirted to the edge of the perimeter fence, to avoid being silhouetted against the white walls of the building, and began to make her way around the edge keeping her body low to the ground. It soon became clear to her that, unless the intruder had managed either to disable the alarm on the main gate or to scale the barbed-wire fence, he or she could only have retreated into one of the three other buildings within the compound.

The laboratory room itself was constantly locked and accessible only with a rotating code, different to that on the other buildings.

A lock had also been installed onto the residential block, by Doctor Nicholson, shortly after the disturbances had started. It was, of course, entirely possible that the figure in the refectory had been one of the scientists but Jennifer's instincts were telling her otherwise. If the residential block was out then that only left the outside store room unless, Jennifer thought briefly, she included the derelict lighthouse which was technically accessible, albeit only after scrambling over a lot of rock, rubble and sand.

Deciding to check out the store room first she made her way around to it, keeping to the grassy edge of the compound and off the crunch of the gravel.

The door of the stone room was closed and showed no signs of any recent disturbance. Jennifer looked down at the iron handle. Thick droplets of rain still sat where they had pooled upon the metal. Jennifer grasped the iron but did not pull it. She removed her hand and inspected the handle again. The water had come away onto her hand, leaving the metal dry behind it. Reasoning that the door had not therefore been opened by conventional means within the last ten minutes, she moved on.

Jennifer considered the laboratory block again. It was an unpromising hiding place because of the lock on the main room however, as she did at least know the code to access the foyer and common room, Jennifer punched the combination into the steel buttons and let herself in through the heavy front door.

It was very dark inside and freezing cold now. The foyer smelt musty and she wondered if something had gone off or spilt in the corridor, as she had not noticed the horrible sour odour earlier.

Shivering, she moved quietly down toward the laboratory doors at the end of the corridor and peered in through the glass. The smell was worse here. Through the glass, however, Jennifer could make out the pressure and temperature sensors on the floor where she and Mac had left them. They were still all in place and undisturbed. Nothing looked amiss so, given that the sensors had not tripped, she made her way back along the wall towards the door to the common room, which was half ajar, and listened for a few moments without moving.

The building seemed to be deserted and the icy cold corridor was as silent as the grave. An unfortunate analogy, Jennifer told herself. The foyer smelt like rotten eggs now and it was so cold that she had goose bumps. Get a grip Jennifer, she told herself, angry for feeling so unsettled. The rational part of her brain wondered how it could be colder inside the building than out.

She moved a little closer towards the common room door but, as she did so, Jennifer became progressively more uneasy. She looked around. Nothing was obviously wrong, or different, but she felt tiny beads of sweat forming on the back of her neck and a wave of nausea hit her physically as she got nearer to the door.

Jennifer paused to catch her breath. Her pulse was racing and she was suddenly assaulted by an intense feeling of despair and unhappiness. Whilst her brain tried to function and restore some rationality, her heart began to thump harder and her instincts screamed at her to turn around and run. Irrationally, she became convinced that the room beyond was not unoccupied and that whoever, or whatever, was inside should be left undisturbed.

Jennifer, whilst generally a very brave young woman, had always been morbidly afraid of the dark and so she was fighting every instinct in her body when, taking a deep breath, she put her head fearfully into the common room.

It was empty. At least, it looked deserted and nothing was moving around. The room was deathly quiet. When her eyes gradually accustomed themselves to the dark, she noticed the coffee table. Whilst everything else had been tidied away at the end of the game, somebody had left an object on it. Something about it bothered Jennifer but she could not work out what it was until, looking again, she realised that it had clearly been positioned intentionally, exactly squarely, at the centre of the table.

Its position was too perfectly aligned to be accidental and the unnatural precision of it added to her existing tension. She was so cold now she could barely feel her fingers. Steeling herself, Jennifer strode quickly into the room and snatched up the object from the table. It was a rusted old oil lamp and it was so cold that Jennifer, gasping, felt her fingers burning from its touch. She dropped it with a horrible clatter onto the table.

The stench in the black room was unbearable and Jennifer's breath was frosting heavily now as she exhaled. Her legs felt stiff, frozen and heavy and her fingers had gone completely numb. Looking down at the lamp, and at her numb hand, she suddenly felt terrified. On the edge of panic, she turned around to get back to the doorway.

What she saw there made her freeze. She tried to scream, but no sound came out of her mouth.

An unnaturally tall figure of a woman was blocking the doorway. It had its back to Jennifer and was silent, stick-thin and utterly unmoving. Jennifer found herself unable to move and her heart was hammering so hard that she felt about to explode. The rotten stench was horrific and another wave of nausea suddenly gripped her insides. Unable to prevent herself, she doubled up with her face and neck boiling with sweat before vomiting copiously over the floor. After retching, Jennifer watched in horror as the figure slowly turned around, as if aware of her presence. It pivoted unpleasantly like a doll, without moving its feet, until it seemed to look directly down at her. Faint light from the outside corridor was visible through its head. Jennifer thought that she could make out the outline of a uniform before her head, sweating and cold, sagged back down to the ground.

She tried to process what she was seeing but all thoughts of the figure were displaced as a brutal flurry of intense stabbing pains suddenly hit her in the stomach, combined with a coldness in her face and limbs the like of which she had never known. She fell onto her back, crying, and felt her eyes closing.

After what felt like an eternity of despair Jennifer found herself, mercifully, drifting away from the hospital and away from the island altogether. She found herself swimming in a dark and cold sea, so she kicked out hard away from the pain, away from Devon and struck out instead towards a warm and sun-drenched shoreline that she could see on the horizon.

For the first time since she was fifteen, left crying at his graveside, Jennifer felt the presence of her father.

As she swam for the shore, she felt him kissing her head and whispering words from her childhood softly into her ear which, she realised with a shock, she had quite unforgivably forgotten. She tried to swim harder in response, but the shoreline was now much further away. The land became distant and grew darker until, finally, Jennifer was alone in the freezing water with nowhere left to go. At least she was numb now.

With the pain finally gone, she looked down on herself as her vital organs stuttered and slowly began to freeze, before shutting themselves down one by one. She felt strangely peaceful as her tired and failing body gave itself up, with only a few regrets, to the ice and the darkness.

Her last thought was that her father might, after all of the pain, actually be waiting to meet her. Planning what she wanted to say to him, Jennifer finally drifted away into oblivion.

Chapter Seventeen

"Toothbrushes"

"Bloody hell! Is she dead?!"

It began like a muffled booming through a thick wall but gradually, as if a dial were being slowly rotated within her head, the voice became sharper, louder and more distinct. The pounding in her head receded and, sensing warmth and light around her, Jennifer Pettifyr cautiously opened one reluctant, painful eye.

Barbara Porter, clad in a dressing gown with her hair tied up in a bun, was staring down at her with a concerned frown on her face. Jennifer decided to risk it and opened her other eye.

Her ears, still retuning, now picked up another sound. A steady and repetitive buzzing was coming, loudly, at about five second intervals from somewhere far away. A different female voice carried in from the ether somewhere.

"Can't you shut that BLOODY alarm off Martin? For God's sake!" The voice was familiar but Jennifer, from the floor, was unable to place it. She attempted to sit up but thought better of it as her head began to spin. Barbara Porter squatted down next to her and brushed Jennifer's damp hair away from her eyes. She rested Jennifer's head onto her lap and brought up a glass of water to her dry lips.

"Can you hear me, Jennifer? It's Barbara. Doctor Porter. Drink some of this and we'll try to get you up, OK?" Jennifer sat up and sipped gratefully at the water. A pair of heavy practical shoes appeared in her eye-line and, looking up, she found Doctor Nicholson, sporting a tattered but very warm-looking burgundy dressing gown, peering down at her through her thick spectacles.

"Goodness me" said Nicholson quietly, deftly avoiding the pool of Jennifer's vomit which was dangerously close to her right foot. "Are you alright, dear?"

Jennifer, feeling a little happier after the water but more than a little embarrassed by the vomit, made more of an effort to sit upright properly. This time her head allowed her to do so. She sipped a bit more of the water. "I'm sorry... I..." she began but ground to a halt, realising that she had absolutely no idea how to proceed. Her brain was still trying to process what had happened to her. The room felt warm now and was brighter than when she had arrived. How long had she been on the floor?

"Sorry... what time is it now?" she asked the scientists.

Barbara Porter consulted the clock upon the wall.

"It's three o'clock, Jennifer. We came down when Mac raised the alarm." Jennifer rubbed her forehead. She must have been out cold on the floor for at least an hour. "Mac's tremblers went off ten minutes ago!" said Barbara Porter excitedly. "He's in the lab now, getting all of his tapes and readings together. You MUST have heard them, Miss Pettifyr. They're loud enough to raise the dead!"

After ten minutes and a large cup of strong tea Jennifer felt, almost, back to her usual self.

She wanted to talk to MacKenzie and get a look at his video footage but the combination of the Professor being busy in the lab and Doctor Nicholson's insistence that she, Jennifer, needed to rest, won the day.

Barbara Porter escorted her back to the residential block, insisting that she spend the remaining few hours of the night getting some sleep.

Locking the door of the Leightons' room, Jennifer undressed down to her knickers and clambered into the warm bed. She was about to switch off the bedside lamp but then, as an afterthought, she opened the bedside drawer to see whether it contained any aspirin. She had a banging headache. At first she thought that the drawer was empty but looking more closely she noticed a large piece of paper, or card, lying face down at the bottom. Jennifer lifted it out and turned it over.

She found herself looking at a photograph of a girl, taken in what appeared to be a forest. The model was clearly a brunette but was otherwise unidentifiable as, although her voluptuous body was displayed very clearly in all of its naked glory, the girl's face had been entirely scratched away. Jennifer returned the photograph to the drawer and switched off the light.

The sharp plunge into darkness momentarily brought back the panic that she had experienced earlier, but under the blanket at least she felt warm and safe, using the material to drive away the shadows which might otherwise provide her subconscious mind with the ammunition which it perpetually seemed to seek in order to undermine her self-confidence.

Jennifer hated the dark. It frightened her horribly, a position made intolerably worse because she was intelligent enough to understand that her fears were both baseless and childish. Pulling the blankets up around her neck, and her toes up closer towards her body, she found herself thinking about Simon again. Jennifer wondered where he was and what he was doing. What it would feel like if he were with her now.

But he wasn't. He was probably in Nancy's bed. She wished that she could turn the clock back and erase the stupid things that she had said but, not for the first time in her life, she chose instead just to berate herself for her stupidity. She had, yet again, simply reaped what she had sown.

Jennifer shivered despite the warm blanket. It wasn't the encounter with the intruder in the refectory which had scared her particularly. She could deal with people and, on that front, Jennifer felt that she had at least made some progress. It seemed highly possible that the figure in the kitchen was the same person responsible for the graffiti and damage. No, it had been the common room. That overwhelming sense of despair and terror was a sensation she never wanted to experience again. Her brain tried to rationalise what she had seen but her stomach just continued to churn away as her body remembered the unnatural cold which had enveloped and overcome her.

Needing the toilet again, Jennifer contemplated making the journey back over to the main block but she was not brave enough now. Ashamed, she used the sink as quietly as she could, running the tap to disguise the noise. She washed the sink and her hands.

Looking down at the twin pair of toothbrushes, in their little enamel stand, Jennifer felt more lonely than she ever had since her first night at boarding school. She realised how much she just wanted a cuddle. Being Jennifer Pettifyr, however, she was unable not to remind herself that, at twenty-nine years of age, she didn't have anybody that wanted to cuddle her. Not one.

Chapter Eighteen
"Comprehensively pissed on"

Daylight crept its way stealthily up the outside wall of the residential block until, finally reaching the blinds of Jennifer's window, it found her lying tightly wrapped up in her blanket with her body bathed in sweat. At nine o'clock, sounds of activity from an adjoining room had woken her up, with a start, from the small measure of fitful sleep which she had been able to manage. Digging out some old tracksuit bottoms and trainers from her bag, a fragile Jennifer padded out of the residential block and across in the morning sunshine to the main building.

The double doors to the refectory were swinging as she entered through the front, signalling that somebody had just passed through to the eating area. Peering through the glass panel, she was faintly surprised to see that Nancy had arrived, before remembering that Nicholson had told her she sometimes came over at the weekend. The girl was again dressed effortlessly stylishly, this time in faded-blue denim and a white T-shirt which made her look younger than the racier outfit of the previous day.

Perhaps because of her experience in the night, and her current state of heightened anxiety, Jennifer was so relieved to see another human being in daylight that she resolved to make friends with the girl. It was not, after all, Nancy's fault that Simon was such a shallow and insensitive bastard as to have his head turned by a large pair of boobs. Jennifer took a deep breath and went through into the refectory.

Nancy was tidying up the tables and turned at the noise of Jennifer entering. She straightened up and put the dishcloth in her hand down onto the table. Jennifer stuttered over to her and smiled.

"Morning, Nancy. Sorry if I disturbed you…"

The girl looked at her, briefly flicking her eyes up and down as if taking in Jennifer's rather baggy (and a bit smelly if she was honest) tracksuit bottoms and old trainers. Jennifer could not shake the sensation that there was laughter behind her girl's blank eyes. As if she had come out of the toilets with her skirt tucked into her knickers and none of the other girls had the kindness to let her know. Nancy picked up her cloth and began a lazy wipe of the table-top.

"It's no problem, miss…" she drawled on in her slow Devon burr. "I was just doing some tidying up. Can I get you anything?"

Jennifer waved a deprecating arm to indicate a negative and sat down instead at one of the nearby benches. Nancy went back to her cleaning for a few minutes before, putting the cloth down again, she turned around to Jennifer.

"Did you sleep well then?" she asked lightly.

The question was entirely innocent but the girlish lilt in Nancy's voice just seemed to re-ignite the terrors of the night which Jennifer was trying desperately to put behind her.

"Not really, no." Jennifer rubbed some sleep out of her eyes.

"Oh. That's a shame" said the girl lightly, just standing still now and watching Jennifer. She picked up her cloth and gave the table another wipe. She put the cloth down again. "Simon and I had a lovely time last night, by the way…"

Jennifer paused before looking up, slowly, to find Nancy looking straight at her, but the eyes behind the hurtful statement appeared guileless and devoid of any emotion. She was, Jennifer thought with a sigh, just making conversation. Nancy, she decided, was extremely beautiful but possibly also a bit simple. More fool bloody Simon, she thought.

"Did you? Great" she managed, affecting disinterest. "Do anything nice?" Nancy smiled down at her.

"Lots of things, Miss. But a lady never tells…"

Jennifer stared down at the table, trying her best to keep the pain away from her face and out of her voice. The girl picked up her cloth and, turning her back, returned to wiping the surface of the table and treating Jennifer to a display of her backside which just seemed to reinforce her innuendo as to how she and Simon had chosen to spend their evening. Jennifer felt like she had been punched in the stomach.

Nancy put the cloth down again and turned around. "Actually, Simon suggested that maybe you could come out with us next time…" she burred.

Jennifer's heart rose slightly. He had at least been thinking about her then despite the horrible way in which she had spoken to him. Maybe she could make it up with him after all. She resolved again to visit him to say hello as soon as she could get back to the mainland.

"Really? That would be nice."

"Oh yes," continued the girl, turning her back on Jennifer once again and returning her attention to the table. "He said that you were a bit sad and lonely and it would do you good to get out and meet some different people." She drawled on, ever so slowly wiping the same area of the table-top. "You know, people more your own age. There are a few older guys at the Feathers I know who've been single for years. I bet they would love to take you out." She stopped wiping and turned around, wearing the same blank expression on her face, as if daring Jennifer to react. Finally, apparently satisfied with her work on the table, she bobbed and stalked off out to the kitchen.

Feeling comprehensively pissed on, Jennifer stomped out and went to the toilet herself in somewhat less ostentatious style (although probably generating superior volume, she told herself, as it felt like she was going solidly for a summer) before venturing outside for some much-needed fresh air.

Looking over at the laboratory, now standing quiet and innocent in the sunshine, it was as if the events of the night had never occurred. She imagined herself walking confidently up to the doors and exploring inside without a care in the world. Certainly, she reflected, the daylight made a difference.

The photograph in the Leightons' room disturbed her. Her first thought was that it must have been put there by John Leighton for, presumably, his own personal enjoyment. The more she thought about that, though, the less likely it seemed. It was a ridiculously reckless hiding place for something of that nature unless, perhaps, both of the couple enjoyed that sort of thing to spice up their love life a bit.

Jennifer's main concern was why, if the picture was a harmless bit of erotic fun, the face of the girl had been obliterated. It came across as either a destructive act by an unbalanced mind or some attempt to prevent the model's identification. Neither of which made much sense if the picture belonged to either Leighton.

The voluptuous body in the picture was clearly not Linda's and bore no obvious resemblance to anyone whom she had met so far, with the possible exception of Nancy who was better stacked than Tesco (and cheaper, thought Jennifer nastily, smiling to herself before remembering that it was Nancy's drainpipe and not her own that Simon was clearly interested in shinning up).

No. Jennifer told herself off for her continual fixation on Nancy. She had to forget about Simon and do her job properly. The photograph was however, she felt sure, tied in somehow to the disturbances at the institute. She needed some time to think that one over properly.

Her immediate priority lay in front of her. It was squatting quietly and significantly less threateningly in the warm morning sunlight than it had in the dead of the night.

Jennifer was contemplating the lighthouse.

Unless the refectory intruder had retreated into the residential block, which would narrow the field down quite nicely in Jennifer's mind, the lighthouse was the only other place in which he or she might have disappeared. The stone store room had been untouched and the laboratory and the common room had been empty. Well, she shivered, empty of anything of sufficient substance to carry a pint of milk around. She had inspected the perimeter fence and it was both intact and not scalable by any normal human.

Jennifer made her way across the gravel toward the rocks and rubble that separated the main grounds from the short pathway leading up to the lighthouse. Watching her footing carefully, she clambered over the various obstacles and made her way slowly down the track towards the main door. It was locked however and, presumably just on the off-chance that skeleton keys made their way back into fashion, a large wooden plank had been nailed across it for good measure. Neither the lock nor the plank showed any sign of having been interfered with in the last few months, let alone in the last few hours.

Looking up from the door, Jennifer could see a small window about two thirds of the way up the structure, facing back towards the main building and the mainland. It was far too high up, however, to be accessible from the ground.

Slightly crestfallen, Jennifer turned away from the door and made her way gingerly around the perimeter. On the far side of the lighthouse however, at the point nearest and rather dangerously close to the cliff's edge, she came upon another window.

It was recessed into the stone, with a sill roughly at the level of her head. The window was significantly larger than the one on the other side and, from its position, was not visible either from the institute buildings or from the mainland at all. She looked up. It was broken in and, she reckoned, large enough for a man or woman to gain entry through. It was still quite high up though. She was not sure that she could reach it and pull herself up unaided.

Jennifer looked around for something to assist her but none of the rocks or boulders nearby were large enough to stand on. Then, staring at the wall, she noticed that one of the bricks was missing about three feet up from the ground, slightly to the right hand side of where the window was positioned above her. Using this as a toehold, Jennifer hoisted herself up and gripped onto the ledge.

"What are you doing?"

The loud voice behind her caught Jennifer by surprise and she slipped back, thankfully not tripping in the process as the clearance between the lighthouse and the cliff edge at that point was only a metre or so wide. Jennifer clambered to her feet to find a frowning Nancy standing about ten feet away from her.

"What?" asked Jennifer, frankly in no mood to be pissed around by the girl again.

"I said, what are you doing?"

The insolence and aggression in the tone was more noticeable now, which made Jennifer instantly very curious indeed. Why the fuck, she wondered, should the kitchen girl give two shiny shits if sporty little Jennifer chose to spend her morning clambering about on a fucking building site?

"Problem?" she asked sweetly.

"You're wanted on the telephone" replied Nancy loudly, making no attempt either to move or to return indoors. "In the main building."

"Right! Well I'd better fuck off back indoors then!" responded Jennifer brightly and stomped off past the sullen girl to make her way back over the rubble.

Nancy watched her departing back with the same sour and blank expression she had worn earlier in the refectory. She frowned as the redhead made her way back over the rocks. "Or just fuck off altogether…" she whispered softly, staring intently at Jennifer's back.

Chapter Nineteen
"Gingerbread"

Jennifer made her way back to the main building, passing through the refectory and down along the corridor to Doctor Nicholson's office where, she had noted on the previous night, the telephone was located.

Nicholson was in the room when she knocked.

"Ah Jennifer dear! A very good morning to you. How is the head? Mine's banging like a pile-driver, I'm afraid. I really must have a word with Barbara about her cocktails. I'm starting to think that she cuts them with ethanol from the lab. Anyway, Nancy must have found you then? I worried she might have just buggered off for a fag. You have a telephone call, dear." She gestured down at the desk, where the receiver lay, off the cradle, on its side upon the desk. Nicholson bustled out and closed the door to give Jennifer some privacy. Jennifer picked up the black plastic handset and put it against her ear.

"Hello?" she spoke into the telephone.

The line was crackling and Jennifer was not altogether sure whether anyone was actually on the other end. "Hello," she said again, more loudly, "the is Jennifer Pettifyr. Who is this, please?" There was more crackling, then a low male voice spoke which Jennifer did not recognise. "Jennifer" it said, making it sound like a statement and not a question.

"Yes?" she said again. "Who is this please?"

"Jennifer, Jennifer, Jennifer..." said the voice, rasping eerily through the crackling background like a very old and very faint gramophone recording.

"No, I'm Jennifer" said the lady patiently. "Perhaps you should read the idiot's guide to telephones before starting next time. This is the point at which you reply and tell me who you are." This resulted in a flurry of high-pitched crackling at the other end, to the extent that Jennifer was about to hang up, before the voice came back on suddenly, continuing in a slightly cracked and sing song burr that reminded her briefly of Nancy. It was the accent, she thought. Whatever the voice was, it was local.

"Gingerbread girl..." it burred nastily into her ear. "Nosey little fuck-nose gingerbread... well, well. Maybe we need to bite little gingerbread's head right off..." the voice went on, "...or maybe more fun to gut you out first and watch you squeal like a piggy..." This was followed by a high-pitched, girlish parody of laughter before the line went dead.

A few moments later, there was a short tap at the door. Jennifer placed the receiver slowly back down onto its cradle. Nicholson.

"All finished? Good, good." She shut the door.

"I hope that it wasn't bad news, dear? The man sounded rather grim to me, no offence. I'm sorry, that was rather rude. It wasn't your boyfriend was it, or your family?"

Jennifer just stood looking down at the receiver.

"I don't have one" she said, absent-mindedly.

"No family, dear?"

"Boyfriend. No boyfriend."

Jennifer was still staring at the telephone.

"Girlfriend?"

Jennifer, registering that she was being spoken to, looked up.

"Have you been talking to my mother?" she said, before appreciating the utter inanity of that question. She really did need to pull herself together. The telephone call had unsettled her again. Although, if someone was trying to warn her off then perhaps she was getting onto the right scent. Right now, all she could smell was her own body-odour. She needed a shower.

"Anyway, dear," Nicholson went in for a change of subject, "Doctor Leighton, Linda that is… John's still away… will be back this afternoon, so I'm afraid we're a full house again. You are more than welcome to stay, of course. I can put you up on a camp bed in here, if you like? It's really quite cosy, and I do have a heater if you get cold…"

Jennifer shook her head, explaining that she wanted to return to the mainland and would put herself up at the inn. Being there would enable her to come over without putting anybody out. Also, being honest with herself, the thought of spending a second night alone in the office made her want the toilet again.

She asked Nicholson to thank Linda Leighton for the use of her room, before making her way back to the residential block and up the stairs. She washed in the sink before brushing her teeth and changing into her jeans and a fresh t-shirt. Slipping on her bottle-green jacket, she stuffed her tracksuit bottoms and trainers into her leather bag.

As an afterthought, she took the photograph of the naked girl out of the bedside drawer and put it into the bag before zipping it up. An idea about that was beginning to take shape in her mind and, in any event, if it did belong to the Leightons they were hardly likely, given the subject matter, to start making a fuss and ask for it back. Taking a final look around, she picked up her hold-all and left the room.

Jennifer had intended to head straight back for the causeway but two things stopped her. Firstly, the bastard tide was in so she was effectively stranded, for an hour or so at least, unless she could scare up a boat from somewhere.

A boat, Jennie? Seriously?

Secondly, something about the girl Nancy's attitude by the lighthouse was bothering her so she decided to take another look at it before heading back to the mainland.

Walking back past the main building, she paused to look into the refectory and saw that Nancy had returned and was sitting at one of the tables eating what looked like a bacon sandwich and chatting to Barbara Porter. Good, thought Jennifer, who did not wish to be disturbed a second time.

She made her way quickly back over to the rocks and re-negotiated the boulders and rubble until she found herself, once more, underneath the window from where Nancy had called her back earlier. Putting down her bag, she levered one foot back into the makeshift foothold, gripped the ledge and heaved herself up. The ledge was just wide enough to perch on and the window itself large enough to admit a normal-sized person, albeit with a bit of crouching. Jennifer's physical endeavours did not go unrewarded as, looking down, she was delighted to find herself staring at the very clear impression of a large muddy footprint. Man-size.

Satisfied that her instinct about the lighthouse may after all have been correct, she stuck herself in through the window. Inside, she dropped down a short distance straight onto a winding stone staircase. It was damp and gloomy inside but the window granted sufficient light for her to see quite well. The stairway stretched up and around the wall in a spiral to her left whereas a short stretch led down on her right to the front door which seemed to be as equally effectively barricaded on the interior. A plank of wood had been nailed across it, similar to the one outside.

Inspecting the entranceway Jennifer noticed that there was, in fact, a second door in the stairwell. It was not immediately visible from where she had been standing as it was tucked in underneath and behind the steps. It was about half the size of the main door, too low to admit a standing adult but large enough for anybody to get through if they were prepared to stoop. It was panelled in heavy wood, like the front door, and Jennifer assumed it to be a storeroom or, potentially, a basement.

She gripped the handle but the solid door was stubbornly locked. A few firm rattles confirmed that a key would clearly be required in order to open it.

Frustrated, Jennifer retreated to the stairs and began the spiralling ascent, passing the window by which she had gained entry and pressing on upwards towards the top of the lighthouse.

About half-way up she arrived at another door. Presumably, she thought, this was the room containing the small window facing back towards the mainland. The door was also locked. Next time, she thought, she'd bring a fucking locksmith. Jennifer rattled the handle half-heartedly before pressing on until, a short climb later, she emerged out into the disused lamp room and made her way outside onto a narrow walkway which encircled the old beacon.

The wind caught in her hair and whipped it around as she stepped outside into the cold bright sunshine. The three hundred and sixty degree view was magnificent. Jennifer gazed out over the island and back towards the hospital building.

As she watched, she saw the side door of the refectory open and the tiny ant-like figure of Nancy emerge, carrying what looked like a tray. The figure made its way slowly across to the residential block before disappearing inside.

Looking down at the vertiginous drop, Jennifer suddenly felt a wave of nausea and gripped hard onto the cold but reassuring metal hand-rail. She walked carefully around to the opposite side of the walkway facing fully out to sea. The rail had broken away at this point though and Jennifer realised why all of the warning signs had been erected outside.

Without the guard-rail the barrier only came up to knee-height. For a stretch of about three metres there was literally nothing at all to hold on to. Jennifer moved carefully to the broken section and looked down, tentatively.

The drop beneath her was truly frightening. The reason for this was that the narrow walkway protruded about a metre or so actually over the edge of the cliff-top, so directly beneath the broken section of rail there was nothing but an uninterrupted drop of sixty or possibly seventy feet straight down into the boiling sea below which was littered with a wicked array of razor-sharp rocks which leered up like sharks' teeth.

It was from this spot, Jennifer suddenly remembered, that Martine Dupuis had chosen to leap to her death. Looking down at the sea and the rocks, Jennifer wondered quietly about the state of mind in which the poor woman must have found herself. How unhappy must her life have been for her to leave her bedroom, in the dead of night, and make that final lonely trek across the gravel, climb up to the top of the lighthouse and end her life in such a brutal and dreadful way? Looking down at the surf breaking over the rocks below, Jennifer suddenly felt very cold and lonely again.

Preoccupied as she was, and with the wind buffeting her ears and her hair, Jennifer Pettifyr never heard the figure which had been slowly making its way up the steps behind her.

Chapter Twenty

"Catch of the Day"

The scream of a seagull awoke Simon from his rather restless sleep. Disorientated, he gazed around the unfamiliar little bedroom for a few moments before remembering where he was. He lay back and luxuriated beneath the warm sheets with his eyes closed, listening to the sounds outside. It was a couple of minutes before his brain started functioning properly and he thought back to the previous evening and his date with Nancy. He lay for a moment, remembering the smell of her and the softness of her lips. He wondered idly whether he would see her again.

Then he thought about Jennifer Pettifyr and immediately felt guilty. Guilty and worried. He had basically left her stranded on an island with a bunch of complete strangers, one of whom was potentially a dangerous lunatic, on her first night in Devon.

He remembered the look of intense disappointment on her face when he had broken his news to her the previous evening. Their scene had been horrible.

"What do you mean you've got a date?" Jennifer had said.

Simon had taken a shower at the cottage and on emerging had found Jennifer, returned from her long angry walk, deeply contrite and clutching two large shopping bags. She had obviously gone to a lot of effort and been to the shops to get food and a couple of decent bottles of red. She had been upset in the car on the way back from Shercombe and he had thought it best to give her some space.

"Well?"

Jennifer had just stared at him, bags in hand, as he had come downstairs dressed-up for his night out.

Simon had felt suitably embarrassed.

"It's, erm, well Nancy asked me out. You know, the girl from the Institute."

"The scrubber?"

"That's not very nice…"

"Tea girl. IQ half the size of her chest, yes?"

"OK, now that's really unfair…"

"Is it? Oh, I'm sorry."

Jennifer had pushed past him roughly and dumped her bags down on the floor, hard enough to make her point without, he noted, being quite hard enough to break the bottles inside.

"Well, you'd better piss off and enjoy yourself then while I sit on my own all night. Fine."

She had dumped herself down onto the sofa and then, just as Simon had thought she might not be taking it too badly after all, came out with "Going anywhere nice? I won't wait up. Unless of course you don't come back at all. Three's a crowd and all that!"

"We're just having a drink then going to a restaurant, that's all" Simon had protested before deciding to add, entirely stupidly, "I'm not going to sleep with her if that's what's bothering you!"

He had realised immediately that he had said quite entirely the wrong thing.

"Sleep with her?! Bloody hell. Who mentioned that? Not me. Obviously on your mind then. Why the fuck should I care what you get up to, anyway." Jennifer had just carried on, accelerating away from him like a car over a cliff. "Well, bugger off and have fun with her then. Tell you what, actually, you can drop me back at the causeway now. That way, if you get lucky, I don't need to spend all night kept awake by your bouncing bedsprings."

With that, she had sat back and feigned absolute disinterest in Simon and all of his works.

The really stupid thing was that despite her volatility, or perhaps partially because of it, he really would have enjoyed spending an evening with her. He could just imagine them drinking in the pub, getting some fish and chips before... well, before what exactly? He was really quite attracted to the redhead despite her weirdness and her temper. Nancy and Jennifer were so utterly and completely different from each other that they seemed to trigger responses in entirely different parts of his brain.

Jennifer had looked utterly crestfallen as she held her shopping bags. The contrast between her expression and that of his ex-girlfriend, on their final evening together, could not have been more stark. Simon thought back to that horrible night in London, three weeks earlier.

Nicola had been shopping that night too. Not for him though, as he had quite bluntly been informed, because things had 'got a bit same-y' apparently. Well, he thought bitterly, they had since she had started screwing her personal trainer anyway. He had wondered whether she was being charged for that service too, or just for the body-shaming brainwashing which had turned his previously warm best friend into a narcissistic, self-absorbed gym bunny who looked down her nose at anybody who didn't spend three hours a day working out. Simon's pointing out that, if she was exercising that much, perhaps she should be training for something useful rather than just checking out her own reflection, had nailed the coffin shut and kicked dirt onto it.

During their three years together, Simon reflected, Nicola had never once looked upset if he had been unable to spend an evening with her. He had known Jennifer Pettifyr for five minutes and she had looked at him like her puppy had just been shot.

His mind went back to their parting on the previous evening.

"Right" he had just said quietly. "If that's what you want, I'll run you over there before I go. Look, I'm really sorry about the shopping. That would have been lovely, honestly. Maybe we could do it tomorrow? It's just, I've kind of promised her now…" He had tailed off, waiting for some form of response, but Jennifer on the sofa had neither moved nor spoken.

She hadn't spoken in the car either. Simon had sat and watched her trudging with her bag across the long stretch of sand towards that bleak little island. She had looked so forlorn he had almost got out of the car and run after her.

He hadn't, though.

Instead, he had gunned his car and tried to put her entirely out of his mind. Now, in the morning, he wished that he had stopped Jennifer from going over by herself. He realised that he was actually very worried about her. There was something odd about that Institute and the people over there. He got up and opened the curtains. It was a breezy but bright morning and the tide was in which reminded him that the island, and Jennifer, were currently cut off. Once the tide turned he resolved to drive across to the headland and walk across to find her. He then realised that Nancy might be there too which brought back all of his confusion.

Simon threw on some jeans and a loose shirt before padding down into the empty front room. He made himself a cup of coffee in the kitchen and sat down only to be startled by a sharp knocking on the front door. Thinking that it must be Jennifer, perhaps having decided not to stay the night on the island after all, he sprang up and opened the door expectantly.

It wasn't Jennifer on the doorstep.

It was Jack Kendell.

Ten minutes later the two men were sitting opposite each other at one of the wooden pub tables by the waterfront, taking each other's measure whilst waiting for their food to arrive.

Having been assured by the man on the doorstep that he was not there to bust any heads together, but just wanted to have a quiet chat, Simon had cautiously agreed to meet him on neutral ground for a spot of breakfast.

Kendell was dressed more casually than he had been in the lecture hall and, outside of the public-speaking environment, Simon noticed that he had lost the posturing and pomposity that had peppered his oratory. He looked drawn and tired as if he had been up all night. The deeply-etched lines around his eyes spoke of a life spent doing things rather than, like most people, merely commentating upon the actions of others.

"I was actually hoping for a word with your girlfriend" Kendell said, once Simon had sat down. "Is she around?"

"She's not my girlfriend, Mr Kendell, and she's not here at the moment. Can I help you?" Simon was still unclear as to the purpose of the businessman's visit and slightly nervous, given the nature of their first meeting. He frowned at Kendell. "How did you find us by the way?" Simon had not told anybody where they were staying and they were some distance from Shercombe now.

"With this." Kendell reached into his pocket and extracted a small card. He handed it across to Simon. It was one of Jennifer's business cards. Somebody had scrawled the address of the cottage onto the back of it. "Your red-headed friend left this in reception for me yesterday. Just after slandering me very loudly in public, remember?" he added drily but not, Simon noticed curiously, with any trace of malice or anger. Jack Kendell just seemed sad.

Their food arrived.

"I see. Well I'm sorry, Mr Kendell, but I have no idea why Jennifer left you her card. I presume she must have wanted to talk to you. She's looking into some funny-business at the institute down the coast." Simon took a sip of coffee and waited.

Jack Kendell took a few moments, as if he re-assuring himself of what he wanted to say. "Yesterday, your friend said some very hurtful things in that hall. Things which were completely untrue and which, if I were so-minded, I could quite easily take legal action over."

So that's it, thought Simon. Jennifer's in the shit.

"However," continued Kendell, "I have no intention of doing so if the lady will be kind enough to explain to me why she thinks that I may have had something to do with the death of Martine Dupuis. I'd like to know what her interest is in Martine's death and, as it seems from yesterday that she's barking up my tree about it, perhaps she'll give me a hearing so I can set her straight on some facts." Kendell took a sip of his tea.

"Also, for the record, I know that I'm shit at public-speaking, thanks very much. I don't enjoy it and I appreciate that I sound like a total prick whilst I'm doing it. I brought you both a refund." Kendell picked up his bacon sandwich and took a bite. "You see, Simon isn't it? I didn't push Martine Dupuis off that lighthouse to get her house. Quite the opposite. I loved her, Simon. I loved her very much… and she loved me."

Jack Kendell's voice faltered. Simon sat back and stared at him. He seemed to be genuinely upset and a very different character to the man he had seen on the stage.

Whilst contemplating Kendell, Simon found himself distracted momentarily by a small movement in his peripheral vision to the right of the businessman's head. In the distance, far out at sea, something was moving in the water.

Simon glanced at it briefly and thought that it might be a large dog but it was too far out to be playing. Whatever it was it appeared to be struggling in the water but then it disappeared back out of Simon's view behind Jack Kendell's head. Simon went back to concentrating on what the businessman was saying to him.

"So, you knew Martine Dupuis?" he asked cautiously. "You were in a relationship with her?" Kendell took another sip of tea and gazed candidly at Simon. He took a bite of his sandwich, clearly taking his time before responding.

"We were planning our wedding. Only the day before she died we had been talking about it. The whole thing about my getting her house is ludicrous. We *both* made wills. In favour of each other. I didn't leave her everything, you understand. I've got my kids to think about too." He looked up into the sky for a moment, as if remembering something upsetting.

"I left Martine a substantial sum in case something happened to me. She didn't want it, of course, and tried to talk me out of it but I insisted. Eventually, she only gave in and accepted it if I allowed her to do the same. I mean, to make a will herself leaving me something. So, she put the house in it. It was the only thing of value she had. It was just meant as a gesture. Then, the next day, she died and everyone said that she'd killed herself."

He put his mug down.

"And that's bollocks, Simon. She had absolutely no reason to. Even if she did, she was too kind and gentle to leave me like that. With so many questions. It makes no sense at all."

"So, what do you think did happen to her?" asked Simon. "Why would she have gone up to the lighthouse that night?"

Kendell looked distraught.

"I have absolutely no idea. She might have seen something, maybe, and gone up there to investigate? Then slipped, or something. It was wet and windy that night. God knows why she was up there. She got on with everyone she worked with too, no arguments, petty jealousies or anything. She loved those nerds. I can't believe that any of that lot would have meant her any harm. Let alone push her off..." he faltered again.

Simon was about to respond to this when he noticed something behind Jack Kendell's head again. Something rather extraordinary was occurring in the water at the end of the quay. The small object which he had observed in the sea earlier had, apparently, made its way in to the shore with its progress obscured by Kendell's head.

As he watched, the powerful frame of a fully-clothed, and utterly drenched, Jennifer Pettifyr slowly pulled itself up out of the water and landed, panting, onto the sand. It stayed there for a few moments before rising to its feet, with some difficulty, before proceeding to limp its way slowly and painfully up the beach towards them.

Her sodden jeans, t-shirt and jacket clung to Jennifer's muscular little frame like they had been sprayed on and Simon just stared at her, dumbfounded. Her wet hair was gleaming in the sunshine in contrast to her beautiful pale face and, so transfixed was he by the sight of her, it was at least ten seconds before Simon registered the nasty gash running down Jennifer's left thigh.

Now that she had exited the water, it had begun to seep blood out and into the fabric of her jeans. Jennifer staggered up to their table and stopped to shake out her curls (managing to shower Simon's crotch quite comprehensively with water in the process). Her chest heaving up and down, she looked from one to the other of them.

Finally, she got her breath back.

"Which one of you ordered Catch of the Day then?"

Chapter Twenty One

"Awkward"

One hour later, back in the cottage and wrapped up tightly in a warm fluffy dressing gown with a hot towel keeping her vicious curls at bay, the same Jennifer Pettifyr was feeling very much happier with her lot in life.

Firstly, she was naturally happy that the hard shove in the back she had received as she stood looking out from the lighthouse had not (as had, presumably, been the intention of whichever homicidal bastard had administered it) resulted in little Jennifer's premature demise on the rocks below. She had, she reflected, been bloody lucky. By some miracle, she had managed to survive the plunge into the rock-infested water, suffering only a relatively glancing graze to her leg which, whilst painful, had not proven incapacitating and she had been able, thankfully, to swim her way back to the mainland.

Secondly, the handsome Simon was now fussing over her like an anxious mother-hen and, frankly, she bloody well liked it. She liked it very very much indeed. Little Jennifer, she thought, could get used to a bit of this. She would prefer not to have to do the high dive and marathon swim every time to earn it though.

She took a sip of the industrial vat of single malt which Simon had kindly placed into her cold hands and lay back on the sofa, her painted toenails resting neatly upon Simon's lap, feeling inordinately pleased every time she clocked him taking a surreptitious glance at her powerful toned legs. Maybe, she thought happily, some boys do like sporty girls after all. Life, having not been lost at sea, was definitely looking up.

Jack Kendell was playing gooseberry on the chair by the wall. Having helped Jennifer back to the cottage, Simon had run her a bath and put her wet things on to wash. Now that she was back and resting on the sofa, Kendell was relating to both of them the rather startling tale which he had begun at the pub with Simon.

"Martine Dupuis saved my life, Miss Pettifyr. Well, not literally. What I mean is, she got me through a terrible period of my life and, well, without her I reckon I'd have topped myself." He looked at them with large, sad eyes. Here, in the cottage, he was not at all the larger than life character he had portrayed in Shercombe. Jennifer, like Simon, found herself rather warming to him. "I met her when she came here to manage the Institute. At a charity fund-raiser in town. She came into the room there and I thought, well, I thought she was the most beautiful woman I had ever seen in my life."

Kendell smiled and looked wistful.

"She was so classy and sophisticated. Brainy too, Martine was. Really clever. It was love at first sight for me. Well, we got talking and we just clicked, probably because we were so different. We just sparked off each other. The chemistry between us was... well, like nothing I'd felt before. She was the one, and I knew it after twenty minutes of chatting to her." He smiled to himself, clearly enjoying the memory.

"So, what was the problem?" Jennifer adjusted her dressing gown slightly. She had not entirely forgiven Simon for his date with Nancy. If he wanted a bit more of the Pettifyr thighs, she told herself, he was bloody well going to have to take her out first. "Did you ask her out?" she asked Kendell.

"The problem, Miss Pettifyr, was my wife."

"Awkward. Call me Jennifer, by the way."

"Well, what you need to understand, Jennifer, is that my wife Penny had always been a very jealous woman and, well, she was unstable. Mentally, I mean. By this time, I mean when I first met Martine, Penny had been on the pills for depression for about a decade and basically stayed at home drinking all the time. If we ever did go out she would end up getting pissed, crying and just shouting at me. Or worse."

"Worse?"

"She attacked me once with a carving knife."

"Fuckitty bollocks!"

"After that, well, I spent years just trying to manage the situation at home, keeping the family in one piece..."

Kendell looked more distressed now.

"It was really hard. I got her some help, cleaners and the like, so she didn't have to lift a finger, but I guess I threw myself into work too much to get away from her. Probably made things worse. But, eventually, things came to a head, as these things always do. Martine and I met again in town, by accident, one day and the same spark was still there, just like at the charity night. We had lunch together and it was wonderful, like we had known each other for years. We started meeting up for lunch regularly until, well..."

"You started sleeping together" Jennifer finished for him.

"I'm not proud of myself, Miss Pe... Jennifer. We fell in love with each other. It didn't feel wrong for either of us. She made me so happy, I can't tell you. I thought I could have two lives, you know, and make it work. Stupid prick that I am."

Simon, who had been listening quietly, whilst trying not to be distracted by Jennifer's leopard print thong drying innocently upon the radiator, leant forward. "You're referring to your wife in the past tense, Jack" he asked quietly. "Where is she now?"

Kendell looked at him with a faintly surprised expression.

"Sorry. I thought everyone knew about Penny, but you're not from around here. She's dead, Simon. She got drunk one night and... cut her wrists, at home. I'd gone away to Bath on business and I was, to my eternal shame, in a hotel with Martine when she did it. My daughter came home and found her mother. She was dead in the bathtub."

Chapter Twenty-Two

"Playsuit"

"Well, kiss my ginger tits. I did not see that coming."

The request was sadly rhetorical as Jennifer was now dressed, having applied a roll of bandage to her grazed thigh before re-applying the towel to her still-damp head. Jack Kendell had now gone, but not before reiterating that, prior to her supposed suicide, Martine Dupuis had agreed to become his wife. For the sake of Jack's family, and reputation locally, she had insisted they keep things quiet until her contract at the institute was up and they could move away from the area for a fresh start. Without the cloud of his first wife's suicide hanging over them.

Kendell had, also, invited them to a party at his house that evening. It was another fund-raiser and, he explained, several of the institute scientists would also be going so Jennifer would know some other people. He guaranteed that the food and drink would be top quality and, more importantly, gratis. Jennifer, who had rather grown to like Jack Kendell over the last couple of hours, and who was also never a lady to pass up a canapé, accepted graciously on behalf of them both.

Once he had left, Jennifer had tapped Simon smartly on the chest and made it quite clear in words of two-fisted syllables that, as the invite was clearly just for the two of them, any bright ideas which he might be entertaining about shoe-horning little Nancy big-baps in on his arm would result in her wearing his bollocks as earrings. In other words, normal diplomatic relations had been restored.

"Who pushed you off the lighthouse, anyway?" Simon asked this partly out of a desire to change the subject but mostly from genuine concern. Jennifer, who had been lying back on the sofa performing bicycle kicks with her muscular legs, jumped up suddenly, sending the towel flying from her head and releasing a violent cascade of red into the room. The hair had clearly had enough and was back on the bash.

"I have no fucking idea." She disappeared into the kitchen.

"Did you upset anyone whilst you were over there?" Simon called through. He heard the kettle boiling and, shortly afterwards, Jennifer stomped back in.

"I'm ignoring that question, Simon. Of course not. I'm lovely." Simon wisely decided to keep his opinion on that to himself and, instead, allowed Jennifer to continue. "I'll be honest with you, it's a bit of a head-fuck." She sat down. "The worst I encountered over there (other than the hollow woman, of course, which Jennifer was definitely not going to dwell upon now) was a bit of low-level dissing at the hands of your fulsome girlfriend, but I'm putting that down to natural jealousy on her part. Other than that, I thought we were all getting along famously."

The redhead was suddenly thoughtful.

"Unless, of course, they are sore losers. I did kick their butts super-hard at Escape from Colditz, you see. Hmm. That might have rankled. Yes, there could be motive there…"

Simon looked at her dubiously. I bet she was the Nazis, he thought. "I don't think losing at a board game sounds like a particularly strong motive for murder…"

Jennifer stared back at him.

"Are you fucking joking, Simon? Anyway, the real kick in the bollocks here is that the only one of them even quasi-fit enough to get up to that lighthouse and in through a dodgy old window to give little Pettifyr the push, is your Nancy. If, that is, she could manage to squeeze her fat ego and mammaries through the gap, obviously."

"She's not my Nancy, and there's no need to be quite so nasty about her" Simon said patiently. Jennifer scowled, as much at herself for going down this silly road again as at Simon for leaping to the girl's defence. She put up a hand to acknowledge her yellow card before continuing.

"Anyway, it couldn't have been her. About one minute before I got the shove I was around the other side of the gangway, looking down at the institute. I saw Nancy, plain as day, taking a tray of tea into the bedroom block. There is no way she could have made it over in time and, by the way," she turned to Simon and looked seriously at him for a moment. She was so striking and, as she looked into his eyes, Simon found himself blushing.

"Did you tell her I was a sad and lonely old bag?"

Simon was stunned. "What? Of course I didn't! No."

"Good. Because I'm not. I'm just a bit odd sometimes, that's all. I can't help it." Her voice had gone small again and she went back into the kitchen to construct her coffee from the, now boiled, kettle. Simon just stared after her.

Jennifer made her drink in the kitchen, humming happily to herself. It was, she decided, good to be alive today. She smiled at how Simon had clearly been stealing looks at her legs and how his pupils had just dilated when she had looked into his eyes. Maybe, just maybe, she thought, she might have a chance there after all.

Later that afternoon, they were back together on the road. This time, Jennifer Pettifyr was driving. Her good mood in the cottage had lasted a record-breaking twenty-eight seconds before her brain had woken up and she had realised that she now possessed nothing more than the clothes she was standing up in.

Her beautiful leather hold-all was missing, presumed lost in action. She had put it down on the grass before clambering into the lighthouse. The loss of the bag itself was traumatic enough, but Jennifer was more concerned about the current whereabouts of one particular item which lay at the bottom of the bag. Namely her ornate, and rather specially-adapted, pearl-handled revolver called Jessica. As a result, Simon and Jennifer were now powering out of the village. With the car under Jennifer's control, the Devon countryside flashed by. She piloted the little silver roadster around the twisting lanes with a degree of ruthless expertise that Simon found breath-taking.

Jennifer Pettifyr exhibited almost a sixth sense for oncoming traffic and displayed such authority behind the wheel that Simon started to think that she must actually be a professional driver. Or a witch. Both seemed entirely possible.

In truth, being behind the wheel of a fast car always made Jennifer happy and it was the time at which she felt most at ease with herself. Despite her often brusque manner, Jennifer had a somewhat unusual empathy for the feelings of others which, whilst very useful in her profession, was also something of a burden and, since her early teens, she had always longed for solitude simply in order to be able to think properly. Driving gave her freedom from the emotional noise of life and a wonderful opportunity to push herself to the edge. She found the combination intoxicating. Driving was, after all, in her blood.

Jennifer was also extremely angry with herself.

So far, she decided, she had pretty much just been arsing about and she needed to up her game, quite substantially, if she was going to avoid a premature memorial service attended by her mother and probably nobody else. Even her mother wasn't a definite. Jennifer was under no illusions as to how fortunate she had been to escape with her life earlier. She did not put much faith in her luck holding out either. She needed to get back onto the front foot otherwise, she mused whilst throwing the little car around another bend, it was highly probable that she was going to be fucked. And not in a good (champagne and massage first) kind of way. Just in a fucking dead way. She stamped an angry foot down onto the accelerator.

Her passenger, for the record, was also concerned for his own personal safety. Not, however, because of any lunatic running loose on the island but because of Jennifer's driving. The only way Simon could ever have envisaged his car travelling at its current speed was if somebody had dropped it out of an aircraft. He just wanted the ride to stop so that he could throw up.

A shopping trip, Jennifer had decided, was required. Mainly because, in the absence of her bag, she had absolutely nothing to change into and partly because she just wanted to buy a nice dress to wear to the fund-raiser. Thankfully, her wallet had been in the zip pocket of her jacket and had survived intact. She wanted, for once, to make the best of herself and to have a fun night out with an attractive man who didn't, so far, appear either to hate her (unusual) or to be a complete shit (unheard of). In other words, a bit of a catch.

Jennifer drove them smartly into town and parked up. She even paid the meter herself (a life-event that would have got her sectioned if her family had witnessed it). They agreed to split up, for an hour, to do their shopping.

Simon, after spending the initial fifteen minutes sitting quietly on a bench waiting for his guts to settle, located a small gentlemen's outfitters on the High St where, after a bit of slightly too close to the balls inside-leg measuring, he acquired a seriously smart and ruthlessly well-fitting dinner suit. He finished off his ensemble with an elegant pair of black leather shoes. Easy. Job done in thirty minutes. He made his way to the cafe where they had arranged to meet.

Jennifer, on the other hand, was in a world of sartorial pain. She tried on a dress. Too tight. A trouser suit. Too hot. Another dress. Too pink. Another suit. Too butch. Another dress. Too shit. A playsuit? Oooh. Gorgeous, but inappropriate. A jumper. What? Stop looking at fucking jumpers, Jennifer, it's a cocktail party! Concentrate.

Another dress. Too formal. One more. Too slutty. Jeans and a sparkly top? What, so it's an office Christmas party now, is it? Try again. The playsuit. Oh, fucking hell, Jennie, just buy the sodding playsuit.

Shit, as mother used to say, or get your arse off the potty.

One hour fifteen later, an utterly demoralised Jennifer found herself in the wedding section where a nice young girl, having witnessed most of the earlier comings and goings, took pity on her and, sizing her up professionally, flitted through a few racks before pulling out a little black item which, she assured Jennifer, would do the business very nicely indeed. Jennifer, too tired to argue at this stage, stumped up for the dress (and the playsuit) and asked, quietly, if she could also get some help choosing shoes.

So, only a trifling seventy minutes late, Jennifer and bags rejoined Simon, and his third coffee, at their rendezvous point. Conscious of her tardiness, she declined his offer of a drink (whilst appreciating that, to her surprise, he did not mention her lateness). As the pair walked back to the car together, in the late afternoon sunshine, Simon watched Jennifer. She was unusually quiet and he had more time to study her. The bruising around her eye seemed to have cleared up.

As she walked along the busy street, Simon suddenly had an image of Jennifer being pushed from the top of the lighthouse walkway. Somebody had attempted to kill her and the realisation made him stop dead in the road. Jennifer herself just strode on, swinging her bags around like an eight year-old.

Chapter Twenty-Three

"Nonchalant"

Back at the cottage, Jennifer made a couple of short telephone calls whilst Simon sat in the downstairs lavatory trying to work off his second bout of car sickness. Jennifer's motoring back to Bursands had replaced all of Simon's amorous thoughts with a basic desire for self-preservation. He sat quietly, splashing water onto his face, attempting not to vomit.

Jennifer's first telephone call was to the Causeway Inn. The pub was located three hundred yards down the road from Jack Kendell's house. Whilst Simon's cottage and sofa were lovely, she felt that she was now at risk of outstaying her welcome. She did not want to become a nuisance because, and this was a realisation which she found concerning and exciting in equal measure, she really did like him. The last thing she wanted was to mess things up by inflicting too much of her personality upon him too soon. So, Jennifer was booking a room near the party tonight. This had the additional benefit of placing her walking-distance from the institute which, she reasoned, should probably be receiving more of her attention than the six-foot hunk feeling green in the bathroom.

Jennifer's second call was a very short one to London, during which she provided the kindly old lady, in the East London flat, with an update on her change of address and a brief synopsis of her activities in Devon to-date. For the record, that particular call generated a significant flurry of activity at the London end, the net result of which was to land rather heavily upon her doorstep later that evening.

Jennifer sighed and sat down on the sofa. She contemplated another coffee but then had a bright idea. She bounced up and made a third call, this time to the institute. There was an outside chance that her bag might have been found. At the very least if, by some miracle, it was still sitting by the lighthouse she could get Nicholson to waddle over and get it. She dialled the number and waited. After what seemed like an eternity, the line was picked up at the other end. A female voice answered the telephone.

Of course, it would be. Nancy bitch-face.

"Hello? Bursands Institute." The irritating voice drawled at snail-pace and Jennifer instantly took against it. For that reason, she adopted her most unpleasant, supercilious and condescending tone (i.e. her pitch-perfect impersonation of Miranda Pettifyr, her eldest sibling). Take some of this then, you boyfriend-stealing tart. Then, slightly embarrassed, she remembered that she was actually a grown woman of nearly thirty not thirteen.

Oh, sod it.

"Doctor Nicholson, please" she snapped. "It's urgent."

There was a very long pause at the other end of the line.

"Who is this speaking, please?"

"This is Jennifer Pettifyr, Nancy. From the Ministry, yes? Can you fetch Doctor Nicholson please?" There was an even longer pause. It was so long that Jennifer assumed that Nancy must have left the room. After about a minute, the girl's painfully slow voice came back onto the line.

"She's busy. Don't think she would want to be disturbed. Do you want to leave a message?" Jennifer rolled her eyes and fumed. She would happily bet dollar that the little toss-pot had not even bothered to look.

"No, thank you, Nancy. Anyway, it doesn't really matter because I'll be seeing her later at the Kendell fund-raiser." Take that, you little twat.

"Oh. Going to that party then, are you?" drawled the girl.

Jennifer, now in no mood for small talk, went full-bitch.

"Yes, Nancy. Simon and I are, indeed, going to the ball. Together actually. Jack Kendell is a personal friend of ours. Anyway, I'm sure that we both have lots of work to do, don't we? Those tables won't wipe themselves, so, as Doctor Nicholson is clearly so 'busy', I suggest that we both run along now. Bye bye!" She slammed the phone down on the girl. Bloody little cow.

Jennifer stood breathing hard and looking down at the telephone. What the hell was wrong with her? Why had she felt such an overwhelming need to be so unpleasant to the poor girl? Nancy just seemed to bring out the very worst in Jennifer. The girl, somehow, pushed all of the buttons which she had been trying so hard to bury since her horrible school days. Perhaps she should telephone back and apologise.

Jennifer, suddenly, felt utterly wretched. What kind of person was she turning into? Simon emerged from the toilet. He was still looking green, so Jennifer gestured him down to the sofa and disappeared into the kitchen. She returned a few minutes later, carrying a strong sweet mug of tea and sat down next to him. She put the mug into his hands.

"Thank you. Sorry. I guess I'm not a very good passenger."

"Or driver." She poked him on the arm. "Joke." Jennifer gave him another once over before thinking, again, about how badly she had just behaved on the telephone. She made a decision. "Right, I've booked myself a room at the Causeway Inn for a couple of nights, yes?"

"Oh." Simon looked at her. "Right, well, if that's what you want it makes sense, I guess. You're more than welcome to stay here though... please don't feel you have to leave on my account. I, well, it's quite nice having you actually. Here I mean. In the cottage. Having you here. Not, like, having you..." Stop talking now, Simon told himself.

"That's very kind of you, Simon, but I suspect that you're just being polite" replied Jennifer, who was rather touched by his tone. "I am, as I am frequently told, a lot of a fucking nightmare. Thanks for putting up with me so far though..." Their eyes met properly. Jennifer realised that they had, up until then, rather been skirting around each other. "I do appreciate it, you know" she said quietly.

"Really. You've been very kind."

"Kind? Don't be daft. Anyway, you're not a nightmare at all..."

Jennifer showed nothing on her face but was inwardly surprised at the intensity of his outburst and at the way in which he was now looking at her. She felt it right in her jeans and, she reflected ruefully, he wouldn't be on the bloody sofa that night if she had her way. Not unless she was straddling him, anyway. Bollocks, she had booked the fucking room now. Right, anyway, say something Jennifer. This is awkward enough without him thinking that you're a psycho. Play it cool, she told herself. Calm down. The code word, today, is nonchalant. "Stop it, Simon" she said. "Next thing you know we'll be getting married…" Balls on toast.

"I'll run you over" he said softly.

Jennifer had a vision of being smacked into by a maniacal Simon, grinning out of his little car with his foot down, doing ninety. Then she remembered his driving and revised that down to thirty. Fifteen max on the bends.

"To the inn. I'll run you over there now."

"Gotcha, yes. Fine. Lovely! Much appreciated…"

She flapped around for a bit longer.

"Brilliant. Right. A final wee first, though?" Jennifer pointed towards the toilet, as if suggesting they visit it together. "One for the road and all that…" Which was, as she told herself angrily on the toilet two minutes later, a fuck-tard thing to say.

Twenty minutes later, Jennifer and shopping were dropped off in the evening sunshine at the Causeway Inn. Jennifer stood, quietly for once in her life, watching Simon extract her bags from the boot. He gave her a warm hug and made her promise to allow him to ply her with drinks at the party.

Jennifer nodded quickly and, unable to pluck up the courage to give him a kiss, watched him drive away. She felt a pang at being alone again and wondered what was the matter with her. Normally, she just ploughed straight in feet first. This one seemed to be defeating her. With a sigh, Jennifer Pettifyr picked up her bags and went into the pub.

Chapter Twenty-Four

"Pants"

Three hours later, Jennifer had still not turned up. Simon, assuming that she was simply being fashionably late rather than having an actual problem, helped himself to another drink at the bar whilst having a good look around the enormous dining-room. He was trying hard not to break anything. Jack Kendell had a beautiful home and it was furnished surprisingly tastefully. He took a sip of his cocktail and enjoyed the chill of the strong alcohol on the back of his throat. It made him think of Jennifer's red boots, up on the table, and he smiled to himself. He found himself wondering what she would be wearing.

He did not have to wait long. Simon did not initially hear the sound of the heels but the party-goers lowering their drinks around him and looking over his shoulder should have alerted him. As it was, Simon just happened to turn back from the bar, on the off-chance, when he saw her.

Tip-toeing precariously into the bar, balanced delicately upon a treacherously unfamiliar pair of heels, a certain red-headed lady was tottering into the room, one cautious step at a time. She was wearing a simple, yet elegant, black dress and, unnoticed by her, the room into which she had entered stopped moving. Literally.

Everybody who noticed her just stared. For that frozen moment, Jennifer Jane Pettifyr looked as beautiful as a sunset dripping lazily over a Greek island and yet as vulnerable as a new-born foal abandoned on Oxford Street. She had the physique of an Olympic athlete and, as she moved, her black dress clung to her body like the skin on a wet seal. Her thick red hair glistened under the bright lights of the chandeliers and Simon watched, transfixed, as she made her slow and rather uncertain progress across the floor towards him. He had never, in his life, seen anything quite so heart-stoppingly beautiful.

Jennifer, quite oblivious to the attention that she was generating, was genuinely just wondering how normal females managed to get through life if this was the kind of thing that constituted a 'normal Saturday night out'. She could barely walk and her dress made her feel like a self-conscious sausage.

Then there were the shoes.

Fucking death-traps. She had removed them in the pub earlier, having not even been able to get down the stairs, and had actually contemplated walking over to Kendell's house in her pig slippers before remembering that they were lost with the rest of her stuff. She had braved it barefoot, instead, slipping the heels back on in a bush outside.

Simon was now walking up to her, looking annoyingly handsome in his dinner suit, and obviously quite able to walk spectacularly unaided in his shiny new flat shoes. Smug bastard. She hoped he got a blister.

"You look stunning…"

It was all that Simon could find to say. She quite took his breath away. Jennifer Pettifyr, however, was never a lady to pass up the opportunity to piss on anybody's parade. Particularly not when her feet hurt, she was feeling embarrassed and she didn't have a drink in her hand.

"Wind your cock in, Casanova. We've got work to do."

Despite her remark Jennifer was, for the record, actually rather chuffed about Simon's compliment. She was normally extremely self-conscious about her sporty physique (most of the men she encountered in bars generally took one look before asking when her next fight was, to which her usual response was "in about three seconds if you don't fuck off"). Jennifer had therefore decided to play this situation coolly. Particularly in light of the other, somewhat more sensitive, wardrobe issue with which she was currently wrestling.

She tapped Simon on the chest.

"Your very important job this evening," she said quietly, "is to stop me from sitting down. Clear?" Feeling that her point had landed, Jennifer turned her attention to looking around for a passing cocktail. She clocked a nearby waiter and began to study its flightpath.

"What?" Simon asked.

"What what?" Jennifer said, irritated as she had been just about to launch herself towards a passing vessel of alcohol.

"What," said Simon, a little testily, "as in, what the fuck are you going on about? Sitting down?" Jennifer rolled her eyes.

"No pants, Simon!" she hissed like a viper with a tax bill, causing more than a few heads to turn in their direction. She poked him in the chest again. "We don't want Little Jennie Junior putting in a cameo!" She bobbed about for a bit, wriggling around in an attempt to tease a little bit of extra length out of the fabric.

"Right. Yes. Loud and clear."

"I swear, Simon, if..."

Jennifer began her sentence but then she stopped dead. Staring across the room, she noticed something which made her forget her clothing discomfort and, instead, gave her a nasty prickling at the nape of the neck. On the far side of the room, a young man was moving amongst the guests. He was wearing a dark, well-fitted suit and a dark-red shirt.

Jennifer recognised him. The body shape. The posture and gait. The black hair was slicked back, this evening, on the young man that she had first encountered outside the ruined chapel on the cliffs above Bursands. The man, she realised now from seeing him in motion, who was also most definitely the night-visitor to the refectory who had subsequently managed to disappear into thin air. In the panic of finding herself pitched over the edge of a cliff and having to swim for her life, Jennifer had quite forgotten about him. The more she thought about it, the further up her list of would-be assassins this little scrotum started to climb as well.

If a man can disappear from inside a building (and a key to that locked basement door seemed the most plausible explanation), she reasoned, then he could just as easily re-appear to give little Jennifer Jane the unhelping hand in the back.

She was about to set off in pursuit but at that point Simon, for once in his life, surprised her by doing something constructive. He tapped her on the shoulder and handed her an ice-cold saucer of champagne. Jennifer Pettifyr, always the consummate professional, made an executive decision in the field and decided that the man in black could fucking well wait.

Sipping her fizz, she took a surreptitious glance up and down Simon in his suit (very James Bond, she thought). Right, balls to the wall, Jennifer. She dipped her big toe into the murky waters of conventional small-talk.

"So, about the sleeping arrangements later…" she started off brightly enough, before panicking that her crass reference to the bedroom so early on would scupper her game-plan before she even got going. Jennifer, you see, rather fancied a bit of bedroom. She took another deep breath and pressed on nervously. "Thanks again for putting me up, by the way. I know I didn't really give you much choice, and I also know that I can be a chronic pain in the plums at the best of times. It was very kind of you. Anyway, my room at the inn is quite nice actually. You should pop up later for the tour. Huge bed, and a lovely view…" Jennifer smiled shyly up at him, now wishing that she had spent far less time fighting at school and far more time paying attention to the cool girls when they were explaining, after hours, how to attract boys.

Simon smiled back and clinked her champagne glass against his own. He looked warmly at the little redhead and could not help, once again, making a comparison between her and Nancy. His date with Nancy, although lovely, and Jennifer's subsequent emergence from the sea had reminded him that attraction hits you in the guts and not just in the eyes.

Nancy was elegant, intense and her sheer physical beauty was something which he had never experienced before. That said, being with her felt strangely like watching a play. Her actions often seemed intended for effect, rather than driven by emotion. Nancy's mannered-grace made you feel as if a private performance was being staged for your benefit. A deeply flattering experience, but still a performance.

Jennifer, on the other hand, was an absolute Grade-A total nut job pain in the arse. The fact that, in spite of this reality, Simon just wanted to pick her up and spend the night in her strong little arms (and could think of little else but waking up into her thick red hair) told him, he suspected, something probably quite important about himself. The strange little lady had somehow taken his mind completely off his last, really quite painful, relationship in London. He took a sip of his drink.

"Well, actually," he said, clinking her glass again. Just tell her. "I was rather hoping that…" Simon did not get to finish his sentence, however, because at that moment Jack Kendell popped-up between them, looking every inch the game-show host. He was dressed to the nines in a white tuxedo, black trousers and a black bow tie like a budget Humphrey Bogart.

His hair was slicked back neatly with oil. Simon stepped back from Jennifer, remembering that she was, really, here on business anyway. He could speak to her properly after working hours. He owed her that much at least. Instead, he sipped his drink quietly as Jack Kendell spoke to them.

"Thanks for coming, both of you. It means a lot." Kendell shook Simon's hand and kissed Jennifer on both cheeks. The lady was cursing his timing. Unless she was imagining things, which was a possibility that she never completely discounted, Simon had been about to say something important. Whilst she never trusted her instincts where boys were concerned, after too many bad experiences, he had definitely been looking at her fondly. The Pettifyr legs had also been checked out on quite a number of occasions. As soon as Jack fucked off, she would have a deep chug of champagne and attempt a move. She was rusty and nervous, but bollocks to it. You got pushed off a fucking cliff, she told herself, how hard can getting a snog be?

Jennifer re-focused her attention. Jack Kendell had been saying something but, thinking about Simon, she had tuned out and had not been paying attention.

"Anyway, here they are" went on their host. "I'd like to introduce you to my family. This is my son, William." Jack Kendell was gesturing to his left. Jennifer's hackles rose sharply as, suddenly, the youth in black she had identified as the refectory intruder was standing in front of her. Jennifer gathered her wits, quickly, trying to work out how to play the situation. She felt mentally off-balance. As if her heels were not trouble enough.

Her guard being down, the sucker punch that came next was really rather cruel. A second figure had quietly joined their small group. It wore a dark-crimson Chinese evening gown, fashioned exquisitely from silk. The tall, voluptuous figure filled the garment to feminine perfection. The long, dark hair fell in a wave across the large eyes and the slightly angular face.

Jennifer had recognised the creature's scent a lifetime before Jack Kendell confirmed her fears. "And this, although I guess you must know each other already, is my beautiful daughter Nancy."

Chapter Twenty-Five
"Hard-ball"

The two women stood about three feet apart. Nancy Kendell, arm in arm with her (twin?) brother, looked utterly exquisite. Jennifer's heart sank. The girl looked at her with a variant of the disinterested facial expression which characterised their encounters at the institute but, now, it was coloured with something else. On home turf, it carried a more defined arrogance, amplified perhaps by the setting and, possibly thought Jennifer, by the presence of her brother. The two women, so physically at odds with each other, might have been from different species. It was like a mongoose facing off against a cobra.

A very beautiful cobra, Jennifer thought ruefully.

Her attention turned from the snake to its brother. He was an equally striking, if not conventionally handsome, young man with a lean face and long dark hair. He was standing very still and staring at Jennifer, not in a particularly rude or objectionable way, but with a kind of detached curiosity as if she were a laboratory rat being monitored for emerging signs of infection.

The physical similarity between the siblings, when together, was quite notable. The effect was accentuated by Nancy's dress, and the matching choker around her throat, being an identical shade of crimson to her brother's silk shirt.

"Hello, Jennifer" said Nancy.

Even the use of her first name grated upon Jennifer's ears, although that was completely ridiculous in the circumstances. What exactly did she expect? To be referred to as 'Miss' in the girl's own home? Jennifer felt stupid, particularly as she remembered how she had lorded it over the girl earlier in the day on the telephone. Nancy was still speaking to her.

"You disappeared in quite a hurry earlier."

Feeling stupid or not, Jennifer did not like the girl's tone and was also acutely conscious that the young man by her side, upon whose arm Nancy was perching, was currently topping the suspect list for her own attempted-murder.

She decided to play some hard-ball.

"I fancied a swim, Nancy. Lovely view from the lighthouse, isn't it? To die for." Neither Nancy nor her brother said anything but, unless she imagined it, the boy moved his head slightly and a whisper of a frown passed across his face. Nancy just continued her dead, blank stare. Until, that is, she turned to Simon and played some hard-ball of her own.

"Hello, you…" she said, smiling like a supernova. The younger woman extricated herself from her brother, moved her body into Simon's and collected him effortlessly with a confident arm.

"Why don't we leave the old people to talk while I give you the tour…" Simon, unable to object without appearing extremely ill-mannered, allowed Nancy to steer him off towards the French windows. Jennifer watched them leave. Nancy's beautiful dress, cut low at the back, seemed to taunt her as it departed.

She felt alone, suddenly bereft of allies, standing there with Jack Kendell and his rather peculiar son. Jennifer noticed that the boy was also watching his sister leaving the room arm in arm with Simon. The look on his face was hard to read, but Jennifer did not like it. She reflected again upon her experience at the lighthouse. It seemed scarcely credible that this young man might have, for no reason whatsoever that she could fathom, have felt the urge to mount the stone steps and commit cold-blooded murder. It was utterly ridiculous and yet somebody had done exactly that. There was definitely something off-kilter about the two siblings though. For the first time, since arriving in Devon, Jennifer thought that she might be making some progress.

Jack Kendell looked a little embarrassed, presumably by his daughter's rather offensive parting shot which had clearly been directed at Jennifer. She warmed to him again, remembering the affection with which he had described his feelings for Martine Dupuis. Poor Martine, who had apparently chosen to leap to her death in the dark.

Remembering the circumstances of Martine's death, Jennifer immediately felt guilty for her barbed comment to Nancy about the lighthouse. That said, she then looked again at William Kendell who was obtaining a fresh glass of champagne. Somebody had pushed Jennifer from the lighthouse. It was asking a lot to believe that Dupuis had jumped voluntarily from exactly the same spot, supposedly seeking escape from a world that was too much of a burden for her but which, according to Jack Kendell, had actually offered her a future of love, happiness and financial security.

Aware of her scrutiny, William Kendell turned directly to face Jennifer and spoke for the first time. His voice was a lower, more masculine, mirror of Nancy's lilt and contained the same faintly mocking undertone.

"I like your dress. Was it expensive?" He fixed her with an unnecessarily direct and slightly watery gaze. Jennifer wondered, idly, what substances he was taking. Both he and Nancy exhibited the same, slightly off-kilter, symptoms of recreational drug use which were so familiar to her from drinking out in London.

"What, this old thing? British Home Stores' finest!"

This drew a laugh from Jack Kendell but a blank and perplexed frown from his son. Jennifer decided to chance her arm.

"You do look very familiar, you know, Billy. Not just because of Nancy, obviously. Twins are you? Very similar. No, anyway, I could swear that we've met before. But then, of course, I've been stuck over on the island... so that can't be the case can it?" She eyeballed him for any sign of reaction, before carrying on. "Anyway, speaking of the island, a funny thing happened to me there. Fortunately, I don't take milk in my coffee because, and you'll never guess what, I was sat there minding my own business one evening when some jumped up little twat-bag just came down right in the middle of the night and, cool as a cucumber, walked off with the whole pint. Straight out of the fridge. I mean, really, Billy. What about that? Selfish, or what? I might have wanted some cornflakes."

Billy Kendell stared at Jennifer.

She felt the cold chill of his appraisal, but she was satisfied by his obvious wariness towards her. When the boy finally spoke it was again in the soft burr that reminded Jennifer of Nancy (and, come to that, she remembered the disturbing disembodied voice from the telephone call in Nicholson's office). "Maybe you're mixing me up with the ghost, Jennifer? After all, I heard that you did have a bit of a scare last night…" With the faintest of smirks, the young man sipped at his drink.

Jennifer, however, was very firmly back on her front foot. If this tosser had been responsible for pushing her, he must now be wondering how she was still alive and kicking. That thought was probably what made her finish her drink and say the first thing that popped into her head.

"Maybe I'm the ghost, Billy. Back for revenge."

The youth continued to stare at her, without speaking, until the silence became awkward enough that Jack Kendell felt the need to intervene. They talked for a while about his businesses and about the charity. A clearly-bored Billy Kendell left them, gracelessly, and sauntered out onto the terrace. Jack Kendell watched him leave and then turned to Jennifer.

"I'm sorry about Billy. And Nancy, for that matter."

He frowned.

"Since their mum died they've both been, well, angry I guess. To be honest, I didn't expect Billy to turn up tonight at all. Nancy must have persuaded him."

"They do look remarkably similar" observed Jennifer.

"Twins. Take after their mum too, both of them. Nancy is the spit of her mother at that age. I just hope that's where the resemblance ends." Jennifer raised an eyebrow. "Their mother was a deeply disturbed woman with a very violent temper. Nancy, I'm afraid, is a little too similar for her own good. A bit prone to flying off the handle first and engaging her brain later."

"Really? She seems unusually calm to me" said Jennifer, thinking back to the dull, blank-faced girl from the refectory.

"What? Our Nancy?" Jack looked surprised. "Don't believe that for a second, love. Oh, she can be polite enough if you're not in her way, I suppose. Cross her, though, and you'll see a different side of her." He looked embarrassed. "Sorry, you must think that's a terrible thing for a father to say about his own daughter."

He looked over towards the French windows where his guests were now making their way back in from the terrace outside. "Nancy does take after her mother, though. She won't ever be told, and she's as stubborn as a mule when she wants something."

Jennifer thought about this for the moment and her mind went back to the lighthouse. "And Billy?" she asked. A shadow crossed Jack Kendell's face, and he looked sad for a moment. He looked carefully at Jennifer, as if weighing up what her interest really was in this conversation, before finally speaking.

"He can be just as bad. Billy and Nancy are very similar in a lot of ways, not just in looks. Billy clammed right up after Penny died, though, and he won't talk to me about anything. He just hangs around with Nancy all the time, if he's not out prowling on the cliffs."

"At least, I tell myself, he's devoted to his sister and they still have each other. They're like two peas, always together and plotting something or other. Same since they were kids. Inseparable."

"Did they know about your relationship with Martine?"

Jack Kendell looked at her, uncomfortably, and fidgeted with his drink. "Nancy found out, yes. Unfortunately. It wasn't what either of us wanted to happen, not then at least. I wanted to explain things to them both properly, once the time was right, but Nancy saw us kissing one night in town."

Kendell sipped his drink.

"She came to me about it the next day. I tried to explain it to her, and she seemed to take it quite well, all things considered. She wasn't getting on very well with her mum at that stage and, well, I guess maybe she understood why I might want to find some happiness with somebody else."

"She must have known Martine well, working at the institute?"

"Oh no, not at all. She wasn't working there then. Nancy, I mean. She only got that job a few months ago. I don't know why, to be honest. I mean, no offence, they're lovely people, but Nancy doesn't need the money and, for the life of me, I never thought I'd see the day when she would be waiting on other people. I don't like to say this about her but she is, and this is entirely my fault, quite spoilt. Maybe the job will do her some good and teach her some humility. I'm sorry she was rude to you."

Jennifer waved that away and smiled at him.

"So, Nancy lives here then? With Billy and yourself?"

"That's right. It's a big place, so the pair of them have the top floor to themselves. A couple of rooms, a lounge and some kitchen stuff up there. Like I said, they spend nearly all their time together unless they're out. Thick as thieves. At least I still have them at home, even if they don't ever bloody talk to me." He laughed ruefully, but Jennifer could sense pain behind the joviality. She suspected that Jack Kendell's relationship with his children was a source of more soul-searching than he was admitting.

"The gardens are beautiful" she said, sensing a change of subject would probably be welcome. Jennifer had walked through the grounds on her way up from the pub and had admired the garden when she had stopped to slip on her heels.

"Thanks. The place is incredibly old, actually. The property runs from the house here right down to the rocks by the causeway. We fenced off the end when the kids were small, to stop them running off getting hurt. They spent half of their childhood playing in the secret garden and the grotto."

Kendell smiled at the memory. "They loved it. Penny and I wouldn't see them for hours on end."

"Secret garden?" Jennifer asked and Jack laughed.

"Sorry, the kids called it that. It's basically an old maze and some random old stone outbuildings. It's hidden down in the woods near the edge of our property. A complete rabbit warren down there. The historians reckon that, in the old days, smugglers used to come and go around here and used those buildings to store stuff. Nancy and Billy made it into their den years ago. Nobody else is allowed down there. Nancy's orders."

He laughed, presumably reminded of a version of his daughter from a younger and happier time. "I never go down there. I'd get lost in five minutes! Penny used to laugh at me about it. Apparently, anyway, the island over the way was a haven for smuggling. Secret tunnels, all that crap. Probably a load of rubbish to get the tourists down, but the kids loved it. Nancy and Billy used to play at being pirates."

"Tunnels?" Jennifer was intrigued.

"Oh, I don't know. I think it's guff. If there are any, the kids have never mentioned anything. Anyway, can I get you another drink, or are you in training for something?" Jack Kendell nodded at Jennifer's rather well-muscled arms. Inwardly she groaned, but responded graciously.

"Another drink would be lovely and, no, I'm not in training. I just wrestle a lot of bears in my spare time." Kendell grinned and slipped away to the bar. He returned, shortly, with a drink for Jennifer before excusing himself in order to put himself about with his other guests. Jennifer sipped her drink and made her way outside onto the terrace. It overlooked a grand, landscaped garden surrounded on three sides by tall trees and a well-maintained series of hedges.

She stood, for a moment, gazing out across the lawn. It was dark and the garden was lit, rather prettily, by a series of low-level lamps positioned evenly along the edges of the flower beds. At the far end of the garden, Jennifer noticed a break in the hedge and what looked, from distance, like a small archway. It was hidden in the shadows.

She finished her drink and, removing her shoes (which was a blessed relief) and securing them neatly out of sight behind a nearby plant pot, she made her way down across the lawn to the archway. Beyond it lay a narrow twisting path, surrounded on both sides by high hedges. Curious, she went through.

Away from the lights of the lawn, the pathway was dark. Jennifer began a twisting descent which, she presumed from what Jack Kendell had told her, would eventually lead down to the waterfront. The narrow channel was unlit, forcing Jennifer to take care with her bare feet, but she was able to navigate by moonlight for most of the way until, for a few short stretches, the high hedges became overgrown and created archways of dense black foliage which blocked out even the smallest chink of light.

Jennifer, still on edge from her experiences on the island, was thankful that these stretches of darkness were few and far between. The journey through the bushes felt surprisingly long. This must be due, Jennifer reasoned, to the continual twisting and turning of the path back onto itself. Eventually she found herself at the end of the track and facing into a high hedge which seemed simply to bar her progress. Alone on the path for so long, she was slightly surprised to hear a faint murmuring of voices coming from the other side.

Working her way along the edge of the hedge, after about ten yards Jennifer came to a narrow gap. She stepped through it and emerged into an unexpectedly large clearing, at the centre of which stood an ancient stone folly about the size of a small bandstand. The voices were much clearer now.

Jennifer heard a giggle, then a familiar drawling lilt carried clearly across the damp night air to where she was standing at the entrance.

"So, who is that crazy old ginger woman, anyway?"

Nancy Kendell brushed a non-existent fleck of dirt from Simon's dinner jacket and eased herself closer in to his chest. After giving him a quick look at the house, Nancy had brought Simon down to the grotto to have a bit of fun.

Her plan for the evening was going simply beautifully. It had always centred around showing up the ridiculous Jennifer Pettifyr and Nancy had thoroughly enjoyed rubbing the older woman's face right into the dirt, at the house, by stealing Simon from right under her nose. The fact that the stupid bitch was now standing at the entrance to the clearing, over Simon's shoulder where he could not see her but from where Jennifer could definitely overhear them talking, was just a delicious new layer of icing with which to top her cake. Nancy moved her hand, smoothly and deliberately, down Simon's back until it rested possessively on his backside. Waiting until she was sure that Jennifer could see it there, she pulled him in closer. "Is she your mum or something?" Nancy said loudly.

Laughing, she kissed Simon on the cheek and made a show of gripping his backside harder for Jennifer's benefit. Simon was taken aback by Nancy's raw physicality but, at the same time, he felt guilty and defensive as she talked about Jennifer. He could not forget how rudely they had left the redhead back at the house and he was also surprised to realise quite how much, despite the attentions of Nancy, he was missing her company.

Feeling immensely protective of Jennifer, he changed the subject by adopting a deliberately diffident tone.

"What? Oh, nobody. I hardly know her."

Nancy smiled and nibbled at his ear. Her hand gripped his backside harder and she squeezed up so that her breasts and groin were now pushing firmly against him. "Good" she burred hotly into his ear, "because you're mine tonight..." Then she began to kiss him, hard and insistently.

Simon, surprised, kissed her back even though his brain was telling him that it was wrong. It was a stage performance in which Nancy was just going through the motions. She might have learned how to kiss from watching films, she so consciously moved her body into positions designed for visual impact rather than just losing herself in the moment. Despite Nancy's immense beauty, Simon found himself quite unable to connect with her. When they pulled apart Nancy found, to her satisfaction, that she and Simon were alone in the clearing again.

Jennifer Pettifyr had long since gone.

She broke away and, taking Simon's hand, pulled him out of the folly and over to the darkest edge of the clearing. There was another gap in the hedge. Nancy passed through, with a giggle, and led him down a scrub slope densely populated with thick bushy trees. It was almost pitch black, but a few shafts of moonlight flickered as Nancy tugged him along in her wake. Reaching the bottom of the slope, she put a cold finger onto his lips before moving off into the trees.

Simon, with no option but to follow, eventually found Nancy standing outside a small stone building which was almost completely hidden in the dense bushes. They must be quite close to the waterfront now as he could hear the sound of crashing waves and the cry of seagulls in the air. The hut had a door, which Nancy was unlocking with the key suspended on the end of her necklace. She opened it inwards and disappeared inside. Simon, after a few moments of second-thought, ducked his head and followed.

Inside, he found an open wooden trap door. Looking down, he could see the top of a set of steps which blended away into the shadows below. Hearing footsteps on the stones, he followed the sounds and descended into the blackness.

It was a tunnel. Simon saw Nancy, twenty yards ahead, holding a lantern which was throwing out a flickering yellow glow onto the low stone ceiling and the cold damp walls. Simon bent his head and pushed on into the darkness, strangely unsettled by the echo of Nancy's giggles and heels as they played together between floor and ceiling.

Chapter Twenty-Six
"Four cows"

Jennifer Pettifyr sat, unhappily, at a small table in the main bar of the Causeway Inn with a second glass of red wine and the sad remains of a decimated packet of cheese and onion crisps in front of her. She was, she reflected, a prize twat. Always had been since school. This, she told herself, was exactly why she had no friends and why her family barely put up with her.

The sight of Simon kissing Nancy in the grotto had sent her straight back to being a bullied schoolgirl and she had run back to the house, for her shoes (painful, but she'd paid top whack for them), before tottering back to the pub with damp eyes and without even having the good manners to thank her host. She felt stupid and embarrassed.

She had taken her silly dress off, up in her room, and reverted to her comfortable jeans and a non-sexy woolly jumper. Now she sat, sad and alone, trying really hard not to cry into her crisps.

Not that she could blame Simon, she told herself, for his preferring Nancy. It bothered her though. Jennifer had many faults (she had once attempted to list them out but found that she needed a larger notebook and a better thesaurus) however her many years in a succession of tough schools had, at least, taught her how to sniff out a prize sow at a hundred paces. To her nose, little miss Nancy Kendell Mint-Tits stank like a dead badger rolled in turd.

Why she had taken against the girl quite so strongly was bothering Jennifer though. Normally, she trusted her non-romantic instincts implicitly. In her chosen line of work it was important and had saved her bacon on more than one occasion. In Nancy's case, Jennifer was plagued by the fear that her instincts were prejudiced by the girl bearing such a strong physical resemblance to her chief tormentor at school (Caroline 'two-face bitch-face' Mitchell, just to make that clear) and, even less pardonably, from plain old-fashioned envy. Nancy Kendell was younger, prettier, far sexier and Simon obviously fancied the arse off her. Jennifer knew that she hated the girl because of it. Almost as much as she hated herself for being so unable to rise above her pathetic, petty and juvenile jealousy.

She sipped at her wine and felt her eyes getting moist again. This was, she told herself, fucking ridiculous. He was just a stupid young man she had known for five minutes and who, like the rest of them, presumably thought she was a mad and dangerous oddball (with arms like a builder Jennie, don't forget your arms!) who was clearly best avoided like the plague. Why on earth she was getting so upset was absolutely beyond her.

Her stomach was hurting again. She took another gulp, finishing her wine, then got up slightly unsteadily. Maybe the champagne at the party had not been such a bright idea. It was late now, too. Perhaps she should just go to bed. Jennifer sat down with a bump and promised herself, faithfully, that she would not, under any circumstances, start crying. Maybe a small scotch would help. Or maybe a very large scotch. Maybe the bottle.

At this precise moment, outside in the street, a large white transit van was parking up. At least, it was attempting to do so. The driver, finding all of the spaces occupied, uttered a foul expletive before reversing the van up the narrow road and onto the dirt verge by its side. Having achieved this, a far worse expletive followed as the man now found himself completely unable to open his door wider than five inches into a hedge. After a considerable amount of progressively more exotic swearing, the passenger door suddenly slid open and possibly the largest individual ever to set foot in Devon stepped down onto the road.

Unbeknownst to Jennifer Pettifyr the cavalry, in the form of Richard 'Brick' Shilton (known as 'Brick' due to a striking resemblance to the outdoor lavatory of legend) formerly of Her Majesty's Armed Forces, had arrived in town. Armed, apparently, with a pork pie.

He rolled his way down to the bright lights of the pub.

Ricky Shilton was a significantly enormous man, six foot six in height and with a frame not so much muscular as being what you might end up with if four cows, a pair of jeans and a loud shirt ended up in a cement mixer.

Adjusting his glasses, Ricky squeezed in through the door of the pub, which was no mean feat in itself given that double-beds generally had an easier time of it. The big man was greeted by the sight of Jennifer Pettifyr sitting by herself and talking, apparently, down to an empty wine glass.

The big man grinned and snuck up quietly behind her. "Alright, Jennie?" he shouted loudly into her ear whilst play-punching her on the side of the head. "Got yourself a boyfriend yet?"

Chapter Twenty-Seven

"Stone"

Simon followed the subdued glow of Nancy Kendell's lantern. It was difficult, underground, to maintain a clear sense of direction but, wherever they were headed, it was no small distance. Eventually, the passage widened out into a large room in which he was able to stand up properly.

Nancy stood holding the lamp. She had a wild look in her eyes and the lamp-light accentuated the sharp cuts of her strong cheekbones. The room was unexpected. A king-sized bed, complete with metal frame, stood incongruously against the back stone wall, next to a small cabinet and an old wooden wardrobe. There was a full-length mirror in the corner. A series of ornate, thick-piled burgundy rugs had been thrown across the floor to warm up the cold stone. On the far side of the room Simon noticed a second door.

Nancy placed the lantern down onto the bedside cabinet and walked into the centre of the room. It was impossible to read her expression with the light now behind her. Suddenly, with one deft movement, she undid her dress at the throat and let it fall in a pool around her feet. She stepped out of it, clad in nothing now but her shoes, stockings and a beautiful set of black-laced underwear. The girl regarded her reflection, by candlelight, in the mirror. "This was mother's place" she said, quietly. "Before I made it mine." She was entirely still as she spoke.

"Your mother?" asked Simon. He was disturbed by Nancy's casual decision to undress. Ironically, the intimate act of removing her garments seemed to have increased the distance between them.

Nancy continued to stare at herself in the mirror. "I followed her once. When I was little. After a nightmare, I think, I got out of bed and was looking out over the garden, trying to calm down. It's peaceful at night and you can hear the waves on the rocks if the tide is in. I thought that listening to the waves would help me to sleep. I was looking out and, suddenly, mother was crossing the garden. She was wearing a long coat and I watched her cross the lawn to the archway. As if she was heading to the grotto. To my den, at the folly. I was so angry. She had no right to go there, you see?" She turned, briefly, to look at Simon, as if checking that he agreed with her. "She was trespassing on my space, so I put on my slippers and followed her. I ran downstairs and out across the lawn. I wanted to shout and scream at her to stay out of my den, but when I caught her up she wasn't in my den at all."

"She was down in the trees, down by the horrible stone hut. Mother always kept it locked. She told us rat poison was inside, and we had to stay away from it."

Nancy returned her attention to the mirror.

"She went inside and didn't come out. After ten minutes I got scared and went to check if she was alright. Because of the poison. I found the trapdoor. Then I found this room." She sighed and ran her fingers through her long black hair. "I heard noises and hid by the doorway. Mother didn't notice me watching. She was far too busy on the bed, with two men from the village, to notice me."

The girl was standing utterly still but the shadows, as they flickered and danced around the walls, confused the eyes and made her look as if she were twitching.

"I'm sorry, Nancy" said Simon quietly. "That must have been terrible for you." The girl turned her head around.

"It was the most wonderful thing that I ever saw. She was in ecstasy. I had never seen her so happy in all of her life." Nancy turned and her face was now in shadow. "Get on the bed" she said coldly. Simon did not move, so Nancy walked over and pressed her semi-naked body up against him.

"I said," this time the demand was softer, "get on the bed…"

Deeply uneasy, Simon sat down. He continued to watch Nancy, whose expression remained unreadable, as she walked over to the bedside cabinet. Simon thought about Jennifer Pettifyr again, drinking cocktails and laughing. She seemed a lifetime away.

"Cuff me" said Nancy, coldly.

She held out an arm from which metal was dangling.

Simon was a broad-minded young man but he was now simply calculating how to extricate both of them from the room with minimum embarrassment. He looked into Nancy's cold face and tried to rationalise her behaviour. The girl barely knew him at all, yet she was now in an isolated room and asking to be hand-cuffed. If you have a joint-mortgage, Simon reasoned, you might trust that your partner is not going to leave you to rot or start to dismember you. Not so, strangers in tunnels. He still could not read Nancy at all. Was she high, or drunk and just hiding it better than most?

Nancy grunted angrily and slammed one of the cuffs onto her own wrist. She turned around and, placing her arms behind her back, shouted at him.

"Do it!"

Reluctantly, Simon took the spare bangle and clipped it into place on the girl's other wrist. She tested the restraint and, apparently satisfied, turned on her knees to face him. The intensity in her eyes was like a blazing fire, and a heavy bead of sweat rolled slowly down her hairline onto her cheek.

Simon did not recognise the voice of the girl that spoke next.

"Now punish me…"

Simon put out his hand, gently, wondering how to speak to Nancy now without offending or making her angry. He wanted to choose his words carefully. Then he heard the footsteps.

The second door opened, very suddenly, and the tall figure of William Kendell entered the room. The young man stood, completely still, with his eyes fixed upon his sister on the bed.

For a few moments he did not look at Simon at all. Eventually, however, his eyes shifted. As with his sister before him, his expression was unreadable.

"This is not," said Simon slowly, "what it looks like..."

On the bed, to his horror, Nancy suddenly began to cry out and struggle. "Oh Billy, thank God, thank God! He was going to... oh thank God you're here!" She broke down in tears on the bed. Simon was incredulous.

"That's a bloody lie!" he shouted, then turned to Kendell who was staring at him. "She brought me here and told me to put those on her. She needs help. A psychiatrist, or something. She's not well!" Kendell had been stock still, but at Simon's last words he stepped forward and the barely-restrained violence in his face stopped Simon from talking. The two men faced each other in the flickering candlelight. Billy Kendell barely appeared to be breathing.

"Calling my sister a liar, are you mister?"

He stared at Simon from beneath his long black fringe, which had fallen down over his eyes. The brother had the same accent as Nancy and the same insane fire in his eyes. The pair of them, thought Simon, were cracked. A knife had appeared in Billy Kendell's right hand.

"Well, she is lying now..."

Simon stood very still. Time passed slowly, until Billy Kendell suddenly moved, with the same feline grace as his sister, over to the side of the bed. The dark-haired boy stood, looking down silently at his sister who was still crying in her underwear.

After a few moments he reached down and touched her exposed throat, so tenderly as if it were a piece of fragile porcelain. Simon was aware how bad this looked for him. He was in good physical shape, and could handle himself, but Kendell looked hard, lean and nastily insane. He did not fancy his chances against the knife.

For what felt like an eternity, William Kendell just stared down at the bed. Nancy looked back at him, then she suddenly stopped sobbing. Eventually, Billy spoke. "A liar she is…" he said, very quietly. It was almost a whisper, so much so that Simon thought that he must have imagined it, but Nancy, who had been staring up into her brother's face, transformed.

A horrible, unbalanced grin spread over her face.

It was horrific. She arched her back and began to scream into her brother's face as if she had been stabbed. She rocked violently back and forth on the bed, emitting a hideous high-pitched giggling which chilled Simon to the bone. The rocking and the noise continued until, suddenly, she went silent. Then she spat hard into her brother's face.

Billy Kendell wiped her spittle from his face and stepped back from the bed. He turned and pointed, with his knife, towards the passageway. He looked at Simon. "Come near my sister, or this place, ever again and my friends will make you pay. Ask Crawford how he likes his chair if you don't believe me. Now piss off…"

Simon ran and did not stop running until he was gulping cold air, up in the woods outside of the hut. He stumbled his way back up the slope through the trees and made his way back to the house.

Chapter Twenty-Eight
"Wasps' Nest"

Ricky Shilton, looking very much like a third-choice midwife (during a rail strike when the local rugby team had stepped up to cover for the midwife), cradled Jennifer's sobbing head and considered his position. It was not, to his mind, ideal.

The Pettifyr had been manhandled upstairs to its room and no one had actually accused him of punching her. Which was good. Little Jennie was still busy bawling her eyes out like a toddler with its nuts in a wasps' nest though.

This was not good. This was, indeed, very bad.

The badness was on two fronts. Firstly, he'd known Jennie Pettifyr since she was a thirteen year-old girl and he had only once seen her cry. Now, he had seen her make an awful lot of other fuckers cry and he had also seen her get battered onto her arse repeatedly in the boxing ring, but he had never witnessed anything like these waterworks. This was new territory for Ricky and he wasn't, as a rule, a man who enjoyed paddling in uncharted waters.

Secondly, he loved the little ginger bugger. Her being upset, and his not being able to sort it out for her, made him both deeply unhappy and deeply inadequate.

"There there…" he patted her big red head again with a large awkward paw. "It can't be that bad, Jen? Why don't you tell your uncle Ricky all about it? Then, I can go and break the bollocks of whichever little fucker has upset you, can't I?"

As a bedside manner some might have felt that it left a little to be desired, however in Jennifer's case it actually seemed to do the trick. She snuffled suddenly, lurched up vertically and then twisted around to look at him, all red-eyed and snotty. She smiled widely, through her tears, then punched him on the arm.

"Sorry…" she said, looking down at her feet. "Red wine and black mood…" Jennifer tailed off, then got up onto her feet and balled herself over to the bathroom, returning a few seconds later clutching a thick wad of tissues. After blowing her nose very loudly (and a lot closer to Ricky than he would have preferred), Jennifer dumped herself back down and looked at him through narrow, red eyes. "What are you even doing here?"

"I thought you'd never ask…" Shilton sat back and, via a progressive series of buttock-shuffles, made himself a little more comfortable. "Basically," he started, before breaking off as he noticed the bottle of single malt on the corner shelf. A long, broad arm secured it.

Adjusting his spectacles, and scratching his scraggy beard, he continued. "Basically, Jen, I received a telephone call from a certain little bird this morning who suggested to me that his favourite little cocksure adventuress might, just possibly, have got her head a little bit below the waterline and need bailing out…"

"Fucking cheek!" Jennifer exploded, jumping up.

"Of all the arrogant little shitty…" she began, before clocking that Ricky was grinning at her. She sat down.

"Piss-taking bastard."

"I've missed you too, Jennie. Lovely to see you too."

After a few hugs, Jennifer felt much better and more than a little embarrassed. She knew that she was prone to bottling things up, but that did not make her feel any better when she had to pick up the pieces after one of her tantrums.

After another bathroom visit, she sat down again and poured out some wine. She waved away Ricky's suggestion (quite reasonable, she knew) that she had probably had more than enough already. "This is a happy drink, not a sad one."

Jennifer raised her glass.

"It's really good to see you Rick. How's things?"

"Well, your sister is still busting my balls, twenty-four seven, so no fucking change there. She's only gone and bought a fucking puppy. Cute little thing, I'll give you that, but it's no job for a man, carrying a dog the size of a teddy bear around town on a Saturday. I get looks."

"Fuck knows how you put up with her Ladyship."

Jennifer grimaced.

"Oi! That's your sister you're talking about," said Ricky, wagging a fat finger, "and we both know I'm not brave enough to agree with you. As I was saying, I got a call."

"I thought that was a joke!" Jennifer huffed.

Shilton raised a placatory hand.

"It was love, it was. Settle down. He knows that you're well capable. We both do. The point is, Collins has flagged up that a rather unpleasant little narcotics operation has recently appeared upon our radar. It appears to funnel-in from this neck of the woods. That's what I'm doing here, Jennie. I'm not your fucking babysitter. Anyway, Collins didn't like the coincidence. He did not like it at all, which is why I'm looking you up. The gentlemen in London think that your 'something funny' at the nerd-farm might be related to the drugs but, between these four walls only, they haven't got one shiny iota of anything useful to take upstairs. So, they politely suggested I pop down here and see if you might like a bit of, well…"

"Well..?"

"Backup."

"So I'm still in charge?"

Ricky Shilton, well used to this, sighed and took a drink. Pettifyrs, he reflected sourly. You can't live with them, but apparently it's frowned upon in polite society to cosh them, bundle them up in a sack and sink them quietly in the Thames. You could do it, but you'd need a fucking good brief to get you off. Luckily, Ricky knew the very best in the business. Sadly, that lady was also this little ginger bugger's sister.

"Yes, Jennie love" he said, forcing a saintly patient smile onto his big face. "You're still in charge. Now, if you've quite satisfied yourself that you've still got the biggest dick in the room, and we've all stopped crying, how about you tell me what all this famous five shit is about, then? How's that for a plan?"

Chapter Twenty-Nine
"Bad boys"

One hour later, Ricky left Jennifer tucked up in bed and tabbed his way down to the bar. He had listened, patiently, while she briefed him on the island (bunch of nutters, he had thought), glossed over the incident with the hollow woman ("Fuck me Jennie, how much had you 'ad?"), and he'd raised a suitable eyebrow when she reached the point of being heaved over the side of the lighthouse railing ("what, so you were just standing there like a fucking lemon then?")

He acquired a pint of beer and some scampi fries from the, now quiet, bar and requisitioned a corner booth for a bit of a think. Ten minutes later a tall young man, wearing a somewhat incongruous black dinner suit and carrying a somewhat very familiar brown leather hold-all, entered the pub.

He looked around, as if trying but failing to identify somebody specific, before approaching the barman. "Excuse me," said Simon, once he had attracted the man's attention. "Do you have a lady staying here? A Miss Pettifyr. Red hair."

Ricky Shilton, whose ears had pricked up at the sight of the bag, studied Simon carefully from behind his pint as the barman consulted a book tucked behind the bar.

"Yes, we do. Would you like me to call her room for you?"

Simon thought for a moment, then replied in the negative. It was late, and he wasn't at all sure what reception he would receive if he woke Jennifer up now. Castration, most probably. She had left the party without saying goodbye to anybody and, frankly, he had deserved no better. He felt completely and utterly stupid.

"No, it's OK. Could I leave a message for her though? Can you tell her that Simon has her bag, though? Simon. I will bring it over for her tomorrow. Thanks." He turned to leave but found a medium-sized asteroid blocking his way.

"Oi…" said the blockage, "James Bond. I want a word." Ricky Shilton was not a man to argue with, unless for some reason you enjoyed extreme pain, so Simon followed him back to his table where he received the once-over through a thick pair of spectacles. "Well, get some drinks in then, you plum. Beer please, not a vodka martini." Chuckling at his own wit, Shilton sat down. Simon, thinking it best to do as he was told, as well as being too tired to argue, bought two pints and returned to the large man's table.

"I'm sorry, but do I know you?" Simon was wary that this man might be tied in with Billy Kendell. Had Nancy's brother changed his mind about breaking his legs, after all, and farmed out the job to an over-sized professional? Shilton rolled his eyes at this and, for a horrible fleeting moment, Simon was quite bizarrely reminded of Jennifer Pettifyr.

"No son. I think you'd remember, wouldn't you? I know all about you though." Ricky sipped his pint, then pointed down at the hold-all. "Now, how's about you start our date by telling me where you got that bag?" Simon looked down.

"It belongs to a friend of mine. She's staying here. She dropped it recently and I wanted to return it to her." All of which was true. Simon had returned to Jack Kendell's house to look for Jennifer, after getting out of the tunnel and away from the Kendell twins. In the dining room, he had encountered Margaret Nicholson. Jennifer had disappeared from the island without saying goodbye to anybody and leaving her bag behind. Nicholson had found Nancy in the refectory with it and, recognising the bag, had confiscated it and brought it across with her to return to its rightful owner. Simon had promised to return it to Jennifer. It had not seemed quite the right time to point out that Jennifer's abrupt departure was, in fact, due to her being shoved off a cliff.

"I know who it belongs to, son" said Shilton, giving Simon a hard-man stare. "The lady in question is asleep upstairs and, between you and I, she's quite a little bit upset. So, let's leave her to her beauty sleep and have a nice little chat instead."

"Are you a friend of Jennifer's?"

Ricky Shilton pushed his glasses back up his thick nose. His face betrayed nothing, but the question was, in fact, a deeply poignant one to him. He had served hard and long days and nights, showered, got shit-faced and watched best mates die with Jennifer Pettifyr's dad. Then, just when both of them, by some miracle, had gotten themselves out of that hell in one piece they had lost Marty.

Ricky had lost his best friend but little Jennie had lost her dad that day. Just when the poor little bugger really needed him. She had cried herself to sleep, on Ricky's lap, on the day of the funeral.

"You might say that, yes Simon. I've known her for a very long time. Which gives me every right, I might add, to take you outside right now for a bit of a slap. I mean, you seem to have upset her Simon. Not a very nice thing to do, was it?"

"Look," Simon was dog-tired and did not want a second round of trouble. Billy Kendell had been bad enough. "I came here to return Jennifer's bag and to apologise to her. I've been a bit... stupid. I wanted to say sorry, that's all." He stopped, as he realised that Shilton was looking at him intently and making him feel deeply self-conscious. "I like her a lot, OK?" he finished, quietly. "I just wanted to tell her that."

Shilton put his beer down and then laughed, very loudly. "I see... you've only just met her then. Right. Anyway, let's have a look in the bag." The big man gestured to the hold-all and Simon passed it across. "Shouldn't you wait for Jennifer?" Simon asked, as Shilton unzipped the bag and peered inside. "She might have private stuff in there."

"It's her private stuff I'm interested in..." Ricky delved into the bag, then seemed to realise just quite how dodgy his last statement had sounded. "I don't mean her pants, Simon. I'm checking that she hasn't lost anything more important than those." From inside the bag, on top of the limited assortment of clothes and toiletries, Shilton pulled out the glossy photograph which Jennifer had picked up from the Leightons' bedside table.

He adjusted his spectacles and inspected it. For the record, he inspected it for an awful lot longer than was strictly necessary. "Blimey!" was his professional opinion. "Look at the size of those bad boys..." He passed the photograph across to Simon, who just stared at it in shock. Shilton chuckled. "I'll have Exhibit A back when you've finished with it, son. I've had a long drive."

He continued rummaging through the bag, but the item he was seeking was quite conspicuous by its absence. Little pearl-handled Jessica, it seemed, had gone absent without leave. Ricky pondered this fact. He did not like it at all. Simon was still staring at the photograph.

"Alright, son. Fuck me. You look like you've never seen a pair before" said Shilton. Simon, however, wasn't listening. Despite the absence of the face he knew exactly who the girl in the photograph was. It was Nancy Kendell.

He passed the picture back to the larger man.

"Now" said Ricky. "Any idea why little Jennie should be lugging around a defaced picture of an unusually well-developed naked girl? Besides the obvious one which, despite what her mum says, I don't believe for a minute." He pushed his perpetually sliding glasses back up his nose and looked across at Simon, who had been thinking it through.

"She must have got it at the Institute. She works there. I mean, the girl in the photograph works there." Simon was thinking, again, about the unstable siblings in the tunnel. Who had taken that photograph? Had the same person been responsible for rubbing the face out so violently? Was Nancy at risk?

Shilton raised his eyebrows, skirting the question of how Simon recognised a naked girl with no face. The obvious answer was, clearly, that he was a lucky little bastard. He poked a finger instead and returned to the main issue on his mind which was not, for once, mammary-related.

"Jennie's gun is missing."

"Gun? Jennifer has a gun!?"

"Had. She told me it was in the bottom of this bag, and it isn't. Ergo, someone has half-inched it. Wouldn't be you, by any chance, would it Jimbo?"

"Of course not! I never looked in the bag." Ricky believed him. His surprise at the photo had been entirely genuine.

For his part, Simon could not believe that the short-sighted Margaret Nicholson had been rifling through Jennifer's possessions either. What had she said to him at the party? That she had found Nancy with the bag. Had Nancy taken the gun? Simon could believe that. He could imagine her going through Jennifer's bag and taking anything of interest. Perhaps, he thought coldly, Nancy had believed that Jennifer would not be in a fit state ever to return for it.

The photograph was puzzling though. Why would Nancy have left it in the bag? Had she actually placed it there? After the stone room, nothing about either Kendell sibling would surprise him. The disappearance of Jennifer's gun was a serious matter. Given the disturbances on the island, the thought of someone, Nancy Kendell or anybody else, running around with a revolver was an unpleasant one.

There was something else though, something which Billy Kendell had said earlier, that he needed to investigate. Simon looked over at Ricky Shilton, who was watching him carefully. He decided to trust him. Simon began to talk and, once he had explained himself, the big man nodded sagely.

"Now that, Mister Bond" he said, "sounds like a plan."

Chapter Thirty

"School disco"

Jennifer, waking up to the sound of seagulls in a warm and sunny room the following morning, felt unexpectedly refreshed and happy. Until she remembered the previous evening. Then she covered her face with her pillow and wished she was dead. Another, she told herself, Pettifyr fucking-special.

Eventually, once she had realised that her mood was not going to improve by moping about in bed and taking pot-shots at herself, she got up and showered. After a brutally strong cup of instant punishment coffee, she made her way downstairs and outside for some fresh air.

Hitting the quayside, the first thing she saw was Ricky Shilton's dirty white van, parked up against a hedge. Jennifer smirked. Feeling charitable, however, she trotted to the bakery on the corner which opened early for the self-caterers and bought a large bag of pastries and two takeaway coffees before returning to the van.

Raising a fist, she hammered mightily upon the doors.

Ten seconds later the doors flew open revealing rather more of Ricky Shilton, clad only in his underpants and a sleeveless stained white vest, than Jennifer Pettifyr would have preferred to see. Particularly on an empty stomach.

"Sorry to disturb, sir" she barked into his face, "but we've had reports from the neighbours that an unlicensed East London gobshite has been seen roaming the area. Apparently he knows it all, thinks he's God's gift to anyone not sporting a penis and, and this is the really sick part, some of the local pasties have gone missing. Abducted in the woods, apparently. You wouldn't know anything about this, would you sir?"

"Jennifer love," said the big man, very quietly but with not inconsiderable menace, "It's a fucking good job that I like you because, just between these four walls, there are flyovers being propped-up by lesser cunts than you. Now, did you want something, or were you just worried that I had forgotten you're a twat and wanted to remind me of that fact? Oh, and whilst we're doing this, don't ever bang on my fucking van. It's rude. For all you know, I might have had a lady in here."

"If you had, she'd need a priest. I'd suggest an air freshener, Ricky, but you need a fucking exorcist in there…"

Jennifer wrinkled her nose.

"Anyway," she went on, "we both know that this is the closest you'll ever get to being banged in the morning by a Pettifyr girl, so try to relax and enjoy the experience." She smiled sweetly. Shilton frowned darkly and pointed a fat finger right into her face.

He spoke very quietly indeed.

"Jennifer. If you have not already got my breakfast sorted out, now would be a very good time for you to get the fuck out of my line of sight and do so... if you don't want to be damaged. Badly."

"Don't you point your finger at me, Ricky Shilton. Or anything else, for that matter." Jennifer gestured at the underpants. "Stop moaning, put some trousers on, and get your fat arse out here. I've bought pastries!" She waggled the bag in front of him to emphasise the size of her carrot.

The stratagem proved to be quite entirely successful, as Shilton emerged from the van, two minutes later, wearing jeans and a quasi-clean shirt. He trotted over to Jennifer, who was sitting enjoying the morning sunshine. To her delight, she realised that he was clutching her Italian leather hold-all.

"Yay! Come to Mummy! You pooooor little thing... what have all those nasty, horrible people been doing to you then? Yeeeeeessss..." Shilton looked dubiously at her, whilst Jennifer fussed over the bag and kept stroking it, obsessively, as if it were a rescue kitten. Not for the first time in his life, Ricky wondered whether the Pettifyrs were really quite right in the head. Seeing Jennifer with the bag, however, reminded Shilton of its contents and, looking for an opportunity to avenge the van-bang, he went in with an exploratory jab to the lady's chin.

"Your busty young friend is still there, in case you were worried. Safe and sound. Fuck me love, don't let your mum catch you looking at girlie mags again. She doesn't need any more ammunition."

"Those magazines weren't mine!"

"Whatever, Jen." Shilton took an enormous bite of his pastry. Having satisfactorily tested his reach and range, he followed up with a more testing shot to Jennifer's stomach. "Your friend, what's his face, dropped it off last night." He munched away, eyeing the redhead closely through his spectacles.

"What? Did he?" Jennifer looked up sharply. Ricky was genuinely surprised by the flush in her face. Blimey, he thought to himself. Has hell finally frozen over and little Jennie Pettifyr actually been bitten on the arse by the love-bug? Murky waters indeed.

"Did he, well, did he say anything?" Jennifer asked, extremely cautiously, as Richard 'Shit-Head' Shilton was not someone from whom she needed a royal piss-take from on the subject of her feelings for Simon. The big man feigned spectacular disinterest.

"Nah."

"What?"

"Just dropped it in my lap, then fucked off."

Ricky then started work on Danish number two.

"What?!" He must have said SOMETHING!?"

"What? Oh yeah, we might have exchanged a few words. Yeah. He might have said a couple of things about you, actually." Another sip of coffee, then Ricky returned to his pastry. Slowly. Very, very slowly indeed.

In case the reader feels that he was being insensitive to Jennifer here, it should be noted that Richard Shilton had waited over ten years for an opportunity to wind little Jennie 'know it fucking all, and happy to tell you about it' Pettifyr up about fancying a boy.

This was a priceless opportunity and one which he certainly had no intention of passing up.

"Well WHAT WERE THEY?!" Jennifer hissed at him. She had forgotten how much of a dick Ricky Shilton could be. The big man, however, sighed and took pity. He remembered her tears of the night before. Jennie, twat though she could be, would never not be, to Ricky at least, the little lost girl who deserved some happiness in her life.

"Just some fluff about him being sorry and that he really likes you" he said and smiled at her. Hopefully this piece of news might cheer the little bugger up a bit.

In fact, it did not. Jennifer exploded in his face instead.

"Oh, FUCK YOU Ricky Shilton! Wind me up, will you? Well, bollocks to you! Choke on your fucking pastry and I hope you get your balls trapped in…" she looked around for inspiration, "a lobster pot!" She crossed her arms and sank back onto the bench. Was it not, she felt, bad enough that she had to put up with herself without everyone else thinking it was open season for a good laugh at her expense? She felt her eyes tearing up again, so she grabbed her coffee and hunkered down behind it to hide. Feeling miserable enough, to cap it all she realised that Ricky Shilton was now actually laughing at her. Fucking unbelievable. She slammed her coffee down, but he held up a big hand to prevent her from springing across the table and belting him in the face.

"Jennie, Jennie..." he grinned into her furious face. "Calm down. I'm not pulling your chain, love. I promise. The lad, Simon, he came over last night after you had gone to bed. We had a nice little chat and, although fuck-alone knows why, he actually does seem to be quite taken with you. Straight up. No bull-shitting. It was actually quite sweet." Ricky returned to his pastry. "Has he escaped from Broadmoor?"

"Really?" Jennifer asked, quietly. She chose to ignore the implication that affection for her was a symptom of dangerous mental ill-health. "So, he said he likes me then?" She began to play with her hair and smile to herself.

Ricky Shilton just stared at her, wondering what had happened to the angry little girl he had taken under his wing and coached for months until he had watched her drag herself up from the canvas, in the eighth round, to knock massive Terri (short for 'fucking terrifying') Dixon spark out with a brutal left hook. With a surge of affection, he realised that she was alive, well and just dealing with a different set of problems today. Somebody would still, presumably, end up getting punched.

"Can we put your sex life aside for one minute, please? As I was trying to say, you've got a bigger problem to worry about."

"Sex life!?" Jennifer squeaked. "I haven't slept with him!" She squirmed in her seat, as that was pretty much all she had thought about doing since meeting Simon. Unfortunately, it also reminded her just how painful it had been watching Nancy Kendell running her hands over his body right in front of her. She felt sick again.

"Obviously not, Jennie. I know that" said Shilton. "He's still able to walk and he's not singing castrato. Clearly, Pettifyr base-camp has not been breached." Ricky held up his hand, lazily, to ward off the vicious slap which Jennifer was now delivering towards his head. His brain idly registered that her blow was far too easily telegraphed. Jennifer needed to spend more time on her martial arts and less on the girlie mags.

To be fair though, so did he.

"Anyway Jennie, as I was attempting to say before you went all school disco on me, you've got a bigger problem." He took another lump out of Danish number two. "Jessica's missing."

Chapter Thirty-One
"No chance"

Simon left his car in the same parking spot that he and Jennifer had used on their previous visit to Shercombe. This time, however, he was alone. The sky was struggling to remain bright and the roads were strangely quiet. Checking his A-Z, he found the street he was looking for and headed out of the car-park. He did not feel like an ice cream today. He just felt sick.

Walking for ten minutes, in the opposite direction to the waterfront, he passed row after row of generic modern housing as found across the entire country. Finding the street he wanted, thirty yards brought him to an unobtrusive little terraced house at number fifty-two. It had a red door and a very well-maintained front garden in which rows of bright yellow flowers were blooming. Simon noted the ramp beside the front step.

He took a deep breath before ringing the doorbell.

After ten seconds, a shadow appeared behind the frosted glass and the door was opened by a woman in her late-forties or early-fifties. Her hair was tied back, into a tight ponytail, and she wore no make-up. She was slim, rather pretty and dressed in faded jeans and a casual cream sweatshirt. Her feet were bare and, Simon noticed, her neat toenails were painted the same shade of red as the front door.

"Mrs Crawford?"

"Yes. Can I help you?"

Her local accent was light and pleasant, if a little uncertain.

"My name is Simon Martin. I wondered if Danny was in?"

"Are you a friend of his?" she asked.

Simon could feel her eyes scanning his face.

"We've never met, no" he said openly and smiled at her. "I just wondered if I could have a few words with him, if that's OK? It is quite important."

"Are you from the police?" She looked at him, warily. Simon thought this was a strange question although, he supposed, they might well have been involved in the aftermath of the attack on her son. He shook his head and opened his palms in what, he hoped, was a disarming gesture.

"No, Mrs Crawford, I'm nothing to do with the police. I'm working with somebody who is investigating up at the Bursands Institute. Some unpleasant things have been happening there, and she is trying to stop them."

"The science people? What's that got to do with Danny?" she asked and then glanced briefly into the room behind the door. The reason for the glance became apparent as a young man, in a wheelchair, rolled himself into view.

"Alright, mum?" The boy looked up, nervously, at Simon.

"Danny? My name's Simon. I was just telling…"

"I heard you." The young man cut him off. "Come in."

He exchanged a look with his mother and, presumably agreeing between them that Simon looked sufficiently safe, the boy wheeled himself backwards and into a room off the hallway.

Mrs Crawford opened the door properly and Simon stepped inside. The house was tastefully decorated in neutral tones with a pale-cream carpet. Simon made a move to slip off his shoes, but Mrs Crawford just waved him through.

"Don't worry about that. None of us bother any more. Come on through and I'll put the kettle on." She led Simon into the front room where Danny was now sitting in the corner. The television was on, showing a football results round-up programme, and the young man in the wheelchair muted the sound with the remote control in his lap.

"What is it that you want then?" he asked, not aggressively. His tone was, if anything, curious. Simon filled him in with a few background details about himself and about Jennifer, focusing on the events at the Institute. Danny Crawford listened with an increasingly perplexed expression on his face. Finally, he interrupted. "Sounds bizarre, but I don't understand what I've got to do with any of this." He gestured down at his legs. "I've not been running around scrawling on walls if that's what you think." Mrs Crawford came in carrying a tray of tea mugs. After she had left, Simon got to the purpose of his visit.

"Danny, have you heard of a girl called Nancy Kendell?"

The reaction from the boy made it quite clear that he had. Simon felt for him, as he began to look uncomfortable and agitated, looking towards the door as if wondering whether to call for his mother. The boy looked genuinely frightened.

"It's OK, Danny. I'm nothing to do with her or her brother. I just wanted to ask you a few questions about your accident."

Simon continued. "You see, Nancy Kendell is working at the institute and it's possible, only possible mind you, that she might be mixed up in the trouble there."

"It weren't no accident" the boy said quietly, staring intently at the silent football on the television. They watched as a Manchester United midfielder rocketed a strike from thirty yards into the top corner of goal. The goalkeeper had no chance. "I can't talk to you about it. I'm sorry but I can't." The boy now had tears in his eyes.

"Danny, I know that someone put you in that wheelchair deliberately." As Simon spoke, the boy turned towards him. The desperation in his eyes was painful. "Was it her brother?" Simon went on. "Did he attack you? Threaten you if you told anybody?"

"I can't talk to you!" the young man hissed. "If I tell anyone what happened, I…" he began, but faltered. "He said he would do things to mum. Terrible things." The boy spoke quietly and rubbed his eyes, before turning back to watch the football. The goal celebration was still ongoing, much to the aggravation of the opposition who now had only minutes to save the match.

"Danny…" Simon said softly. "You don't have to say anything, alright, just nod if I'm correct. Once I leave here, I promise that you'll never hear from me again and you won't need to be involved in anything else. Was it Billy Kendell that attacked you?" The boy looked down at his feet. He nodded briefly. They were interrupted by Mrs Crawford entering the room. She went across to her son's side, but he squeezed her hand and told her they just needed a few minutes longer. She shot Simon a look on her way out. He wasn't going to be getting a second mug of tea.

Simon got up and closed the door, gently, before sitting back down next to Danny. He spoke to the young man very quietly.

"Did he find you with his sister?"

The boy, crying openly now, turned and shook his head vigorously. Simon frowned, then sat back and waited. Danny eventually seemed to reach a decision and spoke again. "Do you promise, really, that I don't have to go to court or anything? Please..." Simon nodded, unsure whether he was in any position to offer assurances. He promised himself that he would do his best to keep Danny Crawford out of whatever happened after this. The boy was now wiping his eyes.

"I was with Nancy. I knew her from school, and her mates had told her that I fancied her. That's a laugh mister because, if you saw her, you'd understand. Everyone fancies her. She's stunning. Anyway, one day after school, she came up to me and told me she fancied me and, well... if I went up to the woods with her she would... you know."

Simon nodded and beckoned the boy to go on.

"Well, we went up there and, well, she started kissing me. Then she stripped me naked and sat on me... then... well, then her brother just seemed to come out of nowhere. He had a cricket bat. I had no chance. He did my legs and smashed me up."

Simon listened to the horrific tale and realised his throat was dry. He thought of the stone room and the barely-contained violence he had seen in Kendell's face.

"Did Nancy try to get help? Did she try to stop him?"

"Stop him?"

The boy looked at him. "After her brother had broken my legs, Nancy Kendell just sat on my chest, laughing her fucking head off. She was still laughing as she went to work on me with his knife."

Chapter Thirty-Two

"Jolly girls' outing"

Pastries and coffee destroyed, Ricky and Jennifer sat in the sunshine deciding strategy. There was some initial disagreement as, to Jennifer's way of thinking, step one was clearly for Shilton to go upstairs and borrow her room ("I'm going nowhere with you until you've had a shit, shave and a shower, buster. In that order please and not all in the bathtub...").

A grumbling Ricky had finally acquiesced and stomped off into the pub. He made a point of stealing Jennifer's complementary toiletries and biscuit as revenge though. Upon his return, Jennifer was waiting by the van.

"I want to take another look at that lighthouse. There's something fishy about it and I don't like the business of the locked doors. I'd bet my bits that someone in all this has a key and little Billy Kendell is top of my shit-list. I'd swear it was him in the refectory the other night. It was dark, but he's a distinctive little bastard and, unless he's shagging one of the doctors and hid in their bedroom, which I admit is possible - horrible to visualise - but possible, that lighthouse is the only place he could have gone. Plus, there was a footprint on the window ledge."

"Well," said Ricky, "if that's the case then he's probably also now tooled-up thanks to you. What the fuck were you thinking Jen, bringing a gun to a fucking tea-party? Who were you expecting to come up against on nerd island? The ghost of Al Capone?"

"Shut up Ricky. And stop taking the piss out of my little brush with the paranormal, will you. I'm not a fucking basket-case. Anyway, I hope for his sake that Billy the Kid... hey, that's rather good... Billy the Kid. Guns, yes? Do you get it?"

Shilton rolled his eyes.

"Jennie. Just carry on with your original answer for once as I am, genuinely, interested to discover exactly who you were planning to plug on your jolly girls' outing."

"Billy the Kid. Fucking brilliant... anyway, my point is that, if he has kidnapped little Jessica, I hope for his sake that he doesn't attempt any foreplay with her."

The big man looked dubious.

"And why would that be then?"

"Because Ricky, like her namesake, she's quite liable to blow up in his face." Shilton let that one pass. He'd had far too much experience of the Pettifyr clan over the years to waste time chasing up and down the alleyways their brains seemed to play in. Generally, he understood about one thing in ten that any of them came out with. And that one rarely meant anything good. For him or anybody else. He scratched his backside, thoughtfully, and was about to adjust the crown jewels for good measure until he realised that Jennifer was watching him. He converted the move into an extraction of his car keys.

"Right. Where to then, boss?" Ricky grinned, displaying a big row of teeth through the stubble. Jennifer stood up, jumped up onto the stone ledge and pointed out over the water.

"Murder Island!" she shouted melodramatically.

Shilton looked at her.

"Tide's in, love."

"What?"

Jennifer, who had been staring over at the island, looked down to where Shilton was quietly pointing with a chubby finger.

"The tide. It is in, Jennie. So, unless you expect us to swim there, we ain't going fuckin' nowhere. Unless, of course, you have a boat..." he added nastily.

"I don't do boats Ricky" Jennifer said darkly.

"Well I guess we're staying right here then, aren't we?"

"Actually," said a third voice from behind them, "I might have an idea about how we could get there. Without getting wet." Jennifer whirled around to find Simon smiling at her. "Hello Jennifer" he said quietly, looking up as she stood on the low wall with her thick red hair blowing all around her face. She looked down at him, rather blankly at first, then smiled shyly.

"You brought my bag back..." she said in a quiet voice.

"I'm sorry I left you at the party."

"And you like me."

"Sorry?"

"Nothing!" She jumped down and punched him on the arm. "I forgive you." With that, Jennifer Pettifyr marched off in the direction of the ladies' lavatory.

Watching her striding away, Simon was reminded just how good she looked in those jeans. Not to mention, he remembered, in the incendiary figure-hugging little black dress of the previous evening. "Eyes up, son" came a low voice in his ear. "Mind on the mission and all that. James Bond never got anywhere just chasing arse, did he?"

"Well, yes he did actually…" replied Simon. "Are you related to her or something?" he asked, although it was hard to credit Shilton being from the same species, let alone the same family.

"No son. Her sister's just rubbed off on me, that's all. Although not," Ricky adjusted his spectacles and looked down at Simon, "as much as I'd like her to…" Simon shook his head and sat down on the wall. Shilton, leaning back against his van, gazed thoughtfully at the doorway to the pub where Jennifer had just gone inside. "How did you get on this morning then?" he asked quietly.

"I found Danny. He told me what happened in the woods."

"And? Was it Kendell?"

"It's worse. They did it together. Sounds like the girl set it up."

"Bugger me backwards."

"They're cracked, Ricky. God knows what they're capable of."

"Right. Well. We'd better do something about it then."

"But what? Danny won't testify. He's petrified of the pair of them. They threatened his mum to keep his mouth shut and they're well capable of making good on it. He knows that and he won't go to the police."

"Now that's not very nice, is it Simon? His old mum indeed."

"So, what do we do?"

"You let your uncle Ricky worry about that one, son. I might have an idea how to flush him out. In the meantime, why don't you tell us how to get over to that island, then? Are we flying?"

He noticed Jennifer striding back from the toilet.

"Watch out son, the old ball and chain's back. Keep your eyes up, yes? This is no time for tits." Simon bit down a caustic response as the lady had now bounded up and, he felt, the optimum moment for refuting an allegation of staring at her chest had possibly passed. Jennifer looked from one of them to the other. "Have a good wee love?" asked Shilton, earning himself a look that Jennifer normally reserved for turds on white trainers.

"So, how are we getting to the island then?" Jennifer began bouncing up and down on her toes, like a dog waiting for a stick.

"Well, I've got a theory. Come on." Simon led them off down the road, in the direction that Jennifer had taken the previous evening to get to Jack Kendell's house. Rather than heading to the front, however, they skirted off the road and around to the back of the property. Ten minutes later they were working their way across shrub-land into a dense area of thick bushes and trees.

"You sure about this, son?" enquired Ricky, after snagging his arm for the third time on a bramble. "It's all getting a bit too geography field-trip for my liking…"

"More of a history trip, if we're heading the right way…"

After about five minutes more they emerged, from the trees, into a small clearing. Simon pointed to his goal. It was the same area to which Nancy had taken him on the previous evening, albeit approached from the opposite direction.

The squat little stone outbuilding stood, unobtrusively, just where Simon had remembered it. The door was closed, but unlocked. Putting his finger to his lips, Simon signalled to the others to keep quiet before gently opening the door and pointing down towards the trapdoor. Hearing nothing below, he raised it quietly and led the way down to the tunnel.

The corridor below was empty, dark and silent. Making their way along it, in silence, they eventually reached the stone room in which Simon had endured his encounter with the siblings. He moved over to the bed, locating the lamp and matches which, presumably, Nancy Kendell had left behind. Once lit, the lantern threw out an eerie set of flickering shadows onto the walls. Jennifer looked around and frowned.

"Well, this is cosy..." she observed, drily. Simon said nothing. Being back in the room, his mouth was dry and he felt sick again. Jennifer walked over to the bedside cabinet and opened the drawer.

"Nice. Very ninety-five..." she observed softly. Wondering what she was blathering about, Simon looked into the drawer. The handcuffs had been returned to their home.

"Hello," Jennifer said suddenly. "What's all this then?"

She bent over and ran her fingertip along the top of the cabinet. A fine sheen of powder was dusted over it. She sniffed at it before dabbing it briefly against her lips. Shilton joined her and repeated the exercise.

"Interesting..." said the big man softly. "Collins is a clever bastard. This could just be recreational, but I'd bet money that Kendell is storing it around here somewhere..."

Simon stepped backwards away from the cabinet and felt his foot touch something soft upon the floor. He picked up the piece of fabric scrunched up at his feet. He recognised the underwear, but it would no longer be of much use to its owner. The sides had been sliced through with a blade. Shivering, he pointed towards his reason for bringing them down here. The second door.

It was through it, and not the tunnel, that Nancy's brother had entered the room on the previous night. Simon wanted to know where he had come from. Putting his ear against the wood he was rewarded with silence, so he cautiously turned the handle. Behind the door was what appeared to be a second passageway.

Picking up the lamp, Simon led Jennifer and Ricky down the new tunnel, stopping once for Shilton to crack his head on the stone ceiling, until after ten minutes they arrived at the bottom of a metal ladder. Simon, cautiously, climbed upwards and found himself inside a small room, little larger than a bathroom. He was joined by the others.

In the cramped space, a small wooden door faced them.

"The lighthouse!" whispered Jennifer excitedly. "We're inside the lighthouse. This door leads into the hallway by the main entrance. I'll bet my knickers on it. We must have walked the entire length of the causeway, but underground." Simon tested the handle, but the door was locked. Looking around, to the left of the door frame he noticed a small key hanging up on a hook. He lifted it off and slipped it easily into the lock. It turned, noiselessly, and a few moments later they were in the foot of the lighthouse stairwell, just as Jennifer had predicted.

The lady was thinking hard.

"This is how Billy Kendell got away that night. He came in here, through the window, and left through the tunnel. That little pair of scrotes are coming and going as they please around here without anyone having a fucking clue. All that crap about the tides and the fence. It's bollocks. It must have been Billy that pushed me off the top, you know. He must have heard me climbing up there and crept up behind me. He might even have been in the room upstairs when I tried the door. No wonder the little bastard looked shifty last night. I must have given him the fright of his life."

Jennifer locked the door and pocketed the key to the tunnel.

"Now, if Billy and Nancy use this tunnel to get on and off the island whenever they want, it's no wonder that nobody could work out what the fuck was going on. I bet they've both been at it."

Ricky Shilton coughed politely and Jennifer looked at him.

"Why though?" asked the big man.

"Why what?"

"Why bother? I mean, what's in it for them? The way I see things, we've got ourselves a pair of deranged and unstable youngsters who seem to get off on finding victims and making them suffer, yes? Granted, with this tunnel leading basically back to their own house it's no surprise to find them making mischief over here, but a little bit of graffiti and property damage? Doesn't sound like their bag of chips to me."

"So what are you saying, then? It wasn't them?"

Shilton shook his head. "Oh no, I reckon the mischief is down to those two. But I'll leave you with two questions, Jen."

"Firstly, what is Little Miss Rich-Bollocks doing waiting on tables here? From what you've said, she's got plenty of money and thinks that the sun shines out of her own back-door.

"Good point" conceded Jennifer. "She doesn't need to be working here in order to play poltergeist at night. With this tunnel she could do that anyway."

"Secondly," continued Shilton, "what are the chances that, if Billy-boy did indeed give you the shove Jen, that he was popping his cherry when he did it?"

"Meaning what?" asked Jennifer.

"Meaning, Jennifer, that everyone seems to have forgotten the prospective step-mother. Jack Kendell's intended. Poor Martine Dupuis who, by all accounts, had everything to live for." Shilton scratched his nose. "Once she stepped into their mum's shoes she was set up for life, wasn't she? Martine is who I am thinking about, Jen, conveniently deciding to end her life by topping herself in what now turns out to be the twins' own little playground."

Chapter Thirty-Three

"AWOL"

They re-grouped outside the lighthouse. Jennifer and Simon had climbed out through the broken window. Shilton, taking one look at the aperture and the drop to the ground outside, had told them to fuck off. He padded back downstairs and, introducing a bit of muscle to the proceedings, ripped away the plank of wood nailed over the front door and, with a couple of well-placed kicks, busted the door clean off its hinges. Job done, he sauntered out into the sunshine to where Simon and Jennifer were waiting, having sensibly retired to a safe distance.

"What's the plan then, Nancy Drew?" asked the big man.

"Well," responded the lady, "I suggest that we go and knock on the front door. Or very hard on Nancy Kendell's face, if she's scrubbing around."

Nancy turned out not to be around, however, for which Simon was secretly rather grateful as he did not really fancy another encounter with either of the Kendells.

The three of them had made their way across the rubble to the laboratory. Inside, Jennifer could see Nigel Whittaker and Linda Leighton, clad in their white coats and goggles, working away at the side bench. Jennifer let them into the common room where they found Barbara Porter and Professor MacKenzie.

"Jennifer!" squeaked Porter, jumping up. "Hello again! More ghost-hunting?" The little doctor peered over the redhead's shoulder. "I see you've brought us men. Good girl. Quite the little huntress-gatherer aren't you? Now, who is this gorgeous hunk?"

Simon was embarrassed, and annoyed in equal measure, that Barbara Porter did not appear to remember him until he realised that she was not actually looking at him at all, but straight at Ricky Shilton. The big man coughed and looked behind him, hopefully, but there was no hollow woman coming to his rescue.

"This is Ricky, Barbara" explained Jennifer, clocking his discomfort and enjoying it enormously. "He's exceptionally good with his hands and, yes, everything is quite in proportion."

Shilton shot her a 'fuck you' look.

"Lovely to meet you all" he rumbled politely. Barbara Porter skipped across and shook his beefy paw, tittering at his size. MacKenzie rolled his eyes, gave a brief nod, and sat down again.

"Barbara, would you do me a very kind favour please and look after the kiddies whilst I go and find Doctor Nicholson?" This earned Jennifer a second sour look from Ricky. The little doctor, only too willing to make a fuss over her new arrival, nodded and shooed her out.

Jennifer strode across the gravel to the main block.

As she was doing so, the door of the laboratory opened to emit Linda Leighton, who walked quickly across to the residential block and disappeared inside. Jennifer had the sense that the woman was upset, but the whole episode was so brief that she could not be certain. She carried on and, firstly satisfying herself that neither of the Kendells were skulking in the refectory, she made her way down the now-familiar corridor to Nicholson's office. As she got closer, she could hear Nicholson speaking on the telephone. The portly director beckoned Jennifer in, excitedly, when she appeared at the open door.

"That's right, Minister. Something of a success we feel too. Anyway, I must dash. I will report again tomorrow. We may have something concrete for you then. Goodbye... yes... to you, too. Goodbye!" she placed the receiver down and looked up an Jennifer. "Pompous little prick" she said, somewhat unexpectedly.

"That's new. I usually get 'aggravating'..."

"Not you dear. Silly girl... how are you anyway? Did your nice young man return your bag to you? It looked very expensive. Italian, yes? Flashy little mare. Very remiss of you to leave it behind."

"Yes he did, and thank you very much for returning it."

"Don't thank me, thank Nancy. She found it."

Unless the Oxford Dictionary definition of 'thanking' had recently been extended to include the gentle art of ramming a red-hot poker up somebody's arse-hole, Jennifer Pettifyr had no intention of thanking Nancy Kendell for anything, however she kept quiet and allowed the doctor to continue.

"Silly of you to leave it in your room like that."

"My room? Nancy found it in my room?"

"Well, Doctor Leighton's room, you know."

"Right. Is Nancy here? I'd rather like to 'thank' her personally." With my right knuckle, thought Jennifer, enjoying again the thought of smacking one onto that prize little cow. The gloves, she reflected, had definitely come off where the Kendell twins were concerned.

"No, I'm afraid not. Young Nancy's gone AWOL today. Probably got a hangover from the party, or something. You know what these young pieces are like, Miss Pettifyr. No stamina." Thanks, thought Jennifer, for not grouping me in with the youngsters then.

"Did she call in sick?"

"No, but I expect she'll be back tomorrow. Can't really crack the whip too hard, we don't pay her very much and I can't see anyone else being prepared to fag over here every day." This prompted Jennifer to remember Ricky's earlier comment.

"I don't mean to sound rude, but why does she? Do this job I mean. She's Jack Kendell's daughter. She can't need the money, so why is she working here?"

Nicholson squinted at her through her thick glasses.

"To be honest, Miss Pettifyr, I really don't know. She's an odd girl. I can only assume that either she enjoys our company (What!? thought Jennifer) or maybe she just likes the island. Some people do, you know. It is quite beautiful just to be out on the cliffs, without having all the tourists around like the mainland."

Jennifer was unconvinced. Nicholson went on.

"It is very peaceful here. Nancy might simply enjoy the solitude (Bullshit, thought the redhead). She doesn't say very much half the time, but she's never complained about the work or asked for any more money. That said, we don't work her particularly hard. My pet theory is that she's not allowed to smoke at home and this job is a rather convoluted method of getting a fag break."

"How did she get the job, in the first place?" Jennifer asked.

Nicholson played with her spectacles whilst considering the question. "I think, and I could be wrong about this, but I believe it was Doctor Leighton's idea (I'll bet it was, the dirty bastard, thought Jennifer). I mentioned, some time ago, that we could use a bit of support with some of the admin work, cleaning and the like. Doctor Leighton suggested Nancy, I think. I believe they had met on the mainland and had got friendly, or went to the same gym, something like that anyway. Anyhow, Nancy's name cropped up (along with his cock, opined Jennifer to herself) and, well, I think a couple of days later, she telephoned me and asked for a job. I didn't know, then, who she was, but she seemed polite enough. I took her on, for a trial period you understand. She has been here since then."

"Have you met her brother?" asked Jennifer.

"William Kendell?"

Nicholson paused and squinted at her before, slowly, adjusting her spectacles. "No dear. I've not had that dubious pleasure." Seeing Jennifer's expression, she continued.

"I'm sorry, Miss Pettifyr. I am well aware that it's quite wrong to pay attention to 'village gossip' and all of that kind of thing. However, he has such a terrible reputation that it is, really, a little hard not to believe that there must be, well, just a little bit of fire generating all of that unpleasant smoke."

"What do people say about him?" Jennifer asked, sitting forward more intently. Nicholson put down the pen which she had been tapping upon her desk. She lowered her voice and removed her glasses.

"That he's evil, Miss Pettifyr."

Chapter Thirty-Four
"Amateur night"

Two days later, big Ricky Shilton was sitting quietly by himself in a corner booth of the Causeway Arms, nursing a pint of ale and waiting to see whether his guest for the evening would turn up. The message he had left at the young man's house had been ambiguous but sufficiently, he hoped, intriguing. He had no idea, however, whether his quarry had taken his bait.

Personally, he rather doubted it. Slightly bereft of other ideas, however, he and Jennifer had taken stock of the situation and, in consultation with a few other interested parties including London, had thought the plan worth a shot. If it failed they lost nothing other than, possibly, the risk of putting their man on his guard. Ricky shot another glance at the doorway. Nothing.

The idea had come to him after twenty minutes of fending off the amorous advances of little Barbara Porter, when he had taken the old Scotsman, MacKenzie, up on his offer of rescue via a tour of the facility. He found most of the technical stuff, as a former serviceman, surprisingly interesting.

What had really got his attention, however, was a little piece of kit which fat Nigel Whittaker had been working on, under the corporate radar apparently, in his spare time. Nigel had collared him and demonstrated the tiny device purely, Ricky believed, because nobody else gave two flying fucks about it. As soon as he realised its potential, however, a plan began to form in Ricky's mind. This was why, now, a tiny electronic listening device no larger than a fingernail was taped, and quite invisible to anybody looking at him, to the inside of his t-shirt collar. He sipped his beer, appreciatively. He then placed it, slowly and carefully, back upon the table.

Billy Kendell had just drifted silently into the bar.

Shilton took his first appraising glance at the lean, young man in the expensive clothes. Cocky, definitely. Whether he had anything of substance to back it up was a different matter. Shilton took nothing for granted, however. He had lost too many good friends not to treat anyone in his path as a potential life-taker. It was time, he thought wryly, to dip his toe into Kendell waters and see what was nibbling. Was he dealing with a shark or a minnow?

William Kendell, dressed in black jeans and a fitted black shirt, scanned the bar and eventually caught Shilton's eye. Ricky nodded at him, briefly. Kendell gave him the once over and, satisfied that he seemed to be alone, sauntered over and slipped easily into the other side of the dark leather booth. He leaned back and considered Ricky with a dead-eyed stare. He folded his arms slowly.

"So, who the fuck are you then?" he said quietly.

"I'm your hairy godmother, son" said Ricky, grinning at him. Kendell reached slowly into his jacket pocket and extracted a blade which he held lazily, in his right palm, just high enough for it to be visible to Ricky without drawing any wider attention.

Shilton looked wounded. "Now that's not very friendly, is it son? Not friendly at all. Unless, of course, you've just ordered us the cheese board. I hear that the Cornish Yarg is quite good."

Billy Kendell did not move. He just sat staring. Ricky waited.

"I'm here, aren't I, so what do you want?" Kendell eventually asked. Shilton coughed and scratched his nose. Here goes nothing, then. He leaned back and took another sip of his beer. Very nice. Water from the moors, so they told him at the bar.

"I've got a job offer for you." Kendell said nothing in response to this, so Ricky went on. "I represent a firm in London, Billy, who are looking for a little bit of, shall we say, local assistance to deal with a problem. A problem in this neck of the woods."

"And why the fuck should I care about your problems?"

"No reason, Billy. No reason at all. Unless, of course, you're interested in protecting your own, rather less than legal, powder-based income stream from being royally fucked. Also, on top of your own self-interest, you would be earning yourself a significant sum of money for your trouble. You see, Billy, our information is that, in addition to your distribution activities, you're also a bit of a hard-lad in these parts. Now, my friends have a job that needs doing and, for reasons which I won't go into, they want to keep their paws well away from the flames on it. So, they are looking for, shall we say, a bit of local talent to do the job for them."

"You're full of shit."

Kendell looked at him and started playing with the blade.

"Maybe Billy, but right now you're the one spouting it. I'm not interested in your hard-man act, son. If I'm wasting my time here, and you're not interested in well-paid work, then I'll just be on my way. No hard feelings. No skin off our nose when you end up doing a stretch inside with your little coke business fucked, is it? Hell, we might even pick up your customers…"

He sipped his beer.

"Who put you onto me?"

Kendell glanced at him briefly, then back to the blade.

"Grow up, son. Nobody deals your product, in volume, without my friends being very well aware of it. Like I said, they're not a bunch of fucking amateurs. As it happens, your activities don't conflict with theirs. There are potential economies of scale, for mutual benefit, actually. Only if you're a bright lad though, and not a tit. Hence my calling upon you personally." He scratched his nose again. "Now, do you want to hear my proposition, or not? Some of us have work to do. I've got a ballet lesson to get to."

Billy Kendell continued to play with the tip of his knife, just looking at Shilton steadily. Ricky waited patiently. He was experienced enough to know that the younger man would, eventually, either bite or fight. He was ready for either.

After a few seconds more, however, Kendell settled the matter for him. He put the knife back into his pocket.

"What's the job?"

Ricky's face betrayed nothing.

He looked around briefly to reinforce, somewhat ironically in the circumstances, that they were in absolutely no danger of being overheard. "There's a woman here. Working with the boffins on that island." He pointed briefly towards the window, beyond which the faint lights of the institute were still visible across the causeway. "Now, for her size, this lady has been causing my friends in London a rather surprising amount of aggravation. As a result, they have now decided that they would quite like that aggravation to stop." Ricky paused for another nose scratch before concluding. "Permanently." Billy Kendell laughed and Ricky thought that he had seldom heard a less pleasant sound.

"You want me to bump her off? Is that your game?" Ricky said nothing, just inclined his head very slightly. Kendell folded his arms and leant back against the wall.

"So what's in it for me?" he asked.

"Ten thousand quid, son. Plus, you get to stay in business."

"Fuck off!"

Kendell rested his pale palms on the table and sat back.

"Keep your voice down" said Ricky, quietly. "Like I said, my friends are significant players. This lady has already cost them an awful lot more money than that, so think of it as an investment on their part. Safeguarding their future earnings. Not to mention yours either because, trust me, if she is sniffing around your ankles then you can bet your bollocks your little operation will be right down the toilet by the time she's finished."

"Who is she then?" asked Kendell, becoming more serious.

Ricky smiled.

"She goes by the name of Pettifyr. Jennifer Pettifyr. And, take it from me son, she's a devious little shit." Ricky enjoyed adding that little bit of colour, whilst acknowledging that he would, really quite definitely (despite it being, in his view, a fairly factually-accurate statement), pay for it later. Billy Kendell unfolded his arms and let out a long, low whistle. Then he began to laugh.

"Something funny, son?"

"Just ironic, that's all." Kendell smirked.

"Why would that be then? Anyway, the description I have says she's got red hair and is a lot more dangerous than she looks. Tasty with her fists…"

"I don't need her description" Kendell cut across him. "I've met her. Although we weren't formally introduced. Not the first time anyway…"

"You've met her? Where?"

"When I pushed her over a cliff" said Billy Kendell.

He might have been ordering coffee.

Shilton looked at him without changing his expression.

"You pushed her off a cliff? Right. Any particular reason for that, then? Blocking your view of the boats, was she?" He scratched his nose and looked bored. Kendell leaned in closer.

"She was sticking her nose into my sister's business. Mine too for that matter, and I don't care for anybody who does that. Anyway, it didn't work. Ginger's still alive and kicking. Back yesterday, larger than fucking life, at my own dad's party."

"What's so funny then?" said Ricky darkly.

"Botched up murder attempts don't generally get laughs where I come from, son. They generally earn reprisals. If she's wise to you, you're probably not the man for this job. Too risky." Ricky sipped his pint and waited, inscrutable.

"Don't worry about that, the stupid mare don't know it was me. You pay me to do her and she won't be drinking any more cocktails, I promise you that. I won't miss a second time." He gave Shilton a sickly leer. "Guess it's lucky for me that she didn't hit the rocks after all, I reckon…"

Ricky smiled back, to reassure the unhinged specimen in front him that he was in the company of a kindred spirit. His mind was working overtime though.

"To be honest son, I'm having doubts. If you couldn't top her with surprise on your side, how are you going to manage it now her guard's up? Also, people don't just fall off cliffs, do they? I mean, fuck me. Nobody's going to believe that and we need this job to look like an accident. This ain't fucking amateur night. If you knock her off, you'll need an alibi too. Thought about that?"

"Don't worry. I know how to make it look like an accident."

"Oh really?"

Ricky waited, sensing that he was starting to get somewhere.

"Yes, really." Kendell eye-balled him. "I've had practice."

"Practice?"

Ricky paused, looking just sufficiently interested, hopefully, to prompt Kendell into showing his hand. He took another, slow, sip of his pint whilst counting in his head.

Eventually, Kendell took the bait.

Conforming to the age-old truism that nature abhors a vacuum, especially a verbal one, the younger man looked around, again, to reassure himself that they were alone, then he leaned across the table. "Mister, I can get on and off that island whenever I fucking please. I've been doing it since I was a kid, and none of those dick-heads have a fucking clue about it." He grinned, unpleasantly. "If ginger gets topped over there, I'll have an alibi as tight as her arse. Just like last time."

Ricky sighed inwardly. Youngsters, he reflected, really just can't help themselves. "Last time? What, when you shoved her off and botched it?" Kendell leaned in closer.

"I'm talking about Martine Dupuis. Look her up. Apparently she jumped off that lighthouse. Poor little depressed lamb. Well, she didn't fucking jump. Me and my sister dragged her up there and taught her a lesson for screwing our dad behind mum's back. That French bitch killed our mum, so we returned the favour. She begged like a dog."

Ricky watched, unmoving, as Kendell played with the blade of the knife in his pocket, apparently unconsciously, while he talked. His tone was horribly light and conversational.

"Begged... then pissed herself before we chucked her off the top. So you see, Mister. We're not amateurs either and you've got nothing to worry about. Say the word, and ginger is history."

Back on the island a small group sat, huddled in the common room firelight, around a large reel to reel tape-recorder and loudspeaker which had been set up on the coffee table. In addition to Jennifer, Simon and the resident scientists, who were all listening intently, was the Chief Constable for South Devon. A uniformed constable stood by the door.

The thin, wavering voice of William Kendell leaked out of the loudspeaker whilst Nigel Whittaker sat in front of the slowly rotating tape, concentrating intently and making continual, tiny, adjustments to the receiver dials in order to hold onto the fragile signal coming from the mainland.

Jennifer listened as Kendell confessed to how he, and Nancy, had taken their revenge on poor Martine Dupuis at the top of the lighthouse, throwing her to a vicious early grave purely, it seemed, to avenge their mother. Conveniently ignoring, thought Jennifer cynically, the not insignificant fringe-benefit of protecting their inheritance from a potential step-mother and any future offspring she might have conceived with Jack. William Kendell was clearly cracked and unstable.

Jennifer wondered about Nancy. Was she equally unhinged, or just financially ruthless? As they listened they heard the occasional, seemingly innocent, prompt from Ricky Shilton as he gently prodded Kendell into burying himself.

Barbara Porter was leaning forward with her tongue hanging out, like an old man in a strip-club, lapping up the grisly details. Margaret Nicholson sat back quietly, her hand to her mouth, with a shocked and deeply sad expression on her face.

Jennifer, having finally sat back down after hopping around (incensed far less by Kendell's references to her impending demise than by Ricky's description of her) looked keenly across at Nigel as he played on the dials.

"Are you getting all this?" she whispered for the tenth time.

Whittaker nodded patiently and continued to make subtle adjustments if the signal appeared to be drifting. The reels continued to turn as the eerie and unpleasant voice of the disembodied William Kendell polluted the room.

"Isn't it fantastic!" squealed Barbara Porter, who seemed oblivious to the horrific content of what was coming through the loudspeaker. "Short-range transmission, via a tiny condenser microphone smaller than a postage stamp!" she rattled off excitedly. "Clear as a bell, too, isn't it? Fantastic!" She re-filled her glass, heavily, with scotch and did the same for Jennifer. "We've GOT the little fucker!"

"Language Barbara!" said Nicholson, biting her lip and looking nervously at the senior policeman who was sat listening quietly to the tape whilst making notes.

She felt inexpressibly sad, thinking of the poor French woman, her brilliant and vivacious friend who had just discovered genuine happiness before having it cut down, so brutally, by this evil young man and his sister. It brought her to tears. She wondered what to do and looked at Jennifer.

"Will the police arrest him?" she asked quietly.

Jennifer looked up.

"The police are going to pick Billy up and start questioning him about Martine's death. I don't know whether this tape is admissible as evidence or not, but it's certainly enough to get them burrowing hard and deep into the little bastard's life and turning it upside-down. Isn't that right?"

The Chief Constable nodded.

"Oh yes, Miss Pettifyr. I'm afraid that young Mr Kendell's life is going to be a few shades less pleasant from here on, I think. These kind of things tend to develop momentum, you know. You start tugging one thread and, lo and behold. No, I don't think that Mister Kendell is going to be walking away from this one."

He sat back in his chair.

"We've suspected his involvement in drugs for some time, he's dabbled in it before, but we've had no evidence to justify spending any significant time on him. This business with the tunnels and the lighthouse, though, puts a very different complexion on things. I think a thorough search might prove fruitful."

Jennifer looked at him.

"And his sister? What about Nancy?"

She risked a brief glance at Simon who was sitting, quietly, listening intently to the tape. She was unable to read his expression. Linda Leighton, who had been sitting quietly in the corner with her hands resting in her lap, suddenly got up. She looked around the room and then walked out quickly.

Jennifer watched her leave and then touched Nicholson on the knee. She beckoned the older lady up, out of her chair, and over to a corner of the room.

"I guess she'll be relieved to have Nancy out of the way" Jennifer said softly, gesturing to the door. Nicholson looked at her blankly.

"Sorry… do you mean Linda?" she asked.

"Yes." Jennifer said. "Nancy Kendell is a nasty piece of work, Doctor. I think she took this job because she enjoys playing games with people, turning them into toys to play with. It can't have been easy for Linda, having to watch Nancy getting her hooks into her husband." She kept her voice down low, as she didn't want the others to overhear the conversation.

"John?" Nicholson still looked blank.

For fuck's sake, thought Jennifer, do I have to put this up in sky-writing? "Yes" she hissed. "John Leighton. Having an affair with Nancy! Can't have been easy for Linda. She must have suspected something when he shoe-horned her into the kitchen…"

Nicholson stared at her. "An affair? That's ridiculous, dear. John's devoted to Linda." Jennifer rolled her eyes.

"Well, if he's that devoted, why did he move heaven and earth to get the girl with the golden buns a job here, then? And, more to the point, why else would she take that job except to be close to him and to stir up shit between him and his wife?"

Jennifer, point made nicely, folded her arms. Nicholson removed her spectacles and wiped them with a cloth before replacing them onto her nose. "Jennifer dear, John Leighton didn't get Nancy her job here."

"But you said…"

"It was Linda."

Chapter Thirty Seven
"Teddy bear"

Jennifer Pettifyr knocked, quietly, on the door of her former bedroom before letting herself in. She was carrying a cocktail shaker and two frosted glasses. Linda Leighton sat, crying quietly on the bed, with her head in her hands. She looked pale and drawn, her good-looks overtaken by the strain of, Jennifer presumed, an unhealthy mixture of work and emotional stress. Hopefully, she told herself, she might be able to assist with the latter. Jennifer set the shaker down, gently, onto the desk then went over and sat down on the bed. Linda turned sadly to look at her.

Her eyes were wet and red.

"I don't know where to start" she began briefly, before beginning to tear up and putting her head back into her hands. Jennifer rested a hand gently onto her knee.

"I'm not the police you know… I work for myself, and I want to help you. Anything that you want to tell me does not have to go beyond these four walls." Jennifer got up and constructed two drinks whilst Linda Leighton composed herself. She handed one to the blonde, who took a large gulp.

"You make an excellent martini…" Linda gave a small laugh through her tears and Jennifer smiled warmly. She sat down and laughed.

"I should do, Linda. I've had enough practice. I drink like a fish with man trouble." Linda wiped her eyes and took another sip. Jennifer looked at her, kindly. "Would you like to tell me about Nancy?" she asked, tentatively. "In your own words and in your own time?"

Linda Leighton took a deeper draught of her cocktail, which made her cough rather sweetly. She was really a very attractive woman and Jennifer felt very sorry for her. At least the strong cocktail seemed to have stemmed Linda's tears.

"I don't quite know how it began, really" she said, quietly. "Well, how it developed anyway. I know exactly when it started, for me at least. It was at the lido… last summer. John was working away in London, so I was at a loose end after working all hours, as usual. I felt like a break, so I treated myself to a spa day. I never do anything like that, so it was a real treat. I had a massage, a go in the hot-tub then I went to sun-bathe, with a drink, by the outside pool. I'd had a few drinks by then, I suppose…" She paused and looked at Jennifer, who gave her a smile of encouragement and sipped at her own drink.

"Nancy was there, with a friend I think. Another girl. I didn't really notice the friend." She paused again. "I noticed Nancy, though. She was wearing a tiny red bikini and was wrestling with her sun lounger, right in front of my eyes. Oh, I noticed her all right…" She faltered again, so Jennifer leaned forward gently.

"It's OK, Linda. I do understand. She is a stunningly beautiful girl." It pained Jennifer to say it, but it seemed to help Linda Leighton to continue.

"She's a monster" the doctor said quietly. "I didn't know that then. Back then, I just thought she was the most beautiful creature I had ever seen." She looked down at her hands before taking another sip of her cocktail. "I was trying not to keep watching her, but I couldn't help it. I was lying there, drinking in the hot sunshine and watching this beautiful thing right in front of me, smiling and laughing. She was utterly bewitching. Anyway, she realised. That I was watching her, I mean. After a while, her friend left and then she came over and started chatting to me. I was so embarrassed and tongue-tied I could barely get a sentence out, but she just made me relax. We ended up having some drinks together. She asked me about my hobbies, my interests and, well, I told her about the photography."

"Photography?" queried Jennifer.

Then it clicked. The pictures on the wall.

"It's my hobby" replied the doctor. "I take pictures. Landscapes, wildlife, everything really. Sometimes a few portraits. Well, Nancy was so excited when I told her. She wanted to know everything about it, begged me to show her my pictures. It was so…well, flattering, I suppose. Nobody has ever shown any interest in them at all, not even John. Especially not John…" she faltered. She looked at Jennifer. "He can't find out about this… it would be the end of us."

Jennifer gave her a reassuring smile and patted her leg.

"It's OK, Linda. So, Nancy was interested in your photos?"

"Yes. She pestered me constantly, so I arranged to meet her again and promised to bring some pictures to show her. We had lunch together in town. That was when she told me about her aspirations to be a model. She was certainly beautiful enough and I told her so. She asked me, then, if I would take some pictures of her. I guess that was where it really started."

Jennifer finished her drink and offered the doctor a re-fill. Linda nodded quickly and continued to speak whilst Jennifer refilled their glasses from the shaker.

"I, well we, started meeting up regularly. Nancy would suggest places we could visit and where I could take photographs of her. She wanted to build up her portfolio, for agencies and the like. So, we went out on the beach, outside hotels, on the cliff top. Just portraits, with different outfits, you understand. It was all perfectly innocent..."

She paused.

"But of course, it wasn't. She knew that and so did I, really. From that first day, my watching her at the pool... it wasn't innocent. Nancy always made a point of being provocative when she spoke to me... suggestive... but nothing so overt that I might be offended by it. She just flirted with me and I found her so desperately attractive... I fell in love with her, I suppose. I felt that I could trust her too, as a friend..." Jennifer returned with two cocktails and placed one down in front of Linda. The doctor took a sip and nodded approvingly "That's really lovely... thank you."

"You're very welcome." Jennifer waited patiently.

"So, anyway, the photography trips went on for a while and then… well… one afternoon we met up in town, as usual, and Nancy suggested that we could go up to the woods. I thought this was a great idea…it is beautiful up there, quiet and undisturbed. I knew that we could get some great pictures and…being honest… I think, deep down, I knew what she was planning to do… and I wanted it to happen."

She took a deep drink and bumped Jennifer's shoulder lightly, as if for reassurance.

"I hired a car and drove us up to the woods. We parked up and walked, with my camera, deep into the centre. Nancy had a small bag with her. Clothes, she said. Anyway, eventually we found a little clearing, really in the middle of nowhere. The light was beautiful, so I got my camera out and set it up on a tripod. When I turned around, to suggest to Nancy what we could use as background, she was just looking at me… and undressing."

Linda's voice faltered again.

Jennifer thought she might be about to stop but, after another sip of her drink, she carried on quietly. "I remember it like it was only yesterday. She stripped completely naked, then walked calmly up to me and told me that she wanted to do some nudes. I was thunderstruck… and shaking I think." Linda wavered briefly but continued after another sip. "She had never suggested anything like that before and, although she was always flirty, touching you know and kissing my cheek… she had never been so, well, overtly sexual... before. She just stood in front of me and I couldn't help but stare… at her body, I mean."

"Anyway, then she walked straight past me, into the centre of the clearing, and ordered me to take pictures." Jennifer took a sip of her own drink. Linda Leighton went on.

"She began posing on the grass. Demurely at first, but then insisting I get closer and closer with the camera. Then she began to...to touch herself. Her poses became more and more obscene until, finally, I told her to stop... that I couldn't do it. That made her angry. She called me all sorts of horrible, really beastly, names and I began to cry. I remember bursting into tears and sitting in a ball on the grass, hugging my knees and feeling wretched. Then, suddenly, I felt her arms around me, cuddling me. Then she was kissing me, really gently. She pulled me down onto the floor with her... and then she made love to me. I can't put it into words... how she made me feel, that afternoon. We stayed there for hours afterwards, just lying naked in each other's arms until it started to get dark."

Jennifer, slowly sipping her drink, digested the doctor's story. After the woods, Linda explained, Nancy's demands to meet became more frequent and, invariably, ended up with them in hotel beds or in the woods having sex. Nancy had also persuaded Linda to take photographs of the two of them, together, for fun she said.

Linda had recommended Nancy for the job at the Institute so that she could see her more frequently and be close to her. She was, she said simply, in love. "I wish I could say that I felt guilty, but at first I really didn't. I wanted her so badly, all of the time, even though I knew how stupid and dangerous the situation was. She was like a drug."

"At times she really frightened me. I think that is part of her charm. When she is angry, Miss Pettifyr, she can be brutal and you can't say no to her when she wants something. She is, well, I think quite capable of anything at all."

"Like murder?" Jennifer asked, quietly but distinctly. Billy Kendell's voice on the wireless had, quite clearly, intimated that both he and Nancy had been instrumental in throwing Martine Dupuis to her death. Jennifer was interested in Linda's reaction to that particular revelation about her erstwhile lover. Had it come as a surprise, or confirmation of a suspicion already held?

"I really don't know, to be honest. The risk of getting caught, going to prison, might stop her. I don't think she would have any moral qualms though. She enjoys playing games. That's all I was to her, I think now. Just her latest game. When I told her I had fallen in love with her, she... well she just laughed in my face. It totally crushed me. I was just a toy to her. A sad, stupid old teddy bear she got bored taking to bed and so decided to pull the arms off instead..."

She coughed and sipped her drink. "When I realised what she really felt, although it hurt like hell, I told her we couldn't see each other again and that I thought she should find another job. That was when things got ugly. She called me the foulest names and started slapping my face. She is physically much stronger than I am and she enjoyed being able to dominate me. When we were first together, I loved that about her. She was so strong and just took what she wanted. Now it terrifies me. It also terrifies me that I enjoyed it so much."

"Anyway, she told me that, unless I wanted my husband and all of my work colleagues to see, in glossy eight-by-ten colour, what demure little Doctor Leighton likes to get up to on her days off, I had better keep my fat trap shut and carry on doing exactly as I was told..."

As she listened, Jennifer felt increasingly sorry for this kind, unhappy, woman whose single, guilty foray into a passionate fantasy had twisted into such a horrible and traumatic experience. She reflected also upon Nancy Kendell, sexual blackmailer. Jennifer could envisage a situation where a beautiful and intelligent girl, growing up in a small community with little to occupy her free time, could grow restless and rebellious. Off the rails, seeking excitement and stimulation in all sorts of places, using the power of her alluring body and charisma to demand attention and interest. Jennifer suspected that such situations were, sadly, probably quite commonplace.

To Jennifer's mind, however, there seemed a quiet note of calculated cruelty in Nancy's treatment of Linda Leighton which struck her as dangerous. Like a child not content to pull the wings off a butterfly without caressing it first. Then feeding it its own wings afterwards.

Jennifer shuddered. Her thoughts were interrupted as Linda deposited a third martini in front of her. "There was some left in the shaker" she said. "Thank you, Jennifer. You are a very patient listener. Sorry, I'm really getting a bit drunk. I'm not trying to seduce you, either. Don't worry. I'm rather off girls at the moment... it's nothing personal."

Jennifer laughed and rested her hand gently on top of the other woman's. "Describing me as 'patient' is thanks enough Linda. If you wouldn't mind putting that in writing and sending it to my mother, I would be much obliged. All she ever wanted from me was a decent school report. I'm a perpetual disappointment." She winked at Linda. "Also, for the record, if you were I'd be immensely flattered. You're a lovely woman and, whatever else I do here, I can assure you that I have absolutely no intention of letting anything that you've just told me leave this room. I will do everything I can to keep you out of this mess." Linda Leighton smiled, then frowned suddenly. "Nancy... she has photographs. Of us together. I know she kept them."

She looked worriedly at Jennifer.

"She... well... she once put photographs of herself in my bedside drawer whilst she was cleaning. John could have found them. When I confronted her, she just said she wanted me to think about her body when I went to bed. She was warning me, though. Warning me to toe the line or risk having my whole life, my marriage and career torn down around my ears. Right now, to be honest, I don't know that I care anymore. John... well, he deserves better though... better than me and better than having my dirty laundry rubbed in his face in public."

"John is a very lucky man, Linda." Jennifer patted her hand, "Let me worry about little Miss Kendell. I am not entirely devoid of a few dirty little tricks of my own, you know. Now, cheer up. You're not on your own any more. If you want to talk again, at any time, just come and find me, OK?"

Jennifer patted her hand again. Then she bounced up off the bed and went out of the doorway. Linda Leighton sat for a while longer, looking at the door and thinking about the strange woman in the red boots that somebody kind, somewhere, appeared to have sent to her rescue. She smiled and, for the first time in a very long time, thought about the future.

Chapter Thirty-Six

"Hello Mother"

Three hours later, following a flurry of short and serious calls made by the Chief Constable from Doctor Nicholson's office telephone (which Barbara Porter quite outrageously, but ultimately unsuccessfully, attempted to tap) William Kendell was arrested at his home and taken into custody.

That evening, Jennifer sat in the bar of the Causeway Inn with Simon, Ricky and most of the scientists, drinking an enormous gin and tonic with her feet up on the table. She was dog-tired but relieved to be away from the island. Jennifer felt desperately sorry for Jack Kendell and wished that she could have spoken to him before Billy's arrest to lessen the shock somehow. She could not imagine how he would react to being told that his own children had murdered the woman he loved and had wanted to marry. She liked Jack and, even if she thought he did bear some responsibility for how his children had turned out after the death of their mother, nobody deserved what he was going through. His life and family had literally disintegrated around him.

Nancy Kendell had also been taken to the police station, to be questioned about her involvement in the Dupuis suicide and the incidents on the island, however the evidence against her was sketchy at best. The Chief Constable had promised that, if any developments occurred, he would get word to Jennifer at the Inn.

Jennifer had not been idle though. Whilst the telephone calls were being made she had slipped away to the lighthouse and, using the key she had pocketed earlier, gone back to the tunnel. On a hunch, she made an exhaustive search of the bed-chamber and, after ten minutes, she found what she was looking for. A stash of photographs, including negatives, in a thick brown envelope had been tucked away between two back panels in the wardrobe. The content of the pictures confirmed two things. Firstly, that Nancy Kendell was an unusually adventurous and broad-minded lover. Secondly, that Linda Leighton had been telling the truth. Jennifer had burnt the envelope and its contents with the candle.

She had no qualms about doing this. In her view, Linda had suffered enough and if her actions weakened the evidence against Nancy Kendell then so be it. Jennifer's conscience would carry that one. Nancy, she decided, would get her comeuppance now that the local police, and her father, knew the score about what she and her twisted brother had been up to. Everybody's guard would be up where the manipulative girl was concerned. Jennifer's priority, as she saw it, was to protect Linda. The Kendell twins had ruined enough lives. All of the scientists, other than Linda who had understandably expressed a desire for an early night and some rest, had come over for a celebratory drink.

Now that the Kendells were in custody, or at least out of circulation, her recent emotional and physical exertions had rather caught up with Jennifer. She really just wanted to go to bed. Devon, she decided, would not be at the top of her holiday list next year. She was even missing her poky little flat in Seven Dials and her psychotic, cat-obsessed landlady. That, she reflected grimly, was a sure sign that she was overwrought and definitely needed to get some sleep.

Ricky Shilton and Simon were drinking pints at the bar and had spent the last hour trying to make sense of Billy Kendell and his motivations. Simon had tried to rationalise Kendell's behaviour by reference to his corrosive relationship with his sister and the trauma of his mother's death. That, he asserted, fuelled by his father's inability to cope with his own marriage breakdown and his seeking solace in the arms of a woman other than Billy's mother, must have sent him over the edge and into a series of destructive, psychotic episodes which, unchecked, had escalated over the years. Ricky, considering all of this thoughtfully, had opined that Billy Kendell was just a vicious little cunt who deserved two bullets in the back of the head. Three pints later, Simon was agreeing with him.

In between that, Simon frequently took the opportunity to look over at Jennifer who was sitting unusually quietly with her large and largely untouched gin and tonic. He had not spoken properly to her since the Chief Constable had arrived on the island and, after the policeman had gone to make his calls, she had disappeared.

When she returned she had stopped briefly for a quiet word with Linda Leighton then, just when Simon had hoped to get five minutes alone with her, she had gone straight out and back across the causeway to the mainland.

Barbara Porter came back from the bar with another round of drinks and clearly on a mission to get Ricky Shilton drunk by hook, crook or Mickey Finn. She positioned an enormous and particularly nasty-looking shot glass full of something black and viscous under the big man's nose. Even from Simon's distance it smelt rancid so, getting up, he picked up his pint and went across to where Jennifer was sitting.

She raised her eyes sleepily as he sat down beside her. She looked done in. He raised his glass in greeting and moved his head in a little closer so that he could talk to her without all the world and her husband listening in. "Are you OK?" he asked softly. "Pretty awful holiday so far."

Jennifer smiled at him and took an unenthusiastic sip from her glass. She put it back down onto the table and pushed it away. "I've had worse Simon. Nobody has actually buried me head first in the sand yet."

"You look tired" he said with concern.

"Thanks very much. Turning on the charm tonight then?"

"Sorry…" He took a deep breath and decided just to come out with what he had wanted to say all night but had not found, or made, the opportunity when everything else was going down on the island. The beer helped. He took another breath. Jennifer was staring at her boots. She looked tired, he thought, but beautiful.

He wished he could pick her up in his arms, wrap her in a duvet and watch her fall asleep. And be there, in the morning, to watch her waking up. "What I wanted to say, Jennifer, was that I'm sorry. Really sorry. About lots of things, actually, but mainly for upsetting you because, well, I think that you're really…"

He was not able to finish his somewhat long-winded and inebriated sentence because, at that point, the barman interrupted them by leaning in and tapping Jennifer lightly on the shoulder. She turned around to him.

"Sorry, but is it Miss Pettifyr?" She nodded. "Sorry to interrupt but you have a telephone call, miss. You can take it through here." Jennifer got up and the barman led her into a back room where, amid barrels of beer and unopened boxes of crisps, a black telephone sat on an upturned crate. Jennifer picked up the handset and placed it to her ear. Presumably, she thought, the Chief Constable had an update for them.

"Hello? Jennifer speaking." There was a short pause at the other end and Jennifer thought that she could detect the sound of breathing. Then a giggle at the end of the line enabled her to identify the caller. She felt sick. "Hello Nancy" she said coldly. "They let you out then?"

"You…" The single word sounded vicious. Jennifer suspected that she was now speaking to the real Nancy Kendell, not the calculating shop window dummy pretending to wipe tables and serving up tea. "I'm going to burn you in your bed, you sad little ginger cunt."

"Oh, hello mother. I didn't realise it was you" replied Jennifer. "For a moment there I mistook you for a mad little local slapper, coked off her tits and making a twat of herself down here whilst thinking she's god's gift to mankind. My mistake..." Jennifer paused. The breathing on the other end was heavier now. "Are we still on for Christmas? Let's talk turkey."

"Funny. So FUCKING funny aren't you? You won't be laughing tomorrow, shit-head. Got some black clothes in your pretty leather bag? Oh, you took my picture though, didn't you? Like it did you? I bet you fucking love pussy..."

"Well, to be honest you know, I thought Nancy Junior could maybe use a bit of a trim. Less is more and all that? But, otherwise yes, very nice. Well done you! Growing them so big..." Jennifer paused again, wondering whether aggravating the Kendell girl was really a very sensible strategy. It was a fun strategy though.

"You're fucked, ginger-nut. FUCKED!" The voice was thin and strained. "When I'm finished with you they'll fish you out of the water and won't know if it's a body or a butchered pig..."

"Don't bust your bra, Nancy. It's not my fault your little brother is such a clueless little prick that he can't spot a wire and keep his gob shut, is it? Still, I suppose being a sad little psycho who can only get it up for his sister can't be much of a life for anybody."

Jennifer waited, trying hard to gauge the breathing at the other end and wondering what reaction her provocation might generate. If she got Nancy Kendell riled enough she might come out from under her current rock and have a go at her.

Jennifer considered it worth the personal risk if she could get Nancy done for attempted murder. She had no doubt, now, that the girl was capable of it. Jennifer had also begun to wonder about the circumstances of Nancy's mother's death. What was it Jack had said? My daughter came home from school and found her mother dead in the bath.

Nancy was suddenly back on the line. Her telephone manner, it is fair to say, had not improved much during the interval. "Think you're SO fucking clever, don't you? You rancid old hag. Let's see how you like this one, then. Let's just see shall we…" There was a pause. Then, to Jennifer's horror, she heard a completely different voice. A frightened whimpering came onto the line which was not Nancy Kendell at all.

"Jen…Jennifer? Help me…" A tiny voice.

Jennifer went cold.

"Linda!" Jennifer shouted down the line. "Linda! Are you OK?" There was the sound of a hard wet slap, then Nancy Kendell came back on the line.

"You took Billy away. I am going to take down EVERYONE that you care about. One by FUCKING ONE!! Then you can kiss my fucking FEET before I put you out of your sad little misery." The girl was breathing hard down the line. "First, I want to watch your little bitch-arse run. So RUN, little Jennifer rabbit. Look out of the window and FUCKING RUN!"

There was a horrible pause.

"My hot little girlfriend here is just burning to see you…"

The phone was slammed down.

Jennifer ran back to the bar and over to the window. What the hell was she looking for? She panicked briefly, thinking it might just be a stupid trap to shoot her where she stood, but no gunshot came and, pulling herself together, she scanned the outside. Then her tired brain engaged itself. Linda. Nancy was on the island. Ricky Shilton had got to his feet and joined her at the window.

"Alright, Jennie?"

Then she saw it. She was staring wildly out over the Causeway where the tide was beginning to creep in again. In an hour or so it would cover the sand. She stared at the building from which they had walked a few hours earlier and to where the little group of scientists were preparing to walk home.

The hospital was on fire.

Chapter Thirty-Seven

"Tank-top"

Leaving Ricky and Simon in her wake, Jennifer crashed out of the pub and started sprinting towards the causeway, her powerful thighs propelling her like a bison down the concrete slipway and out across the wet sand. She had been a county champion runner at school and, as she pounded hard across the damp beach, she tried to summon up all the reserves of energy in her tired body and focus on what was ahead of her. She kept her eyes up and glued to the old hospital where she could now see flames starting to lick up at the windows.

She covered the distance in five minutes of hard running and arrived, chest heaving and drenched in sweat, at the bottom of the concrete slipway. Her thighs burned with lactic acid as she forced herself onwards and up the slope until, panting heavily, she punched the key code into the gate and staggered over to the main entrance.

Through the windows she could see that the flames were now more intense and rising up to the ceiling of the refectory. No alarms were sounding, which Jennifer did not understand as she had seen alarms fitted into all of the rooms.

Forcing her way in through the main door, she ran down the corridor to the refectory where horrible yellows and oranges were flickering through the blackening glass. Crashing into the doors, Jennifer fell back as they remained stubbornly shut in her face. She rattled them hard, but some form of chain or other barrier had been set up on the inner side and she could not get through. She peered through the glass but the smoke was now too thick to make anything out. Trying again, the door would not budge.

Attempting to think, Jennifer ran outside and staggered across to the laboratory block. Punching in the code, she heaved herself into the foyer and picked up the little red fire extinguisher from the floor. Lugging it outside, she dragged it across the gravel to the side of the refectory and up against the wall. Taking a few deep breaths, Jennifer hefted it onto her shoulder and, with a mighty roar, smashed it with all of her remaining strength into the window. The glass shattered and Jennifer used the extinguisher like a battering ram to clear a way in. A sickly stench of petrol hit her nostrils. Stripping off her jacket, she draped it over the jagged shards jutting out from the window frame before heaving herself into the room.

The heat inside was almost unbearable. Jennifer dropped to the floor by the busted window, trying to get out of the smoke, and covered her mouth with her forearm. She looked around, desperately, for any signs of life. Her eyes began to stream but in the centre of the room she thought that she could make out a bundle of rags, or something, lying on the floor.

She crawled towards it slowly and, as she dragged herself closer, she realised with horror that it was a body. The body of a woman. The smell of petrol was intense.

Linda Leighton had been soaked in it.

Simon and Ricky had watched Jennifer lurch out of the door and pelt off down the road like a greyhound. Bewildered, they just looked at each other. Ricky pushed his glasses up his nose and scratched his backside.

"Has she got the shits or something?"

Simon looked out of the window from where Jennifer had been standing before her rapid exit. He saw two things, practically simultaneously. The first, in the distance, being flames dancing horribly in the window of one of the buildings on the island. Secondly, he saw the figure of a woman on the causeway, running like a rhinoceros with the very devil at its back.

"Ricky… the island is on fire!" he shouted.

Shilton put his drink down on the table, peered through his glasses at the younger man, then looked out of the window himself. "I'd better get the van then" he said calmly.

The big man moved smoothly out of the door with more speed than Simon would ever have given him credit for. Simon ran outside and down to the waterfront. He could still just make out Jennifer, in the far distance now, sprinting towards the hospital. Thirty seconds later, Ricky arrived in the battered transit and pushed open the passenger door. The big man gunned the accelerator and pointed the van down towards the slipway.

Out on the sand, Ricky Shilton floored it and sent the protesting vehicle rattling off in pursuit of the redhead. It seemed to take an age, but at last they too ended up at the foot of the slipway on the island side. Jennifer was nowhere to be seen, presumably having already made her way in. Simon and Ricky clambered out and jogged up to the gate. Out of breath, Ricky looked expectantly at Simon. He nodded his big head at the door. "Well, in your own time then, son. Bloody hell!" he said, getting aggravated.

"Shit. I don't know the code!" Simon shouted, rattling the gate. Jennifer was still nowhere in sight and the flames were heavier now. The sky around the refectory was beginning to glow and thick smoke was billowing into the air.

"And he says this now? Fuck me!" said Shilton. "Hang on…"

The big man jogged back to the slipway. Thirty seconds later he slammed the transit, at top speed, right through the gates of the Bursands Institute and powered over the gravel towards the burning building. Simon ran after him through the broken gateway and reached the van just as Ricky was clambering out.

They rounded the corner of the building, together, just as an enormous explosion from inside the refectory turned the air white hot and blew the glass from the windows into their face like molten shrapnel. Both men hit the deck as hot glass showered down like confetti.

They lay there, stunned, for about ten seconds. Eventually Ricky Shilton, sensing that the storm was probably over, rolled onto his back and opened his eyes.

A rather dishevelled but surprisingly happy-looking Jennifer Pettifyr was standing over him, supporting what appeared to be the body of an unconscious woman. She stank like an Esso garage.

"Alright down there?" the lady enquired sweetly, "because if either of you two feel like, you know, fucking helping at some point then just feel free to crack on, yes? I'm sweating like a pig in a tank-top over here."

She lay Linda Leighton gently down onto the ground and checked her pulse. Mercifully, the doctor seemed to be unconscious but not badly hurt or burnt. The flames inside had not reached her, but the smoke can't have done her lungs any good whatsoever. Simon came over, coughing, and bent down to cradle Linda's head in his lap and cover her with his jacket. Jennifer squatted on her haunches and coughed heavily. She felt half-dead. She looked up towards the lighthouse.

A lone figure in black stood on the gantry, gripping the handrail and staring down malevolently at them like the Angel of Death. Nancy Kendell was back and this time, sensed Jennifer, she wasn't making the tea.

Chapter Thirty-Eight
"My world"

"Look after Linda!" Jennifer shouted over her shoulder at Simon as she powered angrily across the gravel towards the tower. Her legs were aching and it was painful, now, for her to scramble over the rubble, although Jennifer was grateful that at least she was wearing her most practical pair of trainers. She ran as hard as she could manage towards the dark front door which Ricky Shilton had blasted open with his feet earlier in the day.

Her sixth sense should have warned her to slow down, but by the time she reached the doorway she had built up far too much momentum to stop. As she staggered inside Nancy Kendell, who had positioned herself behind and to the side of the doorway, swung hard with the plank of wood, which Shilton had removed from the back of the door, with all of her strength.

Jennifer took the heavy blow full in the face like an explosion. She collapsed in a heap, bashing her head onto the stone steps in the process. Nancy Kendell looked down at her with a cruel satisfied smile. She smashed again with the plank until she saw blood appear at Jennifer's temple. Then she crunched her foot hard into Jennifer's ribs for good measure. Bending down, she gripped hair and began to drag the redhead slowly up the steps like a sack of potatoes.

Back by the refectory, Ricky helped Simon make Linda Leighton comfortable then he set off in pursuit of Jennifer, cursing her impetuosity. He reached the open lighthouse door and, cautiously, checked inside. The stairwell was empty, but the plank of wood he had dealt with earlier had moved. He picked it up. There was blood on it. Going cold, he looked around.

Firstly, he checked the door to the underground passageway. It was locked so he began, carefully, to make his way up the stairs. There was blood on some of the steps. Halfway up he reached a heavy wooden door and gently tested the handle. It was also locked, but he could hear voices coming from the other side. He put his ear against the wood and listened.

Jennifer Pettifyr lay panting on the floor, winded and quite unable to stand. She looked through blurred vision to where Nancy Kendell was positioned by the door. The locked room. Nancy must have the key. Around the edges of the room Jennifer could make out wooden crates and open plastic white packets. Her mind went back to the cocaine she had found in the stone room and to what Ricky had said about drugs. Presumably this was where Billy kept his stock. She had a more pressing concern now though. The female of the Kendell species was pointing Jennifer's own revolver into her face.

"Put the gun down Nancy… please" she panted. "Nobody needs to die today." Jennifer's chest heaved. She was barely able to speak. Her eyes were struggling to focus and her legs felt like dead weights. Her ribs burned as if she had been shot.

Simply trying to breathe normally was agony.

Nancy Kendell lurched forward furiously and battered Jennifer on the side of the head with the butt of the revolver. Jennifer collapsed back under the blow and lay, groaning, as hot light danced around in her eyes and fire burned in her forehead. She felt a wetness leaking through her hair and down onto the floor. Blood. Groggily, she tried to focus her eyes. Nancy stepped back and stood, legs akimbo, pointing the gun down at the redhead. Her voice sounded muffled to Jennifer through the ringing in her ears. She tried to concentrate on what the girl was saying.

"You FUCKING BITCH!" Nancy was screaming at her. "Billy is going to PRISON and it's all your fault!" The girl was crying, but still pointing the gun with a furious intensity directly at Jennifer's head. "I'm going to make you PAY!" She took two short steps forward and kicked Jennifer viciously in the ribs again, generating a satisfying crunch and sending the older woman sliding across the floor to crash into the crates piled up by the wall.

Jennifer lay, doubled-up, clutching her side and trying to focus on Nancy's feet or anything, somehow, willing her vision to clear. She had to remain conscious. In the far distance she thought she could hear Ricky Shilton hammering on the door but, without the key, she knew that he wasn't about to perform a dramatic last-minute rescue.

Jennifer knew that she only had one chance to get out of the room alive and, right now, it was looking like a fucking long shot. She lay very quietly, trying to get her breath back and gather some strength.

Her sides hurt like hell, but she didn't think that Nancy had actually managed to break any of her ribs. She wasn't particularly worried about her head, either, despite the repeated assaults. Jennifer had survived enough rounds both in the dorms at school and in the boxing ring to be able to assess her fighting condition. She might be down but she was buggered if she was going out at the hands of this little ponce. She focused on trying to talk.

"Nancy, if you shoot me, you'll go to prison for murder. You'll never see Billy again will you? For fuck's sake, you're a beautiful young woman with your whole bloody life ahead of you...don't piss it all away on this rock. You can get help. Your brother might have fucked up your whole life but..." As soon as those words left her mouth she realised she had made a bad mistake.

Nancy Kendell went mad.

"I don't need FUCKING HELP! You don't know ANYTHING about us! He was my WORLD and you've taken that away from me. Do you think I give a FUCKING TOSS about my FUCKING FUTURE!?" The black-haired girl lurched across the room and brutally slammed her foot in again, forcing Jennifer to cry out in agony. Jennifer was now barely able to see for the searing pain in her ribs.

The muffled shouting and the battering on the door seemed to merge in her ears with the pounding of hot blood in her head like a horrible, insistent drum beat building to an ugly and violent crescendo. She looked up from the floor, with no energy left to defend herself.

Calmer now, as if sensing that the end had been reached, Nancy Kendell steadied herself and pointed the revolver very carefully at Jennifer. "He was my world. My everything. You took that from me" she said, crying. Jennifer tried desperately to raise her head or her arms somehow.

"Nancy... the gun" she managed to get out but talking sent searing bursts of pain through the whole length of her body. She tried to focus. "Don't, please. You'll hurt..." she stuttered, but the younger woman was not listening to her. Nancy Kendell stared down at Jennifer, enjoying the spectacle of the smaller woman clutching her ribs and writhing around on the ground like a broken doll. Taking careful aim, she spoke more softly now, almost talking to herself.

"Bye bye, bitch."

She pulled the trigger.

Chapter Thirty-Nine
"Jessica"

On the other side of the door, Ricky Shilton battered away ineffectually at the thick wood. The roar of the gunshot silenced him. As the echo of the report died away, the narrow stairway became completely silent. Shilton went cold. He put his beefy ear to the door and listened. Nothing. No sound at all. He heard footsteps behind him and found Simon pounding his way up the stairwell to join him.

Ricky resumed his hammering on the door.

"Jennie! Jennifer? Are you OK?! JENNIFER!" He battered until his hands were bruised and there were tears in his eyes. Finally, defeated, he sat down exhausted.

"At last!"

A small voice piped up from somewhere. The voice sounded rather annoyed. Shilton, head in hands, slowly looked up. He looked at Simon, then at the door.

"Jennie?"

"No Ricky, it's Mother Te-fucking-resa!" came a familiar, if slightly frailer than usual, deeply sarcastic voice. "Maybe, if you'd shut the fuck up a bit sooner, you might have heard me!" Ricky rocketed his bulk up and banged on the door again.

"Are you alright love?"

"Stop banging on the fucking door! Of course I'm not all right! Get an ambulance. RIGHT NOW! There's a phone in Nicholson's office!" Simon nodded and raced off down the steps.

"Jennie?" Ricky said through the door. "What the fuck's going on in there?" No answer came, but after a few seconds Ricky heard a key being pushed into the lock from the inside and, shortly afterwards, the door was being pulled inwards by a battered and bruised Jennifer Pettifyr, doubled up and clutching on to her side. Blood was running down the side of her face and was all over her hands. "Jennie…" Shilton moved towards her, helping her gently out of the room and down onto the steps. "Where did she get you?" The blood seemed to be everywhere.

Mentally, Ricky began trying to work out how long it would take the medics to get to them and what he could do to staunch Jennifer's blood loss until then. Shit, he might have to move her. Get her out somehow. Shit, shit, shit. Not little Jennie. Please, not her. Not a religious man, Ricky Shilton offered a silent prayer, to anybody listening, for her bullet wound not to be fatal. There was so much blood though. The blood was everywhere.

"I tried to warn her Rick…" Jennifer sat on the step, panting slowly and wincing as the pain in her sides stabbed her with every breath. "About the gun. I did try…" Shilton looked at her and pushed his glasses up his nose.

"What about the gun, Jennie?" he said softly. "What about it?" Jennifer looked up at him, an immense sadness in her tired green eyes.

"It was my gun, Ricky. Jessica. I tried to tell her it was rigged, but I couldn't get the words out. I didn't mean for this to happen. Please, I never wanted any of this." Jennifer tailed off and put her head in her hands. Ricky Shilton got to his feet and, cautiously, went over and looked into the room.

Nancy Kendell, so beautiful in life, lay unmoving on the cold stone floor. Her right arm had all but disintegrated, from the elbow down, in the blast from the explosive charge packed into the handle of Jennifer's revolver. The burned and bloody stump was slowly pumping a stream of thick, dark blood out onto the floor around her. The remainder of her upper arm was burned, and the right side of her once-beautiful face was a charred and smoking mess. Shilton knelt down and felt for a pulse.

He took off his big shirt and, ripping it into strips, did what he could to stem the river of blood flowing out from the girl's severed limb, then he bundled the remains of his shirt into a ball and positioned it gently underneath her head. He and Jennifer were still there, cradling Nancy's head and talking to her gently, when the doctors from the institute and the paramedics finally arrived.

The following night, a second small gathering took place at the pub. Jennifer, Simon and Ricky had joined the scientists for an evening, muted in the circumstances, to recognise the impending completion of their project. Jennifer had hired the function room, organised some food and stuck some money behind the bar. Money which she firmly intended to recover, suitably disguised, via her expenses claim to Brinkley and the Trinity people.

She was bashed up, bruised and her aching sides had been strapped up. Thankfully, nothing was broken though and a fair few glasses of red were helping her to manage her pain levels.

The evening had started inauspiciously when Professor MacKenzie, clearly several scotches to the wind on arrival, had persuaded the group that sitting through his laboratory ghost footage would be a fun way to kick things off. It was fun, at first. At least, it was fun for the majority of them. One member of the gathering was somewhat less than happy as the first five minutes of footage, once the lights had been dimmed in anticipation, was comprised entirely of the backside of Jennifer Pettifyr seeking clarification of whether, under the strict rules of Scrabble, it really was the case that the youngest participant was only allowed to have one vowel. Jennifer sat fuming, shooting daggers at MacKenzie and throwing vicious, throat-slashing gestures at Simon who had volunteered to man the projector.

Once the footage had moved on from the Pettifyr posterior it became exponentially less entertaining, consisting purely of an empty room and no background sound whatsoever. MacKenzie did try to explain that the emptiness of the room was the whole bloody point, and actually the exciting bit, because the sensors had all triggered. By this stage, however, he was too pissed to fight his corner properly.

The consensus was that he was flogging a dead horse (a dead horse, Margaret Nicholson had observed rather drily, would have livened things up considerably) and, eventually, the lights were tactfully raised.

They had returned to the makeshift cocktail bar set up by Barbara Porter, who was again attempting to slow Ricky Shilton down sufficiently, via alcohol, to enable her to have a crack at his trousers. Jennifer, knowing Ricky's levels of resilience when it came to drinking, rather doubted her chances. Which was a shame, because she thought that Ricky would be much better off with the funny little scientist than mooning around after her A-hole of an eldest sister.

Much later, once everybody had consumed far more food and drink than was good for any of them (particularly the lethal industrial-strength 'Portini' cocktails), a somewhat tipsy Jennifer Pettifyr decided that she could, finally, have her own little Hercule Poirot moment in the sun. Once everyone was borderline present and correct, Jennifer stood up rather unsteadily and, banging the doors closed (to pre-empt any mutinous mid-denouement lavatory trips) she bashed a spoon loudly against a china plate to get herself some attention. Ricky Shilton, having just acquired a ham and mustard sandwich the size of his head, sauntered right in front of her as she started to speak. Receiving a look, the big man held up a hand before sitting down, finally, at the end of a long bench and nearly up-ending its existing occupants in the process.

Jennifer coughed and then she set sail, majestically, delivering a slow, considered and deeply thoughtful exposition of the case from start to finish. Her rapt audience sat silent throughout, hanging upon her every word as she painstakingly and logically set out how she had managed to unravel the tangled threads of the complicated set of events.

She crafted the scene with rich, colourful detail. With engaging and atmospheric language, she teased out the subtle motivations of her characters, dealing with and despatching each adroitly until, finally, she demonstrated how, having successfully navigated the treacherous waters and avoided the red herrings, she had finally uncovered the light of the truth and made this little corner of the world, at least for a time, a slightly safer place.

At least, that was what she had intended. Fifteen minutes in and still arse-deep arguing the toss with Ricky Shilton, about fuck-knows what this time, Jennifer had the hump.

Big style.

She had, she admitted to herself, started poorly. Now, try as she might to get any kind of narrative flow going, nothing was working. The reason for this was Ricky, who was jumping in at every possible moment, apparently on a not very secret mission to undermine her. He was dumping her down onto her backside at every step and pissing on her shoes into the bargain.

Jennifer was fuming. He was at it again now.

Shilton, munching innocently on yet another sandwich, had returned to his favourite activity. Namely, sucking the jam out of her first doughnut in ten cases and sticking a little bit of shiny brown shit back in there for good measure.

"All I'm saying, Jen" said the big man, with deceptive reasonableness, "is that, well, it was a bit off you having a pop at poor old Jack Kendell, wasn't it? As far as I can make out, he's the only blameless member of the whole fucked-up family. Excuse my French, ladies."

He paused to look around the table and, receiving a few nods of affirmation, shrugged his big shoulders at Jennifer before continuing on the offensive. "A bit off, really. After all, the poor man had just lost his lady-friend and all that. So, I'm just saying, maybe a bit insensitive?" Jennifer stared at him incredulously. Her, insensitive? Coming from this fucking lump!?

"Ricky, as I have tried to explain, extremely patiently I might add, I was just trying to stir things up, yes? Make things happen. Rattle some cages and..."

"The wrong cage though, wasn't it Jen? Also, why not just make an appointment with the poor man and have a quiet chat? He's got a secretary. Lovely lady, actually. Brunette. Nice legs." Shilton looked across at Simon, an action which just annoyed Jennifer further. "So, next time, make yourself an appointment through the proper channels and then you might avoid the risk of being up in court on a slander charge, Just a thought, love."

"ANYWAY! Getting back to my earlier point..."

"And, whilst we're at it, it was really young Simon here who tipped me off about Nancy being a bit of a wrong'un, recognising her from that dodgy photo you'd been hiding in your bag"

Shilton ploughed on like a steam-roller, leaving Simon wondering once again whether he must actually be related to Jennifer, given how frighteningly similar they both were at not knowing when to shut the fuck up.

"Tipped YOU off?! You cheeky bastard... I did... hang on!"

Jennifer stopped shouting and suddenly looked very lost.

"What do you mean, he recognised her from the picture? He can't have. Her face had been scratched out."

Shilton tapped his nose. "Had her bangers out though, didn't she! Not to mention her other bits. Distinctive. Highly distinctive. You don't come across a pair of that quality every day, if you know what I'm saying." Shilton looked at Simon again, this time apparently seeking confirmation of his glowing assessment of Nancy Kendell's breasts. He seemed genuinely confused by the look of abject horror on the younger man's face. Barbara Porter was nodding her head vigorously though.

"That's true, Ricky. You can say what you like about Nancy, she did have a spanking pair of puppies." This assertion seemed to receive a general nodding assent from the rest of the scientists at the table. Linda Leighton chose to keep her own counsel.

"Oh, fucking brilliant! Lovely" said Jennifer, wondering how her day was going to get worse. Food poisoning and the shits all night, maybe? "Well, clap-clap Simon. Very fast work and, if I may say so, how genuinely fortunate for all of us that you had the foresight to pay Nancy's oh-so-fucking-fabulous tits such VERY close attention. Wonderful!" Despite feeling like she had just been bested, once again, by Nancy Kendell, Jennifer doggedly attempted to press on. She was going to complete this fucking denouement if it killed all of them. Shilton first, with a bit of luck.

"So ANYWAY, once I had worked out that it was both Nancy and Billy causing the damage, giving each other alibis, and that Nancy actually left that photo of herself lying around to cause a bit of mischief…"

Jennifer briefly caught Linda Leighton's eye and received a quick, thankful smile in response. Thankfully Linda was unharmed, other than a bit of smoke inhalation, and was being fussed over by her husband and colleagues. Jennifer knew full well that Nancy had meant that photograph to be found as a warning for Linda to keep her mouth shut or risk having her infidelity exposed. She wasn't about to break her promise, though, and Linda's involvement had been kept entirely out of it.

"Well, glossing over how lame that sounds," Shilton cut across her rudely, "all I'm saying Jen love is, well, credit where credit's due and all that. It was Jack Kendell came to you with the story about Martine Dupuis."

Shilton went on.

"It was Simon who recognised the Bristols, realised the girl was up to something fishy and that led us, of course, to poor little Danny. Billy the Kid only stuck himself into the shit because of the technical wizardry of the lovely Barbara and Nigel here…" Shilton gestured, magnanimously, across the table towards a now furiously-blushing Barbara Porter.

"You were awfully brave too Ricky…" she tittered back, to which Shilton just smiled and raised a finger to his lips, clearly concerned that news of his superhuman status might get leaked to the press.

"What!?" squeaked a now incandescent Jennifer.

Shilton was not done though.

"And then, to cap it all, you go and get yourself twatted in the face with a plank and locked up in the ivory tower with a complete psycho. All in all, Jen, I'm just not sure that there's much here to shout about."

Shilton paused for a tactical bite of sandwich. Jennifer was incensed, but she was more hurt by the truth in his words. "No, Ricky. I suppose not. Apart from getting pushed off a cliff, beaten up and having seven shades of shit scared out of me..."

"Nancy in a nurse's uniform" she heard Ricky saying, *sotto voce*, which hurt Jennifer more than anything Nancy Kendell had thrown at her.

"Fine. Clearly you and Batman here have been carrying me."

Shilton looked up then, as if genuinely wounded by her tone. "Calm down, Jennie. No need to shit a brick, love. I'm just saying that lessons could be learned here, yes? Mistakes were made and people got hurt. Or don't you think so?" He took another large bite of his sandwich. Jennifer just stared at him.

She thought about Nancy Kendell, lying on the floor.

"You know what? Fuck the lot of you."

With that, she walked out.

Chapter Forty-One
"Dark horses"

The rest of the room, it is fair to say, were a little bit stunned. Simon coughed and, rising, made a move to follow after Jennifer. As he passed along the bench he felt a soft, but highly effective, restraining paw on his arm.

"Give her a few minutes, son" said Ricky Shilton, not unkindly. "She's had a tough couple of days." Simon stared at him, and then totally lost it.

"I know Ricky! So what the flying fucking hell have you just been winding her up for?! She's been through total shit! And she saved Linda's life! The pair of them could have been blown to bits in that bloody building. You smelled the petrol, same as I did. Jennifer must have too, but it didn't stop her going inside to try to help, did it? She was doing her fucking best and she nearly died because of it! Don't you think she deserves a bit of support, rather than you just busting her balls and taking shitty little pot-shots at her from the side-lines?"

He tailed off as he realised that Shilton was now looking at him with a rather frightening expression of benevolent approval. He let go of Simon's arm and motioned him, very gently, to sit down.

"That's good Simon. You care about her. I like that. I understand that. We are, on the caring for Jennie front, both very much on the same page of the same book. Good. Now, the thing is though Simon..." he pushed his spectacles back up his nose, "whether we like it or not, that little lady has chosen to make a career out of doing this kind of shit. Worse still, she's a Pettifyr. Now, that might not mean anything to you, Simon, but what it tells me is that she is not about to stop doing this, or anything fucking else that she wants to, just because you, I or the fucking Queen Mother start getting the liquid-shits from worrying about her welfare." He looked serious and tapped a beefy finger upon the table top. "So, for that reason, I am going to be on her fucking case, and right up her shiny little bum-hole, for as long as it takes her to get fucking bulletproof-good at it."

He stopped tapping and, glancing out of the window, suddenly looked very sad. "You might have noticed, Simon, that this is not exactly a desk job. In Jennifer's chosen line of work, you don't exactly get the opportunity to just muddle through and learn on the job. You have, in fact, to either hit the ground running or hit it with a fucking bullet in your back. So, even if it makes me Captain Unpopular-Bollocks, I am not going to swan around and tell her how fucking great she is doing or, for that matter, put up with any of this Miss Marple bull-shit." Shilton looked very hard at Simon.

"She's got talent, don't get me wrong, and that girl has the heart of a fucking lion. But she is also a bit prone, and you might have noticed this yourself, to a little bit too much hit, hope and fuck-up."

"There are some very, very dangerous people out there, Simon, and Jennie nearly got herself killed, at the end of the day, by just a deeply sad couple of fucked-up children."

He adjusted his glasses again.

"So, all in all, I don't think it's unreasonable for us not to treat this little Devon escapade as a completely unqualified success, do you?" The big man sat back.

Simon thought about what Jack Kendell must be going through, having had his family ripped apart in front of his eyes. His son was in custody and his daughter lying, disfigured, in a secure hospital. He thought again about Jennifer though, and how she had not hesitated to run to the island and climb into that burning room to help Linda Leighton.

He realised that Ricky Shilton was watching him.

"Simon, you're a nice lad. I like you. Your heart's in the right place. More importantly, Jennie likes you. She likes you a lot. Now, you must like her back because, fuck knows, she doesn't give anyone any reason to hang around simply for the pleasure of her company. So, if you've got any sense in that handsome little head of yours, you will adopt a similar attitude to myself. Use whatever influence you have to moderate some of her more fuck-witted enterprises. Then between us, who knows, we might stand a chance of seeing her through to retirement rather than a hole in the ground."

Shilton grinned suddenly. "Now, would that not be nice?" His piece said, the big man got up and returned to the buffet to liberate a pork pie which he had quietly secreted on an earlier sortie.

Ten minutes later, Simon ventured into the gloom outside the pub and found Jennifer sitting, quietly, at one of the wooden tables smoking a cigarette. He sat down beside her and neither of them spoke for a few minutes. On the island, lights were shining brightly from the residual police activity at the refectory and at the top of the old lighthouse. After a while, he turned to Jennifer who was still hunched up into herself.

"I didn't know that you smoked" he said, quietly.

"Well, I didn't know that you'd been off taking brass-rubbings of Nancy Kendell's nipples, Simon. So, I guess we're a right pair of dark horses, aren't we?" Jennifer took a long drag, coughed, then stubbed her cigarette out onto the table. "I only smoke when I'm angry."

"A thirty a day girl, then?"

"Fuck off, Simon" she said, but not nastily.

That one was quite funny, for him.

"Actually, it was the scar" Simon said quietly.

"What?" she snapped.

"Nancy had a small scar across her neck. God knows from where. Her brother's pen-knife would be my bet." He shivered. Simon did not want to think about Billy and Nancy Kendell any more. "I saw enough of her to recognise it on that photograph. Just for the record." He looked around at her, but Jennifer remained inscrutable. Simon looked at the water instead. Then he heard a small voice.

"So, you two didn't actually…"

"No Jennifer." Simon said. "We did not. I'm only sorry that I didn't realise, earlier, how disturbed she was. I've been very stupid and have, pretty much, been making a tit out of myself ever since I got here." Jennifer looked up at the sky and hugged her legs.

"Well, you don't have a monopoly on that. According to Ricky Shit-head, in there, I'm just a useless pile of toss who couldn't find her own butt-cheeks without a road map."

"Not a map of Scotland, though."

"On fire this evening, aren't you? I had to leave in a hurry, actually smart-arse, and I picked up the wrong set. That could happen to anybody." Jennifer ran her fingers through her thick hair. "He's right though, Simon. He's always right." She sounded very sad. "That's why he's so fucking irritating. I've got a shit-load to learn." Simon watched her as she looked out across the water. She seemed, suddenly, so very small and fragile. Thinking, again, about how she had gone in through the window, he risked putting his hand gently onto her arm.

"Maybe. Don't be too hard on yourself, though. You risked your life and tried your best to help a group of people that you barely even know. I think that's pretty amazing."

Jennifer glanced at him.

"Do you really mean that?" Her voice was soft and he wondered whether she had been crying. He smiled and moved his hand so that it rested on top of hers. She was very cold.

"Of course" he said. "I wasn't put on this planet just to blow smoke up your arse, you know."

"Oh, that's a shame. I've got another cigarette somewhere." Jennifer began to pat her pockets. "Don't think, incidentally Simon, that I haven't noticed how much you keep talking about my backside. It's borderline sexual harassment, you know."

"Only borderline? Interesting. Anyway, as you're here I was actually wondering whether you, and the rear-end obviously, might like to go out on a date. With me. Sometime. When I've stopped being a dick, obviously." She glanced up and their eyes met.

"I'll ask bum to check her social calendar. We come as a pair."

"Whoa there. I'm not promising to make you come."

"You're actually worse than me, aren't you Simon? Sex bloody mad. Maybe Nancy rubbed off on you…" She punched him in the arm before realising what she had just said. Jennifer remembered Nancy's broken body on the stone floor and the joke wasn't remotely funny anymore. They looked at each other for a few seconds and Simon squeezed her hand softly. Jennifer stood up, painfully, and looked over at the island. She would not, she decided, be coming back to Devon for a very long time.

"Bloody hell!" stated Simon. Nothing new was on fire, he was just eye-level with Jennifer's posterior now.

"Oh, for fuck's sake get up!" she laughed, despite herself, and dragged him bodily to his feet, totally forgetting about her burning ribs and getting a painful reminder as she did so. Her eyes were red and moist, Simon noticed. She looked utterly beautiful and painfully lost. Then she looked down at her toes, as if unsure what to do next. After a few moments, a small voice came out from beneath the red curls.

"Are you really asking me out? A proper date, yes? Not just a drink and a fumble…"

"Yes Jennifer. In spite of the obvious drawback."

"You cheeky sod. I'm not THAT much older than you!"

"I was referring to your personality" said Simon, which generated an expletive from Jennifer Pettifyr that surprised them both with its invention and intensity. "That's a little bit harsh. I'm not even sure it's physically possible." Simon put his hands onto Jennifer's waist, making her wince again. He moved them, apologetically, and held onto her frozen hands instead. The reminder of her pain sobered him up. "Whilst you get better, maybe I could just spend a bit of time looking after you?"

He said this very quietly and Jennifer lifted her head up from where it had been pressed into his chest. Her elfin green eyes gazed at him and they were wet again. Simon ran his finger, slowly, down the side of her cheek, and bent down to touch his lips lightly onto the top of her head. Her thick red hair smelt of cherries, reminding him of their first trip in the car, a lifetime ago. He spoke softly to her head. "I'd like that very much…"

Jennifer Pettifyr looked up and decided, for just this once (don't go setting a fucking precedent Jennie), to break her habit of a lifetime and to keep her big fat trap shut. Instead, she tugged Simon's face down to her level and, rather nervously, began to kiss him. Softly, at first, but then with such an intensity that she frightened herself. She broke off and looked up, worried that she had stuffed up again. Simon was staring at her. He didn't, she thought, look angry.

Simon gently placed his hands onto her cheeks.

"Miss Pettifyr," he said softly, "I do have one request."

"What's that?" Oh crap, bad breath, isn't it. Bloody smoking.

"Would you do that again, please?"

Jennifer Pettifyr finally smiled. She rested her head into his chest, wrapping herself into him like a warm winter coat. The night, she thought happily to herself, might not be a complete write-off after all.

THE END

However…

Jennifer Pettifyı WILL RETURN!

(She really does need to do some housework first though.
Her bathroom in particular. Honestly, people, it's disgusting.)

Printed in Great Britain
by Amazon